THE
Slippery
Slope

← CORRUPTION

HONESTY →

← GREED

INTEGRITY →

David Crabb

Contents

Also by Author

The Magic Formula published on Amazon

Acknowledgements

Thanks to Helen Sandison, Sarah Ray and Dylan Hearn for their input, guidance and encouragement.

Thanks also to my wife Nikki and my children, Alice and Thomas for believing in me, encouraging me to write and to finish the book even when I doubted myself.

Preface

Geoff is a talented and aggressive executive striving for greatness, riches and the recognition he feels he deserves. Caught up in a string of events beyond his control, he is compelled to do the right thing – yet, could greed get the better of him? The choices he makes will determine his fate, as well as that of the people closest to him. Which path will he choose as he embarks on a twisted corporate career of choices, compromises and events?

Greed runs parallel with righteousness as he powers his way towards the wealth he desires whilst overlooking the corruption that lies in his way.

Meeting those with powerful friends reminds him of the dangers of his new connections as his colleagues start to go missing under suspicious circumstances.

Success in a corporate career has its price tag, and Geoff discovers that the journey is not what he had envisaged.

Tough choices, murder and sexual desire become the junctions that both impede and fuel his way.

Will he follow his values of honesty and integrity? Or will he choose the path of greed and selfishness?

Geoff

Geoff's once dark brown swept-back hair was now a light grey mixture, which looked positively white in places. The wizened salt and pepper look was often described by others as distinguished; everything you would expect of a successful forty-something businessman.

The years of work-related pressure were clearly visible through his somewhat wrinkled complexion, particularly around the eyes. His skin darkened from holidaying in the Maldives three days previously was still glowing and heavily moisturised.

The annual family holiday was the result of expensive spoils from a career that paid well, yet he had little to show from this in the form of savings and investments relative to his income. That said, he had a lovely home that was now mortgage-free and worth a pretty penny, even before the lavishness of its decor was taken into account.

Still tired after returning from holiday, Geoff rubbed his eyes in the way that never seemed to overcome the fatigue. He glanced at his smartphone to see the hectic schedule that lay ahead of him – just like any other week.

As vice president of talent for a global manufacturing and distribution organisation, his job involved both hiring and firing, most of which were on a large scale spanning thirty-two countries. Geoff had seen it all. The years of experience he had under his belt left few surprises for him, yet he was never bored. Every day brought a fresh challenge, demand and aggravation in one form or another. Geoff would have a moan or two about pretty much everything in the comfort and confines of his home, yet underneath this typical human façade he loved it. He was a man who was highly valued, in demand and at the peak of his career, with many professional dependents each with their own agendas, political battles and ready to stab anyone in the back for the right career move.

The departure lounge sign read '2145 to New York', an overnight flight from the UK to JFK with meetings upon arrival. It was a familiar destination for him; the global board met there each month. This was the flagship office and the jewel in the crown offering palatial facilities compared to the further corners of the corporate empire such as Jakarta and Mumbai, which were just two of their manufacturing facilities and shitholes by comparison. Although, to the locals they were a place of wealth, creation and comfort.

The meetings in New York were to plan for the appointment of a new vice president of sales and operations. The position was for emerging markets in South American territories and focusing on the good work of the country managers in these areas, including Brazil, Argentina and Bolivia, typically with poor economies, corrupt politicians and crime-ridden beyond anything Geoff had seen in the suburbs of London.

Given the seniority of such an appointment, Geoff would be conducting the interviews personally. Something he had carried out numerous times. Geoff had arrived at the happy place in life where copious amounts of preparation and planning were no longer necessary compared to earlier in his career. Such meetings had become more of a comfortable transaction for him in recent times.

The interaction with people was the part that Geoff loved. Meetings were an everyday occurrence, but the kinds that involved more politics than anything else were a frustration. A necessary evil in such a networked organisation of backstabbers and ladder climbers. Bitches and bastards the lot of them, yet he could play their game all too well.

The meetings he loved were the senior appointments, working with executives and placing great talent at the top of the tree. He knew he was good; everyone said as much.

Geoff could reduce an executive to a slab of jelly in minutes. His razor-sharp wit and questioning techniques would cut down the most confident personalities. Such behaviours were not always to be nasty, merely to get what he wanted, what the organisation needed. He was quick to think and even faster to dismiss a wallflower that was under the impression that their twenty-five years of experience, a confident smile and some well-oiled charisma would get them the job without any trouble.

Geoff was a talent in himself, a rare and valuable commodity, and was revered by those who knew him, if they were smart enough to recognise it.

He was known by his family as the playful dad, the loving husband and the caring person who would help anyone that needed it. At work, however, this character was unrecognisable. Charming, for sure, yet focused and calculated without the impression of happiness or contentment – except every so often a wry smile would be seen as if to recognise that he had achieved something beyond expectation. Satisfaction for him these days was harder to achieve than twenty years ago. Then, everything he did seemed to be both progressive and enjoyable, fresh and new, with a sense of excitement similar to that of young love.

Now, his work was comfortable, stale, so he needed to create his own enjoyment. Playing with others was his fun, being a bastard to candidates, toying with them to see how they jump when he kicked them, as he so often did.

Business Class and Vodka

The journey to JFK was like any other, always business class, with executive transfer to the hotel, five stars of course. Not that he had time to enjoy the facilities or go sightseeing; he was typically busy and in demand.

Maybe the travel would be exciting and the sights would be appealing when he was younger, but two decades on his method of operation was get in, get the job done and go home. One city looked like any other.

Several glasses of champagne were always needed to relax his otherwise stressed mind, preparing him for the fact that he was a nervous flyer, a non-swimmer and some thirty-nine thousand feet above the Atlantic Ocean trying hard not to think about the statistics of airline safety and shark-infested waters with no parachute.

Starting on the vodka over a bite to eat, Geoff began to read the candidates' profiles. A sure-fire distraction from his fears of travel and playing to his ego of being important in front of the pretty female aircrew.

Oswaldo was the organisation's country manager from Argentina. Not unlike himself, he was said to be a charming, suave chap with proven results in his respective country. With the credentials to take on more responsibility, he had prepared for future promotion through good succession management and his replacement was teed up to fill the void. The accompanying notes highlighted that he was related to the chairman of the audit committee, Peter Parsons, through marriage. Something that was necessary to disclose as nepotism was always a concern in the senior ranks. Only last year, Geoff needed to fire a vice president for employing his live-in lover and promoting them to the dizzy heights of his personal assistant. It was never disclosed and viewed very quickly as both corrupt and inappropriate. This was in Poland, which had been an acquisition into the global organisation and typically harder to integrate global practices. Prior to their ownership, dating the payroll was common practice and more widespread than initially understood.

The second candidate was Julio, a Spaniard living in Italy, and from a competitor. Julio had risen to a senior position through excellent results, yet the competitor was smaller and paid him much less than he was worth. If he were successful at interview, it would have been an inevitable loss for them given that the salary for this position was $100,000 more. Geoff recognised immediately that he certainly had the hunger and desire to earn this. Julio's current role as zone manager took him from Italy to Argentina and everywhere in between throughout the southern hemisphere. With extensive travel, he was never at home or settled in one place.

The third candidate was Ricardo, a Bolivian whose file was limited in detail other than his career history, which was fine in its own right but lacking the detail and ambition of the other two. Geoff viewed this as the wildcard. All interviewers have something similar, a benchmark and an extreme candidate on which to judge the others. Wildcards are typically hard to manage, expensive and unpredictable, yet they are necessary in appreciating the other candidates or raising the bar higher to ensure the organisation gets the best. Geoff had always been such a wildcard in his younger days and never discounted them straight away as other interviewers usually would.

It is usually only the best interviewers who employ these people, as they are often intimidating, super confident and in control. Geoff was the best; he loved wildcards. Sometimes he employed them, other times he played with them – emotionally, that is. His job was a self-satisfying game of sport. When he was feeling down or bored, such games would often remind Geoff of his self-importance, reinforce his self-esteem and bring the candidates down a peg or two if he felt it necessary, which was often.

Geoff was always intrigued by people. Even wildcards would need to pass the test, be accepted by the chief executive or the chief operating officer, although Geoff's recommendation was always accepted as he was more knowledgeable in this area by far. They were typically far too busy running a multibillion-dollar organisation to worry about the detail. That's why they had Geoff.

In any interview process, it was typical to have at least three candidates shortlisted for the final interview. It was important to have a contingency because candidates often pulled out. However, it was strange that there were no notes on Ricardo's file. He had been interviewed by others, so Geoff thought they could have been misplaced. For a large organisation, it may have seemed strange to other people that the file was handwritten notes rather than a soft copy. Geoff was old school and always liked it that way. He was somewhat of an expert in graphology; therefore, he used this in his work to read and interpret the candidate's handwritten letter of application and the notes from his team. This helped him to monitor their mood and state of mind, and decipher a personality trait or two. Some ammunition that he would use on them later.

Although the calls in flight were expensive, Geoff would just claim it back, so he put in a call to the head of HR, Mary Casciani. The call started confident and friendly, but then ended in a state of confusion. Mary offered details that concerned Geoff. Although the notes had seemingly disappeared, the memory of the interview with Ricardo was as clear as the sky beyond the clouds after the initial ascent from his aircraft window.

Mary recalled this super charming young man who was overconfident in nature and at times rather rude. At the interview, he offered an internal reference from the global chief finance officer, Martin Brinstein. Mary could see no connection in his career summary or letter, so she took the initiative to contact Martin in his New York office to make the enquiry. Martin told Mary to put Ricardo through to final interview, even though Mary's views were contradictory to his. Never in a million years would Mary have sponsored Ricardo's application to final interview based on the notes she took.

'What of your notes?' enquired Geoff.

Mary recalled the salient points; after all, someone like Ricardo would not be forgotten that easily. She was confused. 'I'm unsure why you don't have my notes, Geoff?'

Geoff dismissed this quickly because he had simply not received them. The bundle was forwarded by his secretary, Kathryn, so perhaps they had been left on her desk in error. The parting point made by Mary added to the confusion. Martin Brinstein had asked for the notes to be sent to himself first, and then suggested that he would pass these to Geoff via Kathryn. *Strange for Martin to intervene*, he thought to himself. This was neither his remit nor typical of Martin.

Geoff went on, 'Thank you, Mary. Sounds like Martin really likes this Ricardo chap. Perhaps he sees something we do not. Either that or he's losing it completely.' Geoff laughed before ending the call.

Pausing for thought, Geoff sipped his vodka and orange staring out of the window. The sky was now getting darker with every passing minute; it was time to take a nap as tomorrow would be a busy day and an early start.

His first meeting was at 7 a.m. with the executive team. A review of feedback and initiatives Geoff had presented three months ago. His chance to join the global board, he hoped. Although this was not a meeting to discuss his personal career, he always used such interactions to impress upon them how good he was.

Yet he was preoccupied with the strange events leading to Ricardo being put forward for the role. He could not understand why such an obvious decision to reject Ricardo was not taken and that Martin Brinstein had intervened. Why? What was his interest in Ricardo? All sorts of thoughts raced through his mind as he reclined his seat into a relaxed bed position and forgetting that he was above a shark-infested ocean below.

The Right Man for the Job

The plane arrived at JFK. Bleary-eyed and jet-lagged, Geoff wished he were arriving on holiday rather than a two-day business trip. 'Still, it pays the bills,' he muttered to himself. It did as well as super-expensive annual holidays and a decent lifestyle beyond, so he could not complain too much.

Despite needing to be objective, Geoff quickly dismissed the idea of Ricardo as a candidate following his conversation with Mary last night. Her comments were still echoing around his head, so he quickly moved on to think about his meeting with the global executive team.

An uncomfortable feeling swept over him as a lot was resting on this meeting: a seat at the big table one day along with final recognition for his many years of loyalty and hard work. He should have prepared more. But prepare what? How do you prepare for a meeting with no agenda? Difficult, of course, although the hope that they wanted him on the board of directors kept resurging.

Geoff had no appetite for the pastries laid on for the meetings, having eaten breakfast on the plane, although the gesture was appreciated.

Martin Brinstein arrived and was very welcoming to the seasoned traveller who was now shaved and in a neatly pressed suit. No tie though, as the culture was smart casual and the Americans loved trousers and a contrasting jacket. Geoff was British, so he always preferred to stick to a suit even when travelling to developing countries. It was his dress code. Although sticking out like a sore thumb, he stuck to it rigidly.

'No CEO?' Geoff enquired.

'Ah yes, he will be joining us in between meetings this morning, but he doesn't have long,' Martin responded.

Being curious and a confident adventurer, Geoff asked Martin about Ricardo, specifically

Mary's comments regarding why Martin had referred her to himself.

Martin dodged the question with polite corporate chit-chat, offering nothing in return other than general updates and talking about the overall direction of the company. Martin continued to thank Geoff for his loyalty, in particular highlighting words such as *trust*. He also hoped that one day soon Geoff would be sitting with them at the global board meetings and he would be rewarded with a package that would see him wanting for nothing other than a little more freedom to return home and spend more time with his family.

Geoff sat in unusual silence. He had set the question and although Martin was treading a different path, it was one he liked hearing about – his future – so he allowed the distraction to continue.

'The board need to know that we can trust you, Geoff,' said Martin.

'Trust me? Why would you ever doubt this?' Geoff insisted. He had flown thousands of miles each week and lived away from family in favour of doing his job. Sure he was paid well, but why was this being questioned.

'Ricardo,' said Martin, 'he is a well-connected guy and we think he can help us in ways that other candidates cannot.'

Geoff ceased listening and questioned Martin, 'So, you want me to hire this chap?'

'Far be it from me to tell you your job. You know how to spot great talent. All I want to do is help fill in the gaps,' replied Martin.

'Gaps,' said Geoff. 'The missing notes from the interview? I spoke to Mary who told me she was sure that she sent the notes on all three candidates to you before I received these. Why, may I ask, was this the case?'

'Mary is no doubt a good solid team member, Geoff,' said Martin. 'Although, I doubt she will see things as clearly as you and I.'

Geoff listened. He was a little less comfortable than he had expected to be and sought to understand what was meant.

Just then Barry Isaacs, the CEO, entered. 'Hi, Geoff, thanks for coming in. No doubt Martin has updated you on events and the need for your sensitivity on this one?' he said.

Geoff's puzzled look prompted Martin's swift intervention to update his boss on where they were up to.

Barry continued to dominate the conversation for the next few minutes, whereas Geoff felt like a mere bystander watching an unstoppable train pass by a station. Barry also continued to offer the same words such as trust, sensitivity and opportunity.

Geoff could take no more of this ambiguous bullshit. 'With respect to you both, can someone please explain what the hell is going on? I know I live thousands of miles away in the UK, but it seems like you're talking a different language.'

'Okay, Geoff, let me be clear on this,' stated Barry in a stern and direct manner. 'We need you to appoint Ricardo to the position of South Americas VP, no questions, and we need to make sure that this is your decision, uninfluenced by us. The audit committee will have my ass if this comes out. So, I need you to make sure that Ricardo, along with any notes you write, is your choice.'

'But he is clearly not,' stated Geoff defiantly. 'Mary's notes will have highlighted this already.'

Martin handed Geoff the sparse interview notes from Ricardo's meeting with Mary, as well as apologising that they had been misplaced on his desk.

Geoff did not need to look in too much detail to realise that these were not Mary's notes; the notes were reflecting a positive meeting and immediate recommendation for final interview. He froze for a few seconds, which felt longer as his heart raced, looking at Martin and Barry both staring at him as if nothing was wrong. Geoff had to say something. 'Look, I have spoken to Mary, and frankly I'm surprised that these notes do not reflect her true views – her real negativity towards Ricardo. I am just amazed that the notes you have given me reflect such positivity!' Geoff was attempting to dispute that these were Mary's notes.

Barry responded calmly, as if to purposefully ignore the inference, 'Mary's notes are clear to me, Geoff, and this further endorsement of Ricardo's application should clear up your misunderstanding of events.'

Barry looked at Martin and then said to Geoff, 'Are we going to have a problem with this? Can we rely on you and trust you to tow the corporate line?'

Geoff moved his head up and down slowly acknowledging his acceptance of this instruction, yet he felt quietly abused in the process.

'Let's get beyond this, and then we can look forward to seeing where your recent initiatives take us, hey, Geoff. We could use a guy like you on our board at some point. Let's just get through this first,' said Barry.

Unconvinced, Geoff stood silently looking at the table in front of him where his coffee had been left untouched, the mark inside the cup denoting that the hot liquid had evaporated. 'If there is nothing else, I will crack on because I have three interviews to conduct,' he said as if to make a statement rather than a question whilst dismissing himself. He turned around before opening the door. 'One thing though, if I can ask, why is this so important to you? Is Ricardo a relative?' Geoff pushed.

'All I can say is that he is a friend of a friend and his connections will help us without a doubt, trust me,' replied Barry. 'I just need this to happen under the radar, so to speak, away from the shareholders and audit committee, then we are all good.'

Geoff left the room feeling that his once favoured experience had been disrespected at the very least, that his views counted for nothing, but more importantly he wondered what he had missed. Something was rotten, very rotten indeed. Ricardo must be a relative. Why else would Barry want to brush this under the carpet and who the hell would risk their corporate career by fraudulently making up notes and passing these off as Mary's? There was more to this than met the eye. Although very worried, Geoff felt a surge of excitement – something more than he had felt in ages doing his job. As exciting as his job was, he was unprepared for this turn of events. He liked it. He was intrigued and, after all, they trusted him with this. Talk of joining the board was long overdue.

Beyond the excitement, Geoff was thinking like a detective. He loved to solve problems and had always been rather good at it, so this situation was like reading a good book that you just cannot put down. This served as a continual distraction to his other thoughts.

The role of vice president of sales and operations for the emerging markets in the

South Americas would encompass imports and exports of the global trading divisions, managing many staff and reporting to the chief executive for the global group: Barry. This in itself was also unusual as the president of sales and marketing, Bernard Urkhart, would usually take this reporting line. Barry had previously explained that the developing markets was his pet project and wanted to stay close. Yet Geoff hoped that there was something darker about this, but he concurrently had concerns over his personal career if he was being involved in something unsavoury.

Usually, Geoff would remain focused and objective during each senior candidate interview, totally unbiased, yet today he had the answer. He just needed to go through the motions with the other two candidates. 'What a waste of bloody time,' he said to himself. To a seasoned talent spotter, this was like asking a diabetic to eat sugar for dinner; sure, he could do it, but it was not healthy.

The meeting with the first candidate, Oswaldo, started well as each candidate had the right experience. Cultural fit was the main objective and how these people reacted under stress – and boy, could Geoff put them through it when he needed to.

Oswaldo was clearly a superb candidate. His psychometric test highlighted how he would react under pressure; the check carried out by Geoff supported this.

'This job is not for you,' Geoff concluded. 'We need someone who wants the job rather than trying to impress the relatives.' Geoff was referring to Peter Parsons.

The look on Oswaldo's face reflected his distaste at the comment. He responded calmly, 'I think I am beyond that, Geoff. I am a country manager, earning more than Peter could ever dream of. I have managed my team to success and already have a successor. Believe me, Geoff, I am ready.'

Thirty minutes into the interview, Geoff stood up and offered his hand as a parting gesture.

The move was unannounced and unexpected by the candidate.

'Thank you for coming in,' said Geoff. 'We wish you well, but we will not be taking your application further.'

Confused, Oswaldo politely stood up and asked, 'Why have you terminated the meeting?'

Geoff repeated the phrase he had used so frequently. 'You are not the strongest candidate, and therefore you have not been successful.' He needed to be careful here as the person Oswaldo was related to, the chair of the audit committee, Peter Parsons, was not a particularly pleasant chap and known to be rather political.

The words Geoff uttered were not true. In fact, in any other situation Oswaldo was perfect for the role and organisation, yet he could not let the side down. Or could he?

Oswaldo, being suave and fluent in negotiation techniques, would not let go and attempted to understand what in particular was the reason for him not demonstrating his superior strengths.

Geoff was impressed with Oswaldo; he should get the job. He decided to keep him as a warm candidate, as he did not believe that Ricardo, having not even met him yet, would last, so he wanted to ensure that Oswaldo remained interested. After all, if Ricardo was appointed and subsequently left, he would need to replace him.

'Okay, you have impressed me. Let's keep you as a contingency,' Geoff added, sounding somewhat positive and condescending in the same breath.

It was the job of the vice president of talent to keep a pool of great candidates in mind in case the organisation needed someone. As a growing global group, great talent once spotted should not be pushed away.

Disappointed, Oswaldo agreed that one day another opportunity would pop up and he would be ready. He was an internal candidate, so Geoff thought he would understand.

Julio was the next interview. Having already secured Oswaldo's long-term interest and knowing the outcome of Ricardo's interview, Geoff was suitably cutting. His question technique was unnaturally harsh, like a slap in the face upon every answer. Geoff was a skilled interviewer and never allowed himself direct involvement with junior staff, as they would not know how to deal with this. Candidates at vice president level, however, were rather different. They were typically prepared for a tough time, like commercial versions of politicians. Anyone earning $300,000 per annum would not expect an easy ride in their job or at interview either.

Yet, despite this, Geoff could still reduce them to rubble. They earned more than he did, as they earned commission on results, yet they were no match for his talents. He was always successful in getting the answers he needed.

His wife often said that she wondered why anyone would want to work for this organisation having learnt how Geoff conducted his interviews. Geoff would just laugh this off as if she had paid him some form of compliment, which he ultimately knew it was not.

'So, you now feel you want more money, and then in twelve months' time you will want us to pay you more again. We hire people who want the job here, not just the big bucks,' Geoff slammed.

'You are offering a bigger salary; it is not me demanding anything, Geoff. I do want to work for the company,' Julio was quick to retort.

'Okay, so if I offered you the position on less money, would you accept?' Geoff added, stabbing Julio with a question that was painful and difficult to recover from.

Julio could not provide the answer required to satisfy this as Geoff was not intending to listen.

Julio left the interview after an hour, his tail between his legs, emotionally drained and questioning himself.

Geoff was also tired and unusually worried about his next meeting with Ricardo in three hours' time. He knew that his usual skill and attention would be pushed aside to make way for someone else's decision. One that he did not support at all.

Business as Usual

As internal meetings continued in the meantime, Geoff was not his usual self. He used the old excuse of jet lag to explain his otherwise distant demeanour to those who asked.

'Oh shit,' Geoff mumbled under his breath as he walked towards the lift on the seventeenth floor. It was the chair of the audit committee, that Peter Parsons fellow, a fellow Brit who was not that well liked.

'Geoffrey, how are you, old man?' he asked.

He hated being called Geoffrey. His grandmother called him that, and since then only one of his least favourite relatives before she died in a tragic accident – or incident, as the police now say.

'How did it go with my little Argentinean friend this morning, Oswaldo?' Peter continued.

No wonder no one liked him; he could not even refer to his own son-in-law pleasantly.

Geoff was brief in his response. 'Not the strongest at this time, but one day, Peter,' he offered.

Peter was a naturally inquisitive person, which might be another reason why no one liked him that much. The lift doors opened. 'Going down?' asked Peter.

Sadly, Geoff travelled in the confinement of the moving glass box for eleven floors to his next meeting. Peter would not let it go when Geoff informed him that Oswaldo was not getting the job. Peter's political positioning made him appear a bully at times.

Geoff ended the conversation when the doors opened. 'Just let me do my fucking job, Peter, okay?'

Peter looked angry. But other than Geoff being so direct, Peter seemed undeterred to let it go in his usual manner of being a complete ass.

Phew, thought Geoff when he was finally out of the lift and away from him. The claustrophobia in there was nothing compared to feeling trapped with unwanted questions that he was unprepared to answer at this time, particularly from Peter Parsons.

Geoff walked slowly to his next meeting as he pondered on how to sweep the Ricardo detail under the carpet. Peter would still ask awkward questions. It was his job to make sure that the executives acted appropriately and adhered to the values and statutory obligations at all times. Ouch, yes, that was exactly what the CEO and CFO were asking him to do: go against such ethics and obligations.

Later, as Geoff made his way to reception to greet Ricardo, he felt strangely nervous, like meeting a celebrity or royalty. A form of reverence came over him as he approached the reception area, which was filled with many visitors. The receptionist's instructions were not required as Geoff could easily spot Ricardo.

Still sitting when he approached, the short, dark gentleman arose from his chair as if Geoff was visiting him instead. Geoff welcomed him. Ricardo merely smiled as they set off towards the ground-floor meeting room.

Geoff struggled with his usual note taking because he was not expected to record his true thoughts, merely record notes that would support Ricardo's application. Something he would just do later to tick the box.

The conversation was awkward, not a typical situation for Geoff at all, and his one question that needed answers was regarding the relationship between Barry, Martin and himself. 'So, how do you know Barry?' asked Geoff.

The suave Bolivian humoured Geoff and played with his question like a child who abused a toy it no longer wanted. Ricardo eventually replied, 'My family and your CEO are, shall we say, good friends, let's just say that.'

'Well, you have not said much at all really. Can you elaborate?' Geoff demanded.

Ricardo wanted to talk about his connections in the import and export arena. The organisation needed new routes for products in and out of the South Americas, and Ricardo claimed to be able to offer instant connectivity.

'Perhaps he was a drug lord.' Geoff chuckled inwardly as he stared at Ricardo and watched his calm body language. He was actually rather impressed with how Ricardo handled himself. Although, for obvious reasons, he was guarded and reluctant to demonstrate his true interview magnificence – it somehow seemed pointless.

Ricardo seemed unnaturally comfortable with this meeting. He took no notes and asked no questions.

At this point, Geoff snapped, 'You seem completely uninterested in the job, Ricardo, compared to other candidates, and frankly I'm unsure I can recommend you to the board.'

With a raised eyebrow and a turn of his lip, Ricardo replied, 'Are you sure that's a good career move, Geoff?'

In usual circumstances the meeting would have ended, yet he felt powerless. Ricardo was right, but Geoff did not want to let it get to him. Angered, Geoff barked, 'I do not give a shit who your family's friends are. If I do not approve you, you are not employed. Do you get that?'

Ricardo smiled and shrugged. Geoff had seen this in Latin American men previously. Not necessarily rude, it was just their way, but Geoff was still angered by the audacity of this person.

Ricardo noticed Geoff's facial expression before commenting further. 'You seem like a great guy, but we both know that this is a foregone conclusion. So ask your questions, and then we can move on to contracts.'

Geoff was half intimidated and half impressed. No one had talked to him like this in years. Then he quickly recalled the conversation earlier with Martin and Barry, like that was somehow different, which it clearly was not – except the words used. It was the same outcome.

This was hardly Geoff's proudest moment, but he had no option but to accept Ricardo into the organisation and set about the contracts, which were duly signed and filed.

Geoff handed the announcement to his secretary. It contained the usual messaging in such a missive to announce Ricardo's appointment and the organisation's changes this would bring. Despite believing Ricardo's ability to help the organisation connect with its exports, Geoff still felt cheated and somewhat disappointed in himself. He knew that he had completely trashed his own values in favour of following others.

He also had personal ambition in mind, recognition for years of loyalty, hoping that this would soon be forthcoming. A chance to reach the heights of the global board was something he had discussed numerous times with his wife.

Despite travelling once again to New York the following month, neither Martin nor Barry were available to meet Geoff. Had they forgotten their arrangement? Were they ignoring him?

Yes, that was it. They had what they wanted; now stuff everyone else. Although Geoff did not want to believe this, there would come a point when he would need to know the next steps for his career advancement. When should he ask again?

Geoff was never the shy, retiring type, but this situation was rather different to the typical controlled state he always placed himself in.

As Geoff sat at his desk looking through his window on the sixth floor, he fixated on the office block across the road where he could see a business meeting taking place. He had not noticed that he was late for his meeting with the country manager of France, who by this time had become a little aggressive.

'Geoff, are you planning on joining us today?' said Manu walking up to him without a concern for politeness – his name was Emanuelle Meunier, but he felt self-conscious amongst the

New Yorkers in the building who doubted his masculinity with the name of a character from a 1980's soft porn movie.

Geoff apologised and made up some crap about another important project he was working on, yet he had found it difficult to remove himself from Ricardo and the manufactured stories in his head about corruption and deceit. Part of which was clearly reality; he just did not know which part.

As Geoff sat through the meeting to discuss the mass culling of one hundred plus jobs in France, he was acutely aware of a familiar face walking by the huge glass wall of the meeting room. It was Ricardo. He was distracted and eager to detach from the meeting, but Manu had invited him to take the floor and talk through the process of identifying the unlucky staff to be fired. Needing to focus on the job in hand, and watching through the corner of his eye as Ricardo disappeared towards the lifts, he commenced his presentation to the thirty-nine people in the room.

This was not a company built on the last-in, first-out method or fair redundancy practices. This was a modern-thinking, greed-driven corporate ruthless in keeping those it wanted and culling those it did not.

On Geoff's target list were those who had not performed well, were not performing as well as they once did in their late twenties when they were young and hungry, and some who Manu just did not like.

Sexism, racism and general inappropriate decision-making should not have existed in this modern age. Although, contrary to human rights legislation, this is where the rules were broken. These policies were supported by the executives in order to drive better performance and cost savings as long as they kept out of the courts – and more importantly out of the press, for the image. Despite the corporate law team hating such meetings, all were onside as they were every week, as was the case each time they met.

Geoff was the guy responsible for ensuring that they kept the best talent and trashed the rest. Realistically, though, this was never an easy task. Geoff had times when he was performing well, others less so. Including the last few weeks where he had become more distant and lacking the motivation he once knew in himself.

The meeting took much longer than Geoff had hoped. Although it concluded decisively, Geoff was keen to see if Ricardo's visit had led him to the seventeenth floor where Martin and Barry had their executive offices, but he could not find him.

Geoff had a good rapport with the reception and security team. After all, he had provided authority on many occasions to prevent ex-employees from returning via the ground floor.

The security guard regularly received a Starbucks treat from Geoff on his way in, so he was a friendly face to ask.

'Hi, Geoff. Yes, he went up to seventeen for some executive powwow. Left here half an hour ago,' the security guard confirmed.

Geoff returned to his desk and emailed Martin to see how things were going and also to invite him for a drink after work. He was trying to strengthen the bridges between them by getting closer to his boss and hoping to gain the trust needed for further career talks. His email also asked how Ricardo was settling in and hoping, of course, that his 'latest recruit' was doing well. In reality, he was just being nosy and looking for some gossip.

Martin wrote back – in the way you do when you are busy doing other things – short, sharp and mainly in bullet points. He explained that he was busy that evening and highlighted that things were going well in general and that he had not heard from Ricardo for a few weeks.

With a furrowed brow, Geoff read his words a few times over. Ricardo had just been in to see him. What was going on? Why lie?

Perhaps he was unable to make the meeting with Barry today. Yes, that was it, and he did say he was busy. But Geoff was not convinced. His years of perceptive intuition told him that something else was going on. Something darker, perhaps sinister. What were they not telling him?

Alone at the bar of his hotel that evening, an hour passed by without Geoff paying any attention to his vodka and orange, let alone the sophisticated ambiance of the rooftop bar that Geoff had enjoyed so many times before.

The next morning before departing for his flight to Lyon via Berlin, he politely emailed Ricardo to enquire about his first few weeks in the job. Geoff would typically have done this after a month, so it was usual for the process to flow this way.

Ricardo's out of office reply confirmed that he was on business in Afghanistan. Surely he would be busy in his South American territories. Afghanistan was not a territory the organisation had an operation in, which was strange, but Geoff did recall Ricardo's promise of connections in new global areas, so maybe nothing sinister was happening.

Despite recalling this, Geoff still believed that there was another agenda. He was a mixture of being in the dark with Martin and Barry whilst fantasising about a storyline of what could be.

Geoff emailed Ricardo again, this time asking a more direct question regarding his travels, why he was in Afghanistan and questioning his actions. Geoff was aware of his inappropriate questioning to one of his peers, yet he wanted some straight answers.

Arriving on the wet tarmac in a cold Berlin, Geoff had time to kill at the terminal building. He browsed the extensive selection of books on the shelves before heading towards the executive lounge to partake in a few glasses of something cold and sparkling. This was something he usually did regardless of the time of day. Geoff made the most of the hospitality, but he never set a bad example or arrived at meetings too drunk to get the job done.

Fumbling for his lounge pass just metres away from the entrance, he was knocked to the floor by a man running into him. The guy then spun around and steadied himself on Geoff's body as if to stop himself falling in the process.

The man continued his sprint, no doubt late for a transfer to some far-flung place, whereas Geoff had taken a more relaxed stance. 'Fucking peasant,' Geoff said loudly as he brushed himself down. Not that he had any dirt visible on him, he was just conscious of the event and wanted to demonstrate to anyone looking his way that he had not been some idiot lying on the floor.

After a few drinks, consumed at record speed, his flight to Lyon was called. Geoff quickly knocked back the final full glass of Prosecco, holding it in his mouth for a few seconds to appreciate the flavoured effervescence of the free booze.

He saw that a security check had been laid on as he made his way to the departure gate. Geoff was a frequent but nervous traveller and always gained comfort from the extensive security checks at airports, for obvious reasons.

The security staff swabbed his hands for contaminants. The kind of contaminants that might be drugs or explosives. He looked at the others randomly selected to justify his selection.

As he prepared himself to move along towards the departure gate, the security officer halted his movement by raising his left hand. He then requested that he accompany him for a detailed conversation with colleagues.

Geoff was shocked. 'What the hell are you doing? I demand to know what the problem is. What did the hand swab result suggest? I am just a business man!'

He was taken to a nearby room where the contents of his hand luggage were displayed before him, with a dog brought in to sniff the contents.

Drugs. More importantly the illegal kind. The kind that people kill for, lie for and get slammed behind bars for.

Asked to explain the drug test on his hands, he referred security to the incident involving the man.

The security did not look surprised; it was as if they expected it. Showing Geoff a picture of the man, they asked if he knew him. Geoff said that he had never seen him before. Even though he had knocked him over, he did not see his face. The security, along with the police who were also present, suspected that Geoff knew the man, who it seems had been apprehended earlier in the terminal.

The drug swab was not as random as Geoff initially thought. He was being implicated in some sort of drug smuggling.

The police began a new line of questioning surrounding his extensive travels. 'Do you carry anything for anyone else? Could certain items find their way into your baggage or on your person?'

Geoff shrugged not knowing what to say as his mind worked overtime.

Clearly, they found nothing in his bags or about his person, so Geoff knew that he just needed to keep his cool and he would soon be let back on the plane, which he was subsequently in time for departure.

The whole situation was a little scary, but also something he could not wait to tell his family about. *Dad the drug mule, cool!* He smiled.

The episode was over as quickly as it began. He then looked back on it like a welcome break from the draining event that was air travel and extensive waiting at terminal departure lounges.

Geoff had earned his vodka and oranges during the flight. This was a small aircraft and the facilities were not as good as long-haul business class, which made him appreciate them even more along with the efforts of the cabin crew.

He was conscious that other passengers would have seen him being escorted from the security station and attempted to see if anyone was looking at him. To his surprise, no one seemed to look up.

The Mass Cull

In Lyon, with sunnier skies, the meetings with the local team were being planned. Geoff was joined by his HR colleagues who would help with the detail and paperwork that would need to follow. In each country, HR law varied slightly despite the Human Rights Act being more widespread, so having the local expertise was always a blessing and took the detail out of his hands. Something he never enjoyed doing, so he always appreciated their involvement, especially when the shit hit the fan following a dismissal, a potential court hearing or just an angered ex-employee churning out letters and threats.

Manu stayed in New York, no doubt keeping his head down and out of the firing range that was to be created from the changes being made.

'Fucking coward,' Geoff mumbled to himself while shaking his head as the people were invited in to the meeting.

Geoff led the presentation to the entire workforce. He looked upon the hundreds of worried faces, some with hatred in their eyes from previous experiences of such meetings. Geoff was well versed at delivering a presentation or two. He pitched the message just right: reassurance for some who would hear it and a threat to those who deserved it.

'Our business operations in France have fallen below expectations. Despite continued investment, we have not been able to keep our performance here in line with the profitability in other geographical territories. In order to preserve and protect the French operation from collapse, we must effect a number of changes that will stabilise the business in the short term. The changes will include some cost-cutting, which we believe may result in some jobs lost to redundancy.'

The French operation was quite large compared to other developing territories. One hundred job losses would represent seven per cent of the workforce in France, so quite an impact to the team locally. Although, in global terms a mere drop in the global workforce of 100,000 full-time people.

Geoff continued, 'Given the gap from where we are and where we need to be, it is planned to make one hundred redundancies, with these changes being made as soon as is practical. The cost savings in this exercise will protect jobs for those who stay in the coming years to ensure we remain a strong business. Emmanuelle will be joining us during the process. He is currently in planning talks with the board in New York working out the longer-term finance projections with Martin Brinstein our CFO. We will be making our selections based on recent performance records, not length of service. And it goes without saying that those of you who are performing well have nothing to worry about.'

It was a speech all too familiar to him. As always, he needed no preparation or written guide notes.

The one hundred unlucky staff were selected, and the following six weeks were intense with meeting after meeting. HR support was brought in from surrounding countries to help with the emotional journeys, outplacement support for managers and a forceful nudge when needed to those who knew no better, whilst bullying their way around human rights and contractual expenses wherever possible.

Geoff was always amazed at the ease of exiting a junior member of staff. The utter ignorance they showed towards their rights, the acceptance of their poor performance and the loyalty they continued to demonstrate. Like the company was going to change their minds, offer them another role and forget the whole thing just because they were being nice about it. Geoff always loved to take advantage of such people.

Then there were always the rebels, the self-trained lawyers who had watched one series of *Judge Rinder* on television and thought they knew it all. For Geoff, these were always fun to work with. He was extremely knowledgeable on employment legislation and no stranger to the tribunal services throughout Europe and the courts in other territories.

The unions were the thorn in his side when it came to downsizing, but luckily he had the support of Marcus Ricci, the head of support services. What he did not know, he hired in terms of expertise. He was as sharp as a razor. His manner was ruthless and nasty at times. It was as if he had no brake pedal; he kept on pushing, especially when his opponents were on the ropes.

Geoff could be manipulative and sharp, although he was never this nasty. He would always ask Marcus to help him when dealing with heavy losses or senior union lawyers; they seemed to talk the language of being nasty and liked to negotiate with people's lives, like children trading football cards in a school playground.

The French were heavily unionised, so discussions with them were needed. Although, on this occasion Marcus was not required as the unions did not involve their lawyers. Given the lack of forthcoming complaints, it all seemed a little easier this time around, thankfully.

Geoff carefully selected many people who, under normal circumstances, could have been taken down the path of eventual dismissal through poor performance – where a small redundancy payment and solid reference were valuable trading commodities. With the unions championing this as their initiative and claiming wins for their membership, this was something that Geoff let slide. It served him well to do so.

One person, however, did exhibit left-field behaviours. He asked the local HR manager, Cecile, to meet with Geoff personally. His name was Abiola, a chap from Nigeria who had migrated to France several years ago. He had been given notice of redundancy following his two consultation meetings with Cecile and her colleague, so this was unusual given Geoff's seniority.

Geoff refused the request. He asked that Abiola put any concerns in writing, which was of course the appropriate instruction. The employee insisted and asked Cecile again to arrange the personal meeting based on him wanting to appeal to Geoff's better judgement. Again, Geoff refused.

The exercise had been completed. By now, Geoff was exhausted. Even though he had not carried out all the work or attended every meeting, the process of downsizing was draining for him and always squeezed any emotional energy from his brain. However, he was comforted that those who were lost were mainly poor performers by comparison. He felt little remorse for his actions, especially as his job was to retain the talent that would be left unaffected.

A Corporate Whore

Back at Lyon Airport, Geoff was just about to check in when his mobile phone rang. He did not recognise the number so thought it best to answer. His number did not receive random calls as it was generally out of circulation, so it was usually someone internally. The occasional recruiter got through, but the human resources team would mostly deal with those.

It was a familiar voice. Geoff was pleased to take the call given his previous curiosity. It was Ricardo.

Ricardo thanked Geoff for the email and explained that he was enjoying the culture and the job. 'Thank you once again, Geoff, for the opportunity. Have I caught you at a bad time?' he asked.

Geoff responded by telling him that he was flying back to the UK from Lyon and that it was fine to talk.

The conversation continued on to Afghanistan, where Ricardo was open in sharing that he was exploring a new connection for the developing territories in the South Americas.

When Geoff asked about the meeting with Barry and Martin, Ricardo acknowledged that this was merely a progress meeting. Geoff knew that such 'review' meetings in the early days of appointments were rare, but he reminded himself about Barry's special project regarding Ricardo's appointment so was reassured that this was nothing sinister.

Ricardo interrupted Geoff's questioning on the trip to New York. 'Geoff, I need to ask a favour. A good friend of mine has been made redundant, and I would like him to keep his job. His name is Abiola. I am sorry to ask, and I understand you were not able to meet him, but it would be a personal favour if you could reverse your decision.'

Who the hell are you to tell me what to do? thought Geoff. He expressed this sentiment a little more politely, however. 'Well, we have made the decision based on collective agreement and performance grades.' Geoff politely refused on the grounds that his job was finished and that he had moved on from France.

As Ricardo became more persuasive, Geoff recognised a different character – more of the one that his colleague Mary had described previously.

'I do not want to insist, but I need Abiola in France to help me with certain connections,' Ricardo added. 'I cannot say why, but I know you can be trusted to turn a blind eye. And I would not want you to do something you would later regret.'

Geoff was furious. Who was this jumped-up shit to point fingers? The reminder of his previous actions now became acutely uncomfortable. Uncharacteristically, Geoff told Ricardo, 'Go fuck yourself,' and then immediately hung up.

Geoff checked in for his flight. His demeanour now less relaxed than it was upon arrival at the airport. *The audacity of the man telling me who to dismiss*, he thought.

Checking out the brightly coloured departure screen in the terminal building, Geoff could see

DAVID CRABB

that his flight was delayed by three hours. Yet again he would be late home and unpopular as ever to miss another family dinner and a welcome home from the children that he so much looked forward to. Despite his clinically focused and professional manner, he cared deeply for his family, his children in particular.

He took a seat at the bar, one of those open-air places in the middle of the concourse. Not champagne but a cold beer this time. He was feeling rather disconnected from his life and pondered his reasons for living like this. Surely there must be more to life than airport delays, loneliness and isolation?

Well, obviously, there is, but Geoff needed to pay the school fees. He liked expensive tropical holidays and luxury cars every three years – luxuries that came at a price. He felt as if he was paying more for it than just money.

The promotion would take the pressure off. The global execs were on megabucks. He did not see anything more required of him other than more corporate politics, which he was more than familiar with despite not enjoying.

A means to an end, final salary pension and with five years to go before he would jack it all in. It must be worth putting up with. At least that was the message shared with his wife, convincing himself in the process, that by the ripe age of fifty-five he would be free, retired and living comfortably.

Geoff never liked to think of his life as some form of corporate whore, giving up his mind and body for a reward, but at least he had a plan to return to normality after a few more years of pain and abuse. Despite not openly accepting this, deep down he knew what he was.

His usual Face Time call to the family was as clinical as ever. He offered little emotion, energy or information as it was hard to have a truly personal call surrounded by a mass of strangers – most of whom were as bored as hell eager to listen and pry into your personal affairs. Something Geoff did to them in equal measure.

The Face Time call on this occasion was interrupted by his wife answering the door. 'I'll call you back, darling, give me five minutes,' she stated.

Geoff waited for five minutes. It seemed longer as he sat there looking at his smartphone in anticipation of it ringing, just like being cut off on a train going through a tunnel, seemingly endless.

Eventually the phone rang. It was answered before the ringtone was given the chance to operate properly.

Geoff's wife, Nicola, was angry. She had received a package by courier. A small manila padded envelope addressed to her personally from someone she never heard of. Inside was a dead rat.

Hours from home, Geoff felt a surge of frustration. He could feel his face becoming reddened with anger knowing there was nothing he could do.

'I am going to call the police,' said Nicola. 'I have never heard of a man called Ricardo!'

Geoff fell silent. The pause allowed his brain to provide an explanation. Was it the same person he knew? Why had this happened?

He brushed this off on the call to Nicola as a prank, a misunderstanding, suggesting to his wife that she should put this in the outside bin as the police would not be able to act on this. His wife was less than impressed and hung up, leaving Geoff feeling ten times worse than before.

He searched eagerly for Ricardo's number, dialled, then hung up. What would he say? He was about to accuse Ricardo of doing this with just a name, the same name. It was hardly proof. How would he position this so as not to sound unreasonable, crazy or needing to apologise in a hurry. He had too much to lose.

Why would Ricardo do such a thing? This theory was simply ridiculous: Ricardo was a businessman, not the Pied Piper.

Having calmed down somewhat, he did call Ricardo. 'Hi, Ricardo. I feel I owe you an apology for my outburst on the phone earlier – it was uncharacteristic of me. I am just knackered, exhausted and the French business has been a little tricky at times.'

Ricardo acknowledged his apology. 'I understand, Geoff. You are a good man, and I would imagine that you have been under considerable strain over in Lyon. My asking for help was not an easy call to make, so I recognise that it may not have been well-timed.'

At this point, Geoff was sure that questioning Ricardo on his friend Abiola would be inappropriate and once again offered his apology for not being willing to change his view on his dismissal.

Ricardo then wished him a safe flight home and gave his regards to Nicola and the children in London.

Geoff froze. He was never a man to talk about family, where he lived or his wife's name. How did Ricardo know his wife's name?

'How do you know about my wife? I have never mentioned her in any conversation, Ricardo,' Geoff said in a suspicious tone. He was suddenly regretting his earlier apology and polite dialogue.

'Let's just say that my job is easier with friendly faces in certain countries, Geoff,' Ricardo highlighted. 'I would go to great lengths to ensure I get what I need.'

Geoff spoke without thinking. 'Did you send my wife a package just now?' His tone more of a bark than his usual charming style.

There was no answer.

'Answer the fucking question,' was Geoff's retort to Ricardo's silence, even though it only lasted a few seconds.

Ricardo was fast in his response. 'Easy, Geoff. You are accusing me of something, yes? Let me be clear that I do not answer to you on any level, although I can say that you should be nicer to people. Or else, things happen that you will not like in life, my friend.'

'If I find out that you sent the dead rat—' Geoff was about to make a threat but was cut short by Ricardo.

'You will what, Geoff? What will you do? You need to consider your actions, my friend. Look after those who depend on you both in business and at home. Otherwise, your life will become unhappy.' Ricardo then asked Geoff once more to help his friend in Lyon.

The call was silent before Geoff hung up. In a rare event in his life, Geoff was not a man in control; he was confused, unsure of himself and angered like never before.

Geoff looked at the untouched beer on the small table in front of him, now strangely unappetising since the calls.

His only course of action was to call his boss, Martin Brinstein. He rang immediately and left an urgent message for a call back based on a major personal issue. Geoff never left such voice messages. He was self-sufficient and rarely needed input from others, so Martin would have recognised this as unusual when he received it.

A Problem Shared…

Geoff wandered around the shops within the terminal building not looking to buy anything. He was just trying to take his mind off the phone, passing the time, the monotony of waiting around. With his hand firmly on the device, he was ready to react quickly in the event of Martin ringing back and desperate not to miss the next call.

Frustratingly the phone did not ring, despite his attempts to distract himself with the designer shops. He continued to look at the signal strength every few minutes just to make sure.

He proceeded to the departure gate as boarding was in twenty minutes.

Always the last to board the plane, Geoff watched as the people passed through the gate handing over their passes and joined the end of the queue.

The phone rang. It was Martin at last. His voice typically concerned about his message.

Geoff spoke gently as he walked down the gangway to the plane and highlighted the call with Ricardo that surrounded the surprise delivery received by Nicola.

Martin was to the point. 'Geoff, this is not the time or place to talk about this. When are you here next?'

Geoff was not due in New York for another two weeks; he would not wait that long to discuss this urgent madness. Martin was also keen to meet up, so the two quickly agreed to make a special effort to meet in Martin's office in the next few days.

Geoff felt as if a weight had been lifted. Clearly the problem still existed, but he was on a path to greatness. Martin was his boss, his champion, and they had been good for each other over the years despite not being what you would call good friends. It was more a corporate relationship with trust. Yes, trust – as had been mentioned in previous meetings.

They say a problem shared is a problem halved, and in this case it felt so. He knew he had the weight of the global CFO behind him and that Ricardo was in for a complete bollocking. His suave arrogance would soon be clipped, and then potentially Geoff would be able to 'deal with him' in his usual style.

Let's be clear, his usual style would usually be harsh: any executive would be wounded. However, he did need the support of two global directors before commencing such an act on a senior vice president, given the relative seniority and importance of the role.

Few survived the test whenever Geoff went through this type of session. Such high-value individuals would be typically strong and argumentative; often such confrontation was easy for Geoff to plant and execute in his favour. He was a political executioner.

For the first time in months, Geoff felt he was back in the driving seat and excited about being able to curtail Ricardo through his own actions, put an end to his tirade and get his own back for the dead rat incident today.

Geoff was not always a vindictive man, but he was not someone to be crossed with ease.

With revenge creeping into his mind, he could not let this go unpunished.

Now he had a plan to address this, he could once more relax on the plane with his usual drink and look forward to arriving home soon, once this mess was levelled out.

In his acute sense of comfort before the plane departed, Geoff sent an email to Ricardo reflecting on his requests and behaviour and that he looked forward to meeting him soon to clear the air, agree the way forward and ensure that they arrived at an understanding of how corporate behaviours should be adhered to. The note was full of refreshed confidence, strong words and intended outcomes, which if read by a senior business person would be clear despite the ambiguous language that might have first been apparent. For the uneducated, it highlighted that Ricardo was to be put firmly back in his box and Geoff would do what he needed to.

It was Geoff's way of ensuring that there was a record of the day's events – and, just as important, a subtle warning to his opponent that he was going to deal with it firmly.

Once sent, it felt like just another bit of corporate politics gone wrong, something of regular occurrence. Although, he had to admit that the dead rat was a new one even after all these years of downsizing; he had only ever received a few death threats before.

One such event included broken car windows, email threats and a promise to get him dismissed for inappropriate behaviour, which of course never happened. The person was arrested for the smashed windows because they were caught on the CCTV cameras in the office car park. Hardly thought through. Geoff never pressed charges despite having every right to do so.

When this happened, the organisation always supported him, protected him and reassured him of their unwavering attachment to his methods and results. They even paid for his car window repairs on his expenses, which was a rather uncommon business expense and typically an insurance claim.

Geoff had always treated people reasonably well: they got what they deserved. If they deserved to be fired, he would have no trouble sleeping at night, or pulling the trigger himself for that matter.

This particular instance, however, gave rise to some doubt. Despite Geoff knowing and believing in what had to be done, something was missing, something did not feel right – like a crime story where you believe you know who the culprit is, yet somehow there could be a twist of events. Such a twist on this occasion could be beyond his control, and that niggling doubt continued to bother him.

Nonetheless, the email was sent and cc'd to Martin for political completeness. So, with a sense of relief and empowerment, he was able to relax once again and look forward to some much-needed downtime in the familiarity of home.

Before he was able to do so, Geoff received a fast response from Martin. A quick call where he asked Geoff to temporarily reinstate Abiola to help contain the political shitstorm until they could meet. Martin asked politely, so Geoff agreed. Typing quickly, Geoff highlighted that he would be discussing the overall plan with the board and was, for now, reinstating the man he had made redundant: Abiola. Message sent. At least Ricardo would be happy, even if Geoff was not.

An Unpleasant Distraction

After a pleasant weekend with the family, Geoff left early for JFK Airport having arranged a short notice meeting with Martin.

Geoff was exhausted and easily drifted off to sleep in the taxi having left his home in the early hours to catch his flight.

Once settled into the flight, the steward's announcements caused Geoff to wake a little disorientated. He was unsure how long he had been asleep, bleary-eyed and uncertain about the details of the announcement.

Voices of protest were recognised before Geoff finally gathered his mental rhythm once again. 'Why are we diverting?' he asked the passenger across the aisle, who by looks alone seemed to be focused and more aware than himself.

The captain's voice then interrupted the furore. 'We apologise for this inconvenience as we have been diverted to Atlanta. This is due to a security-related matter. Although I cannot confirm the details, we will be able to give you further information once we land. Once again, on behalf of myself and the entire crew, I apologise and hope that we can make your journey a comfortable one.'

Little wonder the voices of unrest were now more prominent than ever. Passengers were now out of their seats demanding to know what was going on and why. Everyone was now a rebel, disregarding the instructions to stay seated and remain calm.

Geoff used the on-board phone to call home, but maybe it was out of order or he used it wrongly in a panic. Either way, he tried again, this time taking greater care when entering his credit card details.

No use, the phone was not working. Geoff looked at the adjacent passenger in row 13C; he was having the same trouble. The man bashed the phone handset on the chair in front of him whilst muttering some expletives, as if to perform a kind of magic chant that might have the desired effect and suddenly make the phones work once more.

Geoff recalled a few hours before he dozed off that someone was using the phone with the usual success, so they may have been disabled.

'Excuse me, miss,' Geoff demanded as a crewmember extracted herself from a conversation with the passenger two rows in front.

She glanced up with a look of discomfort having to deal with everyone's growing questions without seemingly understanding what the hell was happening.

Geoff called out, 'Have the phones been switched off? I am trying to call my—'

'Yes, sir,' she offered without hesitation. 'The captain has disabled the phones for safety reasons.'

'What do you mean?' Geoff demanded.

'That's all I know, sir. Please let go of my arm, sir!'

Without realising, Geoff had restricted her movements with his hand on her wrist. Not something he was proud or aware of, but such panic was creating some strange behaviours.

The man in the seat in front turned around and said, 'This is a fucking terrorist attack, I am telling you! Something is definitely not right. I reckon they have blown up Times Square.'

In the period of time that followed, tempers were frayed, emotions were high and passenger anger was mightily uncomfortable for all. The look of discomfort on the otherwise smiling cabin crew told everyone that they should be concerned, despite their words of support and reassurance.

Geoff was by experience a master of deciphering body language. They were good, but he was better. He knew that they were worried and unaware of events.

The plane began its descent. The announcement from the captain highlighted that they would soon be on the ground and met by the authorities to disembark safely. Also that passengers must remain in their seats until given permission to disembark, even when the doors were opened.

Geoff's patience was in short supply, even though compared to others he seemed calm and contained.

One lady exclaimed, 'I am in need of getting home to look after the grandchildren.'

One chap in a few rows behind shouted, 'Excuse me, miss, how do I get to New York City this morning to see my dying father?'

Such grief, such disruption, yet no one seemingly had answers to the events causing this; nor were any plans made available for getting everyone to their destinations at this time.

Geoff was probably one of the lucky ones. He was on a business trip, so he could pay for another flight, hire a car or take a cab. Money was not the obstacle for him, but for others such options were not necessarily on offer.

The plane landed on the runway, but the usual thud of rubber hitting the concrete seemed different. Geoff, just like others, interpreted every detail with a different level of caution, looking in desperation for facts and answers that were not there.

The reverse roar of those Rolls-Royce engines seemed louder and more distressed than usual. Geoff reminded himself of his heightened senses due to the fear of unknown circumstances that lay around him.

After the plane sat on the tarmac unmoved for over five minutes, the captain once again offered his update. 'Ladies and gentlemen, this is

Paul Sanderson your captain. I apologise for this additional delay while we wait for our slot at gate thirty-seven. We will be moving as soon as I get the okay from Atlanta traffic control. We have been told that the authorities will be keeping us on the aircraft while they board us, and that following their all-clear we will continue our journey to JFK. Once again I apologise for this severe disruption, but I assure you that such decisions are only made with passenger safety in mind.'

The passenger contingent fell strangely silent. Even though the captain had offered nothing of any comfort, his words seemed final and conclusive with a strange sense of inevitability.

As the plane halted, Geoff could see the passengers nervously pressed against the cabin windows, leaning in on others and invading personal space like trapped miners gasping for air through tiny surface holes, forgetting the luxury of space they so eagerly paid for when booking.

Geoff's hearing had developed a honed sense of detection to the comments of others.

The FBI and police were all over the place with cars, people and guns in their masses like only the Americans could do.

Geoff had seen such scenes in many of the movies he loved watching, something that always created a thrill for him and a sense of intrigue. This scene was no different, but the view was not as good as his sixty-inch curved screen at home.

The crew were standing up reminding passengers to stay seated, not to move, not to use the toilet or reach for the overhead lockers for their own safety.

Within seconds of the door opening, the aisle filled with chaps in dark blue jackets with yellow lettering. Geoff could see for himself that they were the FBI and their handguns were unholstered.

Geoff was nervous and excited all at the same time – with such emotions feeling rather contradictory and at times perverse. They were looking for something, or someone, and the detective in him tried desperately to find it before they did.

He noticed an unarmed FBI agent coming onto the plane but failed to notice the agent who had stopped by his seat asking for his name and passport. Geoff froze. He was confused, dazed and the focus of his attention was on the gun aimed at him from a few yards away.

Due to the pause in Geoff's response, the officer repeated his request in more of a demanding tone and then promptly explained his rights.

Geoff was not hearing these words at all in any detail; it was as if they were in a foreign language. He stood up for some reason, there was no logic, just a human reaction, whereby the agent then grabbed his arm, manoeuvred it behind his back and placed the metal cuffs on him. The cold steel dug into his wrist bones. Uncomfortable, restrictive and painful in places.

The other passengers looked on in fear. One was screaming as if their life was under imminent threat.

Geoff was seemingly detached, like an outer body experience he remembered as a child watching himself be moved by his brother due to him collapsing and hitting his head. He felt nothing, just detachment, as though watching his big screen at home, a scene he could pause and switch off at any time. Only this was real life. It was happening, and Geoff was being taken into custody.

Looking at the nearby passengers, he hoped to see looks of support for this obvious mistaken identity that was impacting upon such an innocent man. Instead, he saw a mixture of disgust, annoyance and hatred as if he was some sort of terrorist. That's it, he was being arrested as a terrorist. Geoff recognised that in all the kerfuffle. He had not heard a word spoken to him by the FBI; he was now confused. 'Why are you arresting me?' he demanded.

The agents continued without response, forcing him along the aisle of the plane.

Geoff saw a passenger looking at him and reached out saying, 'I have done nothing wrong, this is a mistake.'

The passenger, a middle-aged man in his mid-forties, replied, 'Fucking scum! Rot in hell!'

Geoff seemed in a daze as he was led carefully down the steps off the plane and into the rear seat of a black Escalade. He noted the others parked around it like uniformed soldiers in a line: black, cold and lacking any sense of hope.

Inside the vehicle, Geoff's discomfort from the cuffs pressing into his wrist bone was the last thing on his mind. His acute uncertainty overwhelmed him: where was he going, why and how could this be happening to a man so typically calm, balanced in his political views and without doubt one of the most law-abiding citizens you could wish to meet? Well, at least that was his self-portrait, as it had been for most of his life. Denial perhaps, yet he felt this.

'Where are you taking me?' Geoff demanded.

'Sir, you seem oblivious to the fact that you have been arrested on suspicion of terrorism and that we are taking you in for questioning. If I were you, I would save it for when we get there,' responded another agent confidently, who Geoff had not even looked at previously.

Geoff could see tall buildings all around him as the car turned in sharply with a loud bump from the suspension as they went over a ramp and then proceeded at speed behind the car in front into an underground car park. The car came to a sudden halt. The door opened from the outside like a sense of celebrity, but there was no red carpet, just another agent ushering him by the collar into an elevator via a security-controlled door where another agent was waiting inside.

The agent selected the fifth floor. Geoff could see that there were eleven in total. It was some sort of office block; at least it was not a military complex. Geoff had read all about people being taken to such places and never seen as free men again. Somehow he felt relieved, perhaps not recognising the trouble he was in.

It was silence in the elevator. The only sensation was the motion of the metal box moving upwards, which seemed to take ages. Geoff had once been to the Burj Kalifa in Dubai, which travelled over 100 floors in seconds. *This was no modern wonder of technology, a 1990's building at best*, he thought, trying to take his mind off the reality of his predicament.

Three seconds after the fifth floor was reached, the doors slid open. Geoff was once again forcefully taken by each arm and moved into a room. It had no windows, two normal-sized doors and small cameras. Geoff expected a mirrored wall, the exact type seen on many a crime movie where the police are watching from behind the safety and anonymity of the special glass. It was not so in this case.

Geoff was placed in a chair, a black plastic chair, cheap and horrid like the ones he sat on at school decades ago. A far cry from the luxury of the plane that he was dragged away from, where he was humiliated in front of the passengers and crew, and no doubt captured on a mobile phone in the process and whizzing around the internet for millions to see for free entertainment.

Geoff waited alone. There was no agent in the room and nothing to look at other than the cameras that were no doubt watching him. It was hugely intimidating to be spied on in such a manner. His mind focused on how many people were looking at him, wondering what they looked like and whether they were using such a tactic to make him sweat for a while. It was working.

Geoff was startled by the door being opened because he didn't hear a noise outside prior to this. *It must be soundproofed. The sort of place where people are interrogated and no one could hear.* His mind once again recalling a CIA movie he had watched recently.

The man sitting down opposite was not at all what he expected. Small frame and physically fit in comparison to Geoff, but not like a military man in his opinion. He placed his glasses on the bridge of his nose and adjusted them by pushing them back towards his face. 'Hello, Geoff. May I call you Geoff?' he asked politely.

Geoff agreed with a nod of his head, somewhat confused with the politeness being offered.

'My name is Special Agent John Maxwell. You have been brought here on suspicion of your connection with terrorism. Under federal law we can detain you here for several days until we can determine the facts for ourselves.'

Geoff quickly contributed that he was just a normal guy on business with no links to terrorists at all and then asked if he could call his wife.

The FBI agent smiled. 'Of course, Geoff. I'm sure we can sort this out quickly, but I will need your full cooperation in order to do this, then we can both go back to our normal routines.'

Geoff nodded quickly in agreement.

'Prior to take off, we received a tip-off from a caller naming you specifically in connection with recruiting, funding and being connected with certain people who are on our watch list.'

Without thinking, Geoff dropped his guard. 'That's rubbish. I do not know any terrorists. I do recruit…but these people are to work for the company I work at. We are not a terrorist group for heaven's sake. Just another corporation trying to make money.'

'Okay, Geoff, I can see that this may take a while,' John responded. 'We've ran a check or two while you were on the plane, and through our intel we can see that you have travelled to three locations where five recent bombs have been detonated – clinically departing within just a few days before each attack. What do you say to that?' he added.

'Oh, you cannot be serious?' asked Geoff. 'That's just a coincidence. You cannot believe that I was involved? I can verify that I was in meetings, genuine meetings, with no spare time to go off meeting terrorists.'

'Tell us about your trip to Lyon, Geoff, and what you were doing there?' John politely asked in a tone that was consistently calm and unwavering in its politeness.

Geoff was feeling confused, but he also believed that he would be back on the plane in no time at all. He calmly recalled, 'I was meeting some people within our French subsidiary, helping to make some redundancies, restructuring resources and doing the sort of shit that the local team could not. No terrorism, no bombs, just normal business things.'

'In the course of your meetings, then, Geoff,' John continued, 'who did you meet with? Is it fair to say that you may have interacted with someone on our watch list?'

'Yes, I suppose so, but only in doing my job. Not for the things you're accusing me of.' Geoff's tone was heightened. His confidence returned slightly, despite still in cuffs. 'And while I'm at it, can you please take these bloody things off me. They are hurting me.'

John nodded to the other agent, who subsequently released the cuffs from Geoff's red and slightly swollen wrists. The other agent who had not introduced himself had been in the room the whole time, not once showing any compassion or engagement with Geoff until this point.

'Thank you,' Geoff politely commented with a half-smile recognising the gesture.

'Do you know a man called Aghamellah Islam?' John asked while passing across a photo of the chap in question. 'Although he may have other aliases, this is him.'

Geoff quickly responded with a no, then a pause set in as he looked at the picture. It was a little difficult to make out, but the features could have been similar to someone he had recently met.

John pushed at Geoff's questionable response. 'So, you know this person?'

Geoff shrugged his shoulders. He acknowledged that he recognised him somehow but could not place him.

'This is not helpful, Geoff. I am trying to help you, believe you even, but how can I do so when you are not helping me?'

Geoff's brain was working overtime. He sat there thinking, trying to place the image from his meetings. Suddenly, he said, 'I think I know. This is a chap I made redundant – fired, you know. It was part of the process to follow to reduce costs and staff numbers. He was one of them!' Geoff asked for his bag so he could retrieve the files, copies at least, where he could identify him.

The FBI seemed uninterested in this; they continued to push on Geoff's uncertainty and weakening defence.

'So, you do know Aghamellah Islam after all?' John concluded in a surprised tone.

'Well, I don't know him; I just met him as part of the downsizing protocols. He was known as Abiola, and I met him a few times only,' Geoff added.

'So, we have gone from not knowing him, this person on the DEA watch list, to having met him a few times… You can see my dilemma here, Geoff, can't you?' John explained.

Geoff thought for a second or two, and then added, 'Contact my boss in New York. He can verify what is going on.'

John did not acknowledge this at all. Instead, he continued to ask Geoff about his other travels, particularly where he had travelled prior to the bomb attacks in various countries.

Geoff and John continued on this path for many rounds of questioning before Geoff said, 'If I was so supportive of Abiola, why would I sack the bastard?' He hoped this would raise an interesting option for John to consider.

John offered Geoff a coffee and left him to check out his story. He contacted Martin, Geoff's boss, who clearly corroborated his account and offered access to Geoff's emails.

A few hours later with Geoff still in custody, the door opened once more.

'Hi, Geoff, sorry to keep you dangling, but you know that we need to do our job and look at the detail, right?'

Geoff nodded.

'Two things, then. I spoke with your boss who helped clarify your reason for travel, your work – and that all seems fine. He gave us access to your emails, which we have been reading, and a lawyer has been appointed to help you. He will be here within a few hours.'

'So I am being detained still?' questioned Geoff. 'Why the hell am I still here? You spoke to Martin for fuck's sake. Why am I still here?'

'Well, Geoff,' John calmly responded, 'you claimed that you sacked the man you know as Abiola, yet before you took off for New York you reinstated him. Why was this?'

'Because Ricardo and I argued about it. Ricardo wanted him reinstated. He obviously talked to Martin and, due to the politics, he asked me to reinstate him,' Geoff added realising how this looked in the eyes of a third party.

'We cannot find these emails, Geoff. You can see how this looks?'

Geoff acknowledged without speaking.

'Let's get you a sandwich and another coffee, and we will talk again after your lawyer has been to see you. In the meantime, Geoff, I suggest you think carefully about your statement.'

After John left the room once again, he was shocked about how nice he was being. The stories of good cop, bad cop were not apparent to him, thankfully.

Geoff recognised the shit he was in but was once again pleased that his boss was behind him by sending a lawyer to assist.

John once more entered the room. The questioning continued about his relationship with Abiola or Aghamellah, obviously now the same person, and Geoff continued to offer Ricardo as the person they needed to talk to.

John made no notes, but it was safe to assume that others were listening in remotely and doing that for him.

This time Geoff's tone would have seemed really clear, concise and believable; after all, it was true. Ricardo was the forceful one, although to the FBI they could not overcome the fact that Geoff had hired Ricardo himself. An unwanted complication that would not go away easily.

John received a message in his earpiece, and then stated, 'Geoff, your lawyer is here. We will be back to talk with you following your brief time together.'

The Mediterranean Lawyer

A few moments after John left the room, Geoff's lawyer walked in. An unaccompanied large man, Mediterranean looking in terms of skin colour and wearing an expensive suit. Not the tidiest of appearances given his obese sizing. Although the outfit may have been expensive, he looked like he had been in it for days.

'Harry Delaney,' he announced as he held out his hand.

Geoff acknowledged him. 'Are you a friend of Martin?' he asked.

'I am just a lawyer sent here to get you out. Let's focus on that, shall we?' His tone was not what Geoff expected: clinical, unfeeling and focused, and not answering his initial question. 'I am aware of your situation, and I do not believe for a minute that you have anything to answer for. Before I talk to the Feds, tell me why they think you are involved, in your words,' Delaney demanded abruptly.

Geoff highlighted the connection with Ricardo and implicated him with the man in the photo who he had sacked, the man of interest to both the FBI and Ricardo.

Delaney thanked Geoff for his input and recommended that he retract his statement to the FBI, which Geoff was not happy about. He was concerned that he would remain incarcerated in custody for longer.

Harry Delaney then offered an explanation. 'Understand me when I say that I can have you released in minutes, Geoff, minutes, so do not worry. The people who we both know have a vested interest in your release. That is to say that you are not expected to announce Ricardo or the company as implicated in this issue. Therefore, I request that in order to get you out, you retract your statement and offer the following instead.' Delaney handed Geoff a prepared statement. It was brief, highlighting some carefully chosen words and retracting his comments based on the FBI not following proper protocol. It seemed that the arrest was not handled correctly, so the lawyer knew how to exploit the system.

Feeling a little uncomfortable, Geoff said, 'I know Ricardo was involved, Mr Delaney, and I would not be acting lawfully by retracting my statement.'

Delaney, being quite an aggressive man, stared at Geoff while he was delivering his explanation about Ricardo and the events leading to him being appointed. 'I am aware of your dialogue with Ricardo, Geoff. Who do you think sent me? Your fairy godmother?'

Geoff suggested that Martin had appointed Harry.

Delaney interrupted, 'Bollocks, Geoff. If you really believe that, then you're not aware of what's going on here. Ricardo and I share the same friends. I am here to help you, Geoff, but also to help Ricardo from not being implicated in your storytelling!'

'What the fuck is happening here, Harry?' Geoff asked. 'I am an innocent guy, being implicated in a situation I am not involved in.'

Delaney quickly retorted, 'You are involved, Geoff, in it up to your bloody neck, my friend. Do you not see just how big this is? Sign the statement and let's get out of here.'

Geoff demanded answers. Delaney offered none other than to confirm that he would remain in custody if he refused.

Seconds seemed like minutes as Geoff pondered his limited options. When John entered the room, Harry Delaney arrogantly took control of the situation using some legal jargon that he did not totally understand, but it did the job.

John read the statement, asked Geoff if he agreed to it and then released Geoff to his lawyer, given Geoff's positive acknowledgement in writing.

As he left the building accompanied by the FBI, John discretely handed Geoff his contact card, whispering for him to stay in touch if he needed him. It was as if John knew that Delaney was somehow not a nice person and that he would soon need the FBI. Geoff quickly and stealthily put it in his pocket taking care not to let his lawyer see, especially given John's attempts to keep this under Harry's radar.

They left through the front door of the building, which was just a normal cold steel and glass building full of offices like any other Geoff had been in for meeting after meeting throughout his career – nothing to denote an FBI building or signs highlighting interrogation rooms this way!

Harry and Geoff walked down the street for a few seconds when an expensive-looking silver sedan pulled alongside. Delaney opened the door and they both got in the back. Geoff did not question this; his lawyer needed transport so he just assumed that this was his driver. It was not a typical scenario, though, as another man occupied the front passenger seat.

The driver continued on his journey, seemingly knowing his route or just driving awaiting further instructions. The man in the front turned around and greeted Geoff. 'Hi, Geoff, glad you are out and free again. We will soon get you on your way to New York. Harry, my friend, thank you for your services once more.'

'Who are you?' Geoff enquired in a less than confident and shaky voice.

'I am acquainted with your bosses; we have a mutual interest. Names are less important than commitment and obligation, Geoff. Do you agree?' added the stranger.

'Well, I suppose so. But you seem to have an advantage in knowing about me, yet I know nothing about you,' said Geoff.

'That's the way we like it. It would be a sad place if it were the other way around, would it not?' replied the man, smiling, confident and unrelenting of any more detail.

'At least tell me who you mean by "we"?' asked Geoff. It was beyond curiosity, more of a demand, yet the man just laughed it off.

As the car pulled over, he asked Geoff to maintain an ignorance towards Ricardo and that his support for the organisation's agenda would be appreciated. He went on to highlight that disloyal people were not his kind of people, people who got what they deserved, and he felt that Geoff was not one of these people.

Geoff just stared on in wonder. *Who is this man? What is he involved in?* Questions that were now haunting him.

After the man got out, the driver continued to the airport terminal. No words were spoken, just silence.

A few minutes later, Delaney spoke. 'You know, Geoff, the organisation needs your loyalty now more than ever. Martin needs your support and there is a lot at stake, Geoff, and a lot to gain. I would advise you to keep this in mind when rubbing shoulders with the FBI, as they will contact you again. Your loyalty will determine what happens next, Geoff.'

'I have always been loyal to the company,' Geoff explained. 'I am a company man through and through – Martin knows this.'

'Talk to Martin, Geoff, he will guide you on what to do.' As the car halted, Delaney handed Geoff his travel documents and dismissed him to get out of the car with a hand gesture.

A puzzled Geoff continued to the terminal building not thinking about whether he would be arrested again or not by the FBI.

It was a tense moment as Geoff gingerly approached the check-in desk. Successfully passing the first hurdle, he then went through passport control and security with no hitches.

Geoff reached for his mobile phone and called his wife whilst buying a drink in the bar.

She answered unaware of his troubles. As Geoff commenced the story of what had happened, she cut him down with a terse response because he had not called her as promised last night. It was twenty-four hours since he had spoken to her, not realising how long he was detained. Tenderly apologising, he continued to explain the events to her, clearly bruised by his ordeal.

His wife, Nikki, pleaded with him to go to the FBI, even though Geoff had given a false statement and retracted his initial truths. How would this look now? They both agreed that the FBI route would have been wise for Geoff's innocence, although thought it best to think this through again after Geoff had met with Martin. This would now be tomorrow afternoon as Geoff had received a diary invite with a meeting time and hotel confirmation from Martin's personal assistant.

Geoff told Nikki how Ricardo had shown his hand over the dead rat incident. Nikki was disgusted and still felt strongly about going to the police. Once again, Geoff reassured her that he would have further answers after tomorrow's meeting.

Saying goodbye until tonight, Geoff felt an extreme sense of isolation, loneliness and uncertainty, more so than the usual separation of wandering around an airport in between home and work. He was uncertain as to what to expect in the meeting; uncertain of what was going on. He was mindful of a connection with Ricardo. He had never before felt trapped by his own actions and the situation he now found himself in – made worse by his retracted statement forced upon him by Harry. So many questions, but Geoff doubted that he wanted to know the answers. Although, for his own sanity, he needed them so desperately.

He kept on thinking about the unnamed man in the front of the car. *Who the hell was he? How did he know Martin?* Geoff began to doubt his long-term future; all he could think about was the dilemma of whether to go to the FBI again.

His flight to New York was not relaxing at all. The numerous alcoholic drinks he consumed that evening had no effect on him. Becoming an introverted self-image like a photographic negative, he wallowed in self-pity and vodka, ignoring the previously downloaded emails on his phone, which was most unlike him.

No witty banter with the cabin crew, no eye contact with the other passengers, his social firewall was impenetrable to anyone in the vicinity.

Geoff always longed to be at home with the family on any flight. This time, being at home was the worst place to be. How could he go home without the full story? Even when he knew the facts, assuming he got them, what would he tell Nikki?

He decided there and then that the only option available was to go to the FBI. Geoff was a decisive person, and now his mind was made up. He was clear of his path and once again in control. Tomorrow's meeting would give him details that he would take to the FBI; he would call John later and arrange this.

Arriving at his hotel overlooking Central Park, it was getting dark. As Geoff put down the phone from ordering room service, the room phone rang again. Geoff answered quickly as he was still standing over it.

It was Ricardo.

'You bastard,' shouted Geoff.

Ricardo quickly demanded that Geoff stay on the phone.

Geoff was of course curious, so he gave him the benefit of the doubt.

Ricardo explained, 'Geoff, look, this is not personal, just business. Your arrest yesterday was—'

'How do you know about that?'

Ricardo continued, 'People I know had it arranged, my friend, just like the other incident. You must be clear that you are involved in something that requires your support. Do not go against us, Geoff; the outcomes would not be good for you.'

'You bastard, Ricardo. What have you done? Why were you involved in my arrest? Have you any fucking idea what it's like to be marched off a plane in front of other people branding you a terrorist. Me, a fucking terrorist!'

Ricardo attempted to calm Geoff's anger. 'I know you are not happy. You will feel clearer after meeting with Martin; although, I must tell you that he will not be openly giving you all the answers. You will need to convince him that he can trust you with the detail. There is a lot at stake here – more than you can imagine.'

'He is going to bloody well tell me, Ricardo, or else I will get the FBI on to you,' added Geoff in a strict tone of defiance.

'Geoff, do not be too hasty here. You have already retracted your statement, which is bad for you, but please do not get confused with knowing all the facts. This is why we are reluctant to share these with you. You must sleep on it, and then convince Martin of your trust and loyalty when you meet him – otherwise, you may find yourself alone and in a darker place.'

'Take your threat and shove it up your arse. In fact, Ricardo, you are acting like the fucking Mafia! Piss off and leave me alone!'

Just as Ricardo commented that Geoff was already involved, Geoff hung up. He realised that this conversation would not be traceable by the authorities. He sat on his bed staring out across the park as darkness fell.

Geoff was starving. With all the things going on in the past twenty-four hours, he had only eaten basic rations provided by the FBI. That said, given his hunger at the time, their basic hospitality was a most welcome treat.

Geoff tucked into his room service. A ritual he had completed many times each month, yet this time feeling some empathy with his Muslim co-workers fasting for Ramadan, truly deserving this meal after a period of nothing. Other than the alcohol he had consumed, but he considered this did not count. At least that was his justification to himself.

He called his wife. Somehow a full tummy was always the best time to talk to her away from home, and he was typically in less of a rush, calmer and ready to listen more intently.

The conversation was full of pauses, neither side doing much talking. The kind of conversation with few words, yet the participants knew the support from the other, something only marriage or long-term partnerships can offer.

Geoff confirmed that he was going to the FBI and he opened up about the call from Ricardo, which only served to inflame the situation and push Geoff further in this direction.

Nikki was supportive, not in general, but of this action. He would soon know about it if she did not agree.

As they said goodnight, Geoff reassured his wife that things would soon be back to normal, offering the meeting with Martin as the stabilising factor.

An Executive Decision

Not a wink of sleep was expected that night, yet somehow Geoff nodded off and woke up at the unusually late time of 8 a.m. Checking his emails, he ignored the sheer volume of messages and selected just a few to read. Geoff felt the need to involve himself once more in matters of day-to-day business, which kept him suitably occupied over breakfast and for a few hours in the office prior to his meeting.

Waiting for Martin in the executive office reception, Martin's secretary, Veronica, brought Geoff a coffee. As she handed it to him, she asked if he was okay following the arrest. Geoff was taken aback by her knowledge of events, but it was clear that she had no idea of the detail from her questioning.

Geoff simply evaded the question by saying that he was taken into custody to help the FBI with a covert sting operation on one of his fellow passengers suspected of terrorism. Clearly Veronica did not believe this given her body language, which Geoff instantly recognised. It was a sufficient detail for an experienced executive PA to know when to stop asking questions. After all, she had been trusted with a lot of confidential information over the years, so Geoff felt no discomfort saying this with her.

The coffee felt unusually hot, burning his lips as he sipped from the large white cup held carefully by its small handle. Geoff gazed out of the window and focused on a nearby building watching people in the distance going about their business. He recognised that beyond the self-importance of his own colleagues, how relatively small he was amongst the dozens of high-rise blocks each with hundreds of people all doing similar things, caught up in their own little bubbles, like miniature worlds of their own, focused purely on their own politics and ecosystems but ignorant to factors beyond this.

The door to Martin's office opened

abruptly. It closed again rather gently after hearing voices, as if their conversation had taken on another unexpected dimension. Geoff felt anxious as though the people inside were discussing him and conscious that Martin knew he was waiting outside.

As usual, Geoff was early. His anxiety was self-inflicted, but this was understandable in his own mind to be feeling such emotions given recent events. Geoff was eager to secure Martin's support, an endorsement perhaps or a paternal pat on the head to confirm that things were still good between them. Not that Geoff typically needed this, although today felt somewhat different.

Just then Paul Newark, the global legal counsel, entered the executive offices where Geoff was sitting. He acknowledged Geoff with a familiar nod and handshake as he moved towards Veronica's desk. 'I need to talk to him,' he said, referring to Martin as he carried on walking.

'He has someone in there, Paul,' Veronica stated.

Paul continued walking towards Martin's office replying, 'Yes I know, he has just called me.'

The look on Veronica's face showed her displeasure that Martin had not informed her of

Paul's unexpected visit. 'Sorry, Geoff,' she said. 'He knows you're here, so it must be important.'

Yes, thought Geoff, *it must be important. It must be about me as Martin has clearly invited Paul to attend the meeting before I go in.* Geoff was aware of his increased heart rate, his anxiety growing as he played out the various scenarios running through his head.

Who else is in the meeting with Martin? He was concerned that it would be someone he did not like, pissing in his ear to suspend him. His thoughts were on his nemesis. A lady who was the cuckoo in Martin's nest and happy to throw out other executives in favour of her own career progression. Carolyn Fraser. *What a bitch*, he thought to himself. A lady, if you could call her that, who had risen through the ranks of corporate life by hopping into other people's roles like a whore jumping beds. It was rumoured that she had slept her way to her last VP role at Jackson, Smith and Cooper, the global advisory firm based in Boston. There were no such rumours in this organisation, yet he still believed the stories.

She was the result of an 'any cost' kind of gal in Geoff's mind, only loyal to her own motives, never giving a toss about anyone else. He liked to believe that Martin saw through this. Opportunistic bitch that she was, Geoff thought she would be the type to make the most of his arrest, looking to use this as an opportunity to self-promote at his expense and jump into his shoes.

Geoff had crossed swords with Carolyn before. He had overheard her talking to Peter Benson, one of his long-term pals in corporate governance, highlighting her personal views about how one of the trading companies was being run and inferring that she could do a better job. *Yeah, right*, he had thought at the time. But it did cause unrest, an investigation and a few sleepless nights for a few of the local leadership team. Geoff entered into a heated discussion about this because he felt that her opinions were politically motivated at the expense of others, which had wasted time and money for the company, was completely unnecessary and just flag flying – her flag, obviously.

If it was her in there, she would be poisoning the conversation with concerns over publicity, share price impact and Martin needing to make an example of him to demonstrate shareholder confidence, suggestions of action and putting the company first.

Yes, no doubt sowing her bitter-tasting seeds of how she could add value in his job. Despite being, in his opinion, of limited leadership talent and lacking depth beyond her overconfident persona. These were no doubt boosted or created from having the most amazing body and model looks that would intimidate the most successful men and be the envy of her female colleagues who dreamt of being her.

Geoff was not typically sexist; he just resented her methods. The previous stories of her career progression, if true, would not have endeared her to him, yet even he had to recognise that she was an attractive person. Maybe this was part of the resentment. He was much older. At her age, he had not reached the dizzy heights of VP in such a large firm. He was always biding his time hoping that his talents would speak for themselves through results and hard work. He had failed to understand, in her generation, how she had become so powerful within the organisation given the relatively fewer years of work she had to offer. It was inevitable that at some point Geoff would become a dinosaur with people like Carolyn, and many others besides, biting at his corporate heels, looking at dragging him down like some unexpected tyrannosaur attack, rendering him redundant.

Geoff was feeling the middle-aged insecurities he had seen so many times in others during his career. He hoped he would never face such a time. Yet old age was that unstoppable train moving towards its final destination, which you were unable to jump off without impending danger.

Geoff took a sharp intake of breath and muttered to himself, 'Snap out of it, man.' He stood up and walked towards the window of the seventeenth floor. Geoff was always able to turn a negative into a positive. He was self-motivated and successful. Moving around would get him out of the rut of sitting in the faux leather chair staring at corporate pictures to help him focus.

Looking through the window, he began to fixate on the ground, which was never a good idea – especially when feeling insecure. To Geoff, it reminded him of falling from a great height. What if he lost his job? Falling from such a great height in career terms would be fatal at his age.

Geoff knew that he was not feeling himself. His armpits were damp with sweat despite the air conditioning doing its job reasonably well. He looked around to see if he was being watched, as his next action was to remove his jacket. Being typically British, he did not want Veronica to notice his dark underarm patches. Even though she was getting on with her job, concentrating on other things, Geoff still felt it appropriate to keep the jacket on. Instead, he casually took his paper handkerchief to wipe his forehead and gave a little attention to his armpit as discretely as he could.

The door to Martin's office opened. It was double panelled, the right-hand side typically used, and out walked Carolyn looking at Geoff as she approached him. She greeted Geoff with a smile and prolonged eye contact, which he was keen to engage with, particularly as reading body language was a sport to him. He could see through that self-centred bitch's divisive manner that she was up to no good. Geoff reminded himself that it was not always good to be right about things given his earlier thoughts on the closed-door meeting taking place.

As she left the executive office suite, with Martin's office door not quite closed, Geoff looked towards the small gap as if his hearing depended on it.

Veronica's phone rang. She looked up at Geoff and acknowledged the caller, which Geoff suspected to be Martin. 'You can go in now, Geoff,' Veronica said with a kind and supportive voice.

He recollected the various times over the years that he had called to talk to Martin in the office. He was sure that she knew nothing of this meeting other than the time and date, something that was both reassuring and threatening to him. Threatening because Veronica may not be aware of any pending dismissals.

His typical confident swagger was lacking as he entered the room. He was greeted by three people, but only Martin looked directly at him.

He obviously expected Paul to be in there, but he was also joined by the CEO, Barry Isaacs. This was a surprise as he was only expecting Martin: his boss for a personal discussion.

Martin took the lead with Paul mostly looking at the floor, only occasionally looking at Geoff without expression, while Barry tinkered with his smartphone, reading emails or something like that, pretending to be detached as he often did but usually tuned in regardless.

Martin poured a coffee for each person as he welcomed Geoff to New York. 'Always too long in between out get-togethers, my friend,' he said. 'Good to see you and thanks for coming in.' Martin went on to explain why Paul and Barry were being involved. 'Since we last spoke, things have happened, Geoff. And such things have caused a bit of a stir, which you can imagine has created some negativity and concern for us.'

Geoff needed to interject. 'Concern for you? I am the one subjected to a bloody FBI interrogation and—'

'We understand, Geoff. I am sorry. Yes, you must have been through an ordeal. Tell us about what happened,' added Martin, this time in a more sincere tone, although no doubt fuelled by feelings of guilt for not asking straight away and jumping in with a selfish corporate guard.

Geoff continued to relay the events of the arrest, focusing on the shock and unhappiness of his mistaken identity, his involvement in the communications with Ricardo and his 'alumni' offering his own interpretations on what was going on.

'Be careful, Geoff,' added Paul, 'you know what it's like to be on the receiving end of false accusations.'

Geoff paused in his verbal tirade and thought about his comments parallel to Paul's. He did understand, but the FBI were looking into something he could not ignore. 'Talking of accusations, Paul, I have one for you. Ricardo is up to his Latin neck in it. He sent a dead fucking rat to my wife as a warning for me to look after one of his homies, and he called me last night to remind me to keep my mouth shut. And, while I'm on the subject, who the hell was that bloody lawyer you sent me?'

'We never sent you a lawyer, Geoff,' Paul added quickly. 'That was nothing to do with the company.'

Geoff's eyes glanced down to the left as he thought about this once more. 'Harry Delaney said that his friend Carlos knew Martin – Carlos being another lawyer,' said Geoff. 'But then you know that already, don't you?'

Martin's stare jumped from Paul to Barry before speaking again. Neither of them said anything to each other. 'Geoff, I want to talk with you rationally, but you coming in here shouting and getting emotional just makes me feel uncomfortable in doing so.'

Even though Martin was still calm, Geoff could tell that he was not trying to be kind. His eyes were portraying his clinical business side. As a CFO, he needed to be calculated and clinical at times; Geoff once more sensed this.

Barry looked up from his previous ignorance from scrolling through his smartphone. 'I thought the reason we were going to get together was to talk through your future, Geoff.' Barry was giving the impression in his tone of voice that he was almost disappointed he was there. 'Instead, I am wondering, Martin, whether we should reschedule to next week when he's in a less shittier mood?'

Martin looked at Geoff as he turned around from the window. 'Two things, Geoff. Firstly, we need to put this FBI thing into context and move on with a degree of certainty. Secondly, to discuss your future as part of this company – meaning that I have put my bloody neck on the line and recommended you for a board seat –

this FBI mess and your attitude have just stirred up a mess that we do not like.'

'What's more, Geoff, your finger pointing towards Ricardo is not helpful in this process and it needs to stop. You need to get over your feelings, or else,' added Paul.

Strong words from a corporate lawyer, thought Geoff, *one who has had so many splinters up his arse from sitting on the fence.* 'What do you mean?' asked Geoff. 'I have always been loyal to the company, Martin – you know that more than anyone. I have always towed the company line, regardless.'

Paul intervened, 'Now, Geoff, can you carry on doing what we ask, regardless?'

'Well, yes, although Carlos the lawyer suggested that I would get answers today from you, Martin,' added Geoff.

Martin looked at Barry; his stare lasting an uncomfortable few seconds as Geoff continued.

'And there was this other chap who picked us up from the FBI office in Atlanta. A man who refused to introduce himself, like some sort of Mafia boss. Actually, it was him who said that you would give me answers. So, are you able to give me something that will explain what is going on?' Geoff was authoritative in his demand. He had nothing to lose as he looked at the others who themselves seemed unsure of what to say to him.

'Okay, Geoff,' said Barry. 'I can see this is a difficult time; we should level with you. After all, only a few days ago we were making space for your promotion. We need to trust each other.'

Geoff smiled and nodded positively. His obvious delight that the talk of promotion had finally arrived was pushed aside by the feeling that something they now said could dent his usual enthusiasm and derail his chances of corporate happiness – if ever there was such a thing.

The conversation continued to flow a little friendlier for the next ten minutes or so. Then they focused on Geoff's retracted statement to the FBI.

'Do you believe this was the right action?' asked Paul.

Geoff knew he should agree, yet his true self-image reflecting back reminded him of how he was his own man, honest and just – not at all corrupt, or tolerant of those who were. Geoff continued nodding politely in agreement. He knew he would not have believed him if he were in Paul's shoes. Neither of the other men were as well trained in the art of reading body language as himself, thankfully. Either that, or Barry no longer had the time or patience for playing such games.

Barry continued, 'You have done a great job for us, Geoff, as VP of talent, and we are proposing that you will take on the position of president of people reporting to myself, dotted line to Martin of course. There are some who expect me to fire you on conspiracy of terrorism,' Barry said with a laugh.

'Carolyn, I assume?' questioned Geoff.

'Yes, among others,' replied Martin. 'Say what you like about Carolyn, she is a tenacious, hard-working woman.'

'Not to mention the nicest arse of any VP in the company,' added Barry.

Geoff loosened up. Such sexist remarks were dangerous in a company like this, not to mention completely inappropriate. Barry opening himself up like this was a positive step. Geoff laughed and began to relax as his own body language clearly recognised these references were designed to put him at ease.

Carolyn was indeed a good-looking young woman, power dressing in stockings with the outline of her suspenders often seen through her tight-fitting skirts. That is if you ever stopped to take your eyes from her red lipstick, expertly applied like a professional window dresser making a statement in an upmarket shop in Milan, which framed her perfectly aligned white teeth.

As the four men continued to break the ice, bond and edge closer to concluding Geoff's promotion, Paul changed the subject. 'We need you to sign this statement, Geoff, just a press release. It talks about your arrest and the misunderstanding, highlighting that you were helping the FBI with their enquiries.'

Geoff read the piece of paper handed to him. There was nothing controversial, although prior to the press release at the top of the paper it denounced any contact with the person the FBI were watching under the terrorism act, an employee of the company, who Geoff had clearly met, sacked and then reinstated.

Geoff calmly hovered his finger over that paragraph and stated to Paul that this may not be entirely correct. He attempted to make his point known in a light-hearted fashion.

Paul asked Geoff to sign it as the company would not want any trace of a board member associated with such a person, and once again throwing in a reference to Geoff's imminent promotion.

The men continued to laugh as Geoff reluctantly signed the statement and press release. They knew that, just like the statement he retracted to the FBI, he had no other option.

Barry looked at the paper, smiled and suggested that Paul take care of the press release and internal documents while they all took an hour to take care of a few things. They were then to meet for lunch at Barry's usual venue where he entertained on a regular basis. This was to celebrate Geoff's promotion.

Geoff grabbed an office and called his wife. Nikki was already awake, anxious to hear from him. She was pleasantly surprised to hear Geoff sounding upbeat, particularly given the events of the last few days as he focused on one thing: the talk of his promotion.

Geoff reminded Nikki that whilst he did not have the offer in his hands, he believed that the promotion would come with stock options or shares, taking away the pending insecurity in his future career. He would be a reasonably wealthy man one day, a thought consuming his behaviour and giving him the rewards he so richly deserved.

'So, what about the FBI, the arrest, the twat in South America?' she asked.

Geoff was a little embarrassed that he was still without the answers. He reassured Nikki that the meeting was continuing over lunch and he felt this was all just a big misunderstanding. All the while, deep down, he was still aware that they had not opened up fully given what he had expected when he arrived that morning.

His wife was suitably unimpressed, her tone saying more than her few words spoken to him. Geoff knew that he was wrong to dismiss the recent events as water under the bridge. He still needed to push hard for answers, but he could not jeopardise his promotion. He would be walking a tightrope of discussion for the next few hours.

Their conversation did not last long as Geoff knew that Nikki would soon show her anger at his current weakness, having forgotten his recent emotions and her hate mail from Ricardo.

Similarly, Geoff wanted to crack on with his lunch meeting, preparing himself for a positive reaction and taking to the calculator to pre-empt his additional disposable income.

Dining with the Gods

Geoff felt hungry once again as lunchtime approached, like his brain had been unburdened somehow following the meeting earlier. In the back of his mind, though, he knew that he still needed to ask some serious questions.

The three men met Martin in the lobby at noon. They chose to walk the few hundred yards to the office block where the restaurant was situated on the top floor. Surrounded by glass windows from floor to ceiling, the eatery demanded a glorious view of the Manhattan skyline and Hudson River, depending on the table location.

Geoff noticed that Paul was carrying his leather briefcase. The once black leather polished exterior now scuffed and showing the signs of many years of battle. He always had it with him, carrying files and heartache scarred by the corporate life they all knew too well.

At the table, Barry was greeted by a smartly dressed and well-groomed man, who he assumed was the restaurant manager. His use of first names reflected a familiarity only seen through good friendships or, indeed, regular large tips.

Barry was more fun in this environment. Like a man freed from the confines of a cell: happier, more relaxed, gregarious to a fault and most likeable.

Geoff was in awe of his charm as he was acknowledged by three other diners, all mature businessmen looking like a million dollars and not concerned about menus without prices. This was not the sort of place Geoff could typically afford despite being a VP on a high salary.

The company expenses policy Geoff knew was far from generous. His position as VP allowed this to be stretched to great hotels and travel, but for some reason entertaining and subsistence expenses were closely watched. Probably for the reasons of preventing corruption; therefore, something Geoff always respected – being the man he was.

Martin ordered the wine with no need to look at the menu. It was a predetermined decision, like buying a train ticket to the same location. No thought was needed. The wine was not a familiar label to Geoff, but it was good for him to experience a taste of the executive life. He deserved it, in his opinion.

The very attentive waiter watched from a distance for the slightest indication that they were ready to order. Geoff noticed this and judged the rating of the restaurant as top quality. He was exclusively attached to their table, far enough away to respect the conversation but tuned in to their needs.

Before the wine arrived, Paul opened his cracked leather case and handed Geoff some papers. There were lots of others still in there.

Geoff took the A4 stapled document whilst glancing at the contents in Paul's case. He wondered whether there was anything else in there that he would be taking away with him, like a person opening a birthday card and shaking the envelope to see if anything fell out. His curiosity was taking over even though the paperwork in his possession was what he had dreamt of for many years.

Paul asked Geoff to read it through, which he did. Surprisingly, every word was read despite noticing the second page containing the juicy terms.

The sommelier came to the table and attended to the empty wine glasses, which Geoff noticed as pure clinical professionalism. The others seemed oblivious to this detail, as though it was commonplace to be served like this every lunchtime.

They continued talking while Geoff took his time reading through the papers. He was delighted to see comments about his deserved promotion and that he was to be based in New York three days per week. He expected this, as did his wife; but this wouldn't be an issue because their marriage was so strong. This was another way of describing a marriage that had allowed them to drift somewhat, with the passion for each other found in their early years together now a distant memory.

He raised the document towards him so his eyes could not be seen easily by Barry as he read the terms of the offer. *Holy shit*, he thought. A $100,000 increase in basic salary, annual bonus representing a 0.1% of net profit and stock options worth potentially $2 million over the next 4 years. Although it was not tangible cash at the moment, the stock options were generous and the payout viewed as conservative.

He realised he was smiling to himself like a Cheshire cat with a bowl of cream as he continued reading about the lucrative pension, which was more than expected. He didn't want to look up until he was able to compose a serious business face. *No good*, he thought. He was not able to do this even as talented as he was. It was smiles galore as the others interacted with him.

Barry took the lead, of course, and made a toast to Geoff's well-deserved success. 'Welcome to the board, Geoff. Good to have you – someone who we know we can trust.'

The word 'trust' seemed to resonate in his head like a disturbing humming sound from a poorly tuned TV. He needed to confront them about the things on his mind. First, however, he accepted the offer with both hands as if he were clinging to a life raft for safety. He had made it to the top.

Laughing and joking with his team of executives, two men were missing. One man in particular: the president of operations, François Bertrand.

'Is François off on some glamorous trip?' asked Geoff.

Barry responded whilst still smiling from the previous part of the conversation. His face slowly turned into business mode again. 'Sadly, we will need your skills once more, Geoff. François may need to move on, although he does not know it yet, which is a difficult decision.'

Looking puzzled, Geoff pushed a little deeper. 'So, what is it, Barry? Can you let me know what has happened and how I can help?'

Barry's eyes were now no longer full of fun and laughter.

Geoff knew how to bring focus to the discussion, and he could see that something was not right. François was a long-term employee, an executive for about five years and a member of the recent management buyout that would have surely bonded them forever.

'I'd like to think that we will be able to rekindle our friendship again one day,' said Barry. 'Even if it may take a few years.'

Geoff could see the discomfort on Barry's face. He noticed Paul and Martin glance downwards at their drinks as if to consciously avoid engagement in the conversation. Well, on that point at least.

'How can I help?' offered Geoff. 'Do you need me to exit him?'

'No, no. I need to do this myself. HR have documented the terms, so that's sorted. I need you to meet his successor, make the offer, etc. You know the drill, Geoff,' summarised Barry in a way that said just get it done in his own style.

'So, the new chap, what's he like? How did you meet him?'

'What's with the fucking twenty questions? Just get him on board and make it happen. I don't want to go through a justification exercise every time I make a decision,' snapped Barry.

'Okay, guys, let's not get grumpy with each other – life is too short,' interjected Martin quickly to diffuse a situation that had the potential for Barry to stand up and walk out. Martin was smiling, but it was false. He was clearly aware of the sensitivity of whatever had caused the split between them.

'So, how do I reach out to the newcomer?' Geoff asked Martin, avoiding Barry for obvious reasons. The lunch was supposed to be a celebration not a confrontation.

Paul jumped in, 'I will give you the details of our offer, Geoff. No need to worry. It's a chap called Dimitri Petrov. He says his friends call him Peter, for some reason. He is coming up tonight and staying over for a few days, and then meeting Barry on Saturday morning before he flies home to Ukraine for a few weeks. He will be based with our logistics team in Chicago. He's an MBA graduate, Six Sigma trained to deployment champion level and a big hitter from the Russian equivalent of Panasonic. So a good guy to have on the team, we think.'

Barry was silent, no doubt stewing in the juices of the recent departure of François and whatever the hell happened there.

Geoff continued to follow the flow of the conversation, which was surprisingly led by Paul. The lawyer was not known for his gregarious personality, yet he was clearly capable when needed.

A few drinks had been consumed, with Barry taking on more than the others. As the next few bottles were replaced, Geoff was trying to contain his drinking; yet the expectation and peer pressure was a compelling reason to let things go just a little more.

Over dinner, just as the delicious main course was finished, even though Geoff could have eaten more, Barry continued talking without a prompt. It was as if he had held back until the alcohol had loosened his vocal cords and untangled some difficult messages.

'You remember the MBO, Geoff?' asked Barry. But before Geoff could engage, he continued, 'Well, look, it's like this. Our funding fell through at the last minute for us to buy out the previous shareholders. It was just so bloody stressful, but I managed to secure funding from a private equity business based in Chicago among other places called International Rescue. The deal is that they put someone on the board in a functional capacity to keep an eye on us but also to help us grow. It's a typical business model with these private equity venture companies. Sadly for us, they insisted that they would be appointing their own director in charge of ops, so I need to fire François. It has made me fucking ill, I can tell you, but it was a condition of the funding, as the other guys will know. What could I do?'

Geoff's respect for his group CEO deepened as he felt his heartache through every word. Barry was a good speaker. He was the leader, so you would expect this, but his emotions were usually less obvious. Passion in abundance, but not sadness and regret. These were new to Geoff from any CEO he had known. It was a rare glimpse of the man inside the role – vulnerable like any of us just doing a job.

Once again, Geoff felt that his loyalty to this man had only improved. He was letting his guard down, exposing his vulnerability. Less loyal subjects would mount an attack if necessary and take him down. In any political environment, such vulnerabilities would never be on offer to most. A reflection, then, of Geoff's new position of trust. Geoff felt for the first time that he had indeed made it to his final career destination. In some ways, this was more empowering and fulfilling than the new terms he had been offered. A real added bonus. Although Barry was an explosive character at times, Geoff felt that he had entered the inner sanctum – an environment reserved for the elite, of which he was now a part of.

Geoff needed to say something while he could. A mark of respect perhaps, or just to let Barry know that he was feeling his pain and supportive to a fault towards him. 'I am here for you, Barry, I always have been. Thank you for sharing this. I will do all I can to help you on this or anything else.'

Barry's head lifted, not just physically but in a way that his eyes seemed to brighten just a little. It was clearly what he needed to hear, and Geoff had played this situation in the best way possible.

Geoff raised his glass and said, 'To François, wishing him well in his next venture.' A pause was felt by all while Barry glanced at him. Looking at the others, he added gleefully, 'And to us.'

The four men drank to the toast. Geoff peered over his glass at Martin, who was feeding on Barry's changing emotions and looking for direction in the conversation. It was friendly, but Geoff could tell that there was more to say – more for him to learn.

In a split second, he wondered about the timing of his appointment. He knew that he would not have been promoted now a new operations director had been appointed by the major shareholder, which gave him a sense of both fear and security. A strange combination flowed through him like an alternating current, changing seamlessly with each millisecond.

'So Dimitri or Peter, whatever he calls himself, can we trust him?' added Geoff. It was a crafty question picking up on the thread of conversation that had just bonded them.

A silence was noted as Martin and Paul abruptly looked at each other.

Barry jumped in without hesitation. 'What do you think, Geoff? He is looking over our shoulders every day talking to the very people who we rely on for our livelihoods. No doubt he will be the next CEO whenever I fuck up, which in their eyes could be anytime. That's why I need my team strong, able to keep him in his place. Even though I cannot keep him out of my operation, we need to make sure that we are more in control of what is happening. More than ever, in fact; I do not want to end up in prison.'

Recognising the body language, Paul gave away an immediate worried look. He, too, was concerned about something. But how could he ask?

'Guys, look, you are clearly worried, and I really should know what is happening. I do not want to join you over porridge making sandbags for good behaviour,' Geoff boldly stated with a false smile.

Only Barry could respond, despite Martin's eye contact prompting him to explain, like a gentle nudge from a parent to its child while giving a comforting nod of approval and encouragement.

Barry glanced at Geoff as he looked around the room and then back to each of his team. Perhaps he was making sure that no one was within earshot. As he opened his mouth to speak, the waiter approached. He had mistaken Barry's look as an opportunity to approach the table.

No one talked as the menus were handed out. The silence must have been uncomfortable for the waiter, but he was well trained on knowing when to back off. He looked at Martin and suggested that he would be ready whenever they were before moving swiftly towards the edge of the room. There he stood patiently and unobtrusively for most of the meal.

Barry once again looked around as he leant forward. Paul and Martin obviously knew the whole story; they were shareholders too. They also leant towards the centre of the table hoping not to miss Barry's comments. Each of them moved the wine and water glasses so as not to knock them over in the process.

Anyone watching from within the restaurant must have been intrigued. The nearby piano music was a good cover for flapping ears as well as a pleasant addition to a lovely dining experience.

Unregulated Pharmaceuticals

Geoff looked from side to side as if to expect an intrigued diner to catch his line of sight. He was aware of a human's ability to read lips having studied lip-reading at a basic level from his days at school where many deaf children attended. He was concerned that their conversation, which he believed to be sensitive, would be open to those not privy to it.

Barry paused for breath before speaking. Seconds seemed like minutes as they leant towards each other in silence. 'Our shareholders have sixty-eight per cent, Geoff. We have put everything we have, including personal debts for the next twenty years, to owning a part of the company.'

Geoff almost felt sorry for Barry as he explained that he had put his multimillion-dollar home as security towards a massive business loan against his shareholding alongside Paul and Martin. In the back of his mind he knew that this risk was fuelled purely by personal greed. He had forgotten why he was sitting down drinking and celebrating his promotion; he was definitely a hypocrite, although it felt better to judge than be judged.

'Their majority shareholding gives them a lot of say in how we do things. Results, bigger results, and favours for favours,' Barry continued.

'Favours? What favours?' asked Geoff.

Barry gestured for Geoff to move in closer.

He could not move any closer as his stomach was pressed firmly against the table, yet he attempted to do so and then edged back slightly due to acute physical discomfort as Barry continued.

'Without their money, we would have lost a lot: our jobs, the company was going downhill, mass redundancies, shares worthless – those previous shareholders really stuffed us all. The deal we have, Geoff, which you will benefit from, is increased shareholdings through future options at a low purchase price. So, over the next five years, if all goes well, we sell up, pay off the loan and live like kings, my friend. With all that on offer, we are expected to not only get results but help their other businesses flourish. It's called corruption, Geoff, with a big fucking "C".

Geoff stared in amazement as Barry went on; there was no holding him back. Paul poured another glass for everyone as the alcohol loosened his tongue and oiled the wheels of disclosure and transparency.

'None of us knew how they would act once they took us over. These guys claim to be a large private equity firm, although they have serious connections that are, we think, illegal.'

Geoff looked at Paul as the word 'illegal' had been mentioned. Not that it was his fault or lookout, just a subconscious reaction.

Paul reacted to Geoff's look. 'We did the due diligence, sure we did. All we saw was the same as the authorities: a number of part-funded corporations with global operations.'

Geoff was about to ask Paul a question, but he was not entirely sure what to ask, even though he felt the ball had been passed to him for return.

Barry just carried on steamrollering his comments over everyone else's. 'Look, we are expected to help them transport goods from A to B under our packaging with their clients being our clients, you know...' This was a statement not a question, even if Geoff was like a rabbit in headlights unable to respond. 'We are talking unregulated pharmaceuticals, Geoff. The white stuff – fucking cocaine!' said Barry, raising his tone despite keeping the volume low.

'Drugs?' exclaimed Geoff.

Martin punched him firmly on the thigh as he was closest.

Barry and Paul attempted to smile falsely as if to give anyone overhearing a sense of comfort and disguise the real topic.

Geoff was acutely aware of his error and apologised as gently as he could. 'Sorry... Shit... What are we going to do about it?'

Barry looked at Geoff confused and frustrated, like a teacher who had explained his subject many times to a needy pupil. 'Have you heard what I've been saying, you fuckwit? We are in it up to our fucking necks. We need to get on with it, make some money and get out under good, favourable terms – but it will take time, talent and strong leadership if we are to keep these guys happy.'

Geoff responded in a concerned but supportive tone. 'Why not go to the FBI, Barry? They would help us surely?'

'Are you really that stupid?' asked Barry. 'We lose everything and go to prison as a best-case scenario.'

'And as a worst case?' asked Geoff, his voice suddenly a little deeper and more sincere.

Martin touched Geoff on the arm, a friendly gesture to assume his attention. 'You end up propping up a bridge somewhere, strengthening the ready-made concrete mix via the building corporation that they own.'

Geoff looked at Martin as he said, 'You guys, you are funny.'

'How long have you known me, Geoff?' asked Martin.

Geoff knew Martin was serious, so his demeanour reverted to one of concern.

Martin continued as he spoke over Barry's attempts to dominate. 'The threats you've received from that twat Ricardo are not coincidental. I am sure it was him who got you arrested on the plane. He is a dangerous, nasty man. Charming and talented for sure, Geoff, but the inside man to the corporation.'

'Do you mean the *Mafia*?' Geoff said the word slowly to be understood.

'At last, he gets it!' barked Barry in his sarcastic tone while looking at Paul, expecting him to pick up the point, but Paul just wolfed back his full glass as an adult necks a spoonful of medicine to avoid the taste but then realises the effect instantly.

'But the Mafia were squashed by the FBI about twenty years ago,' stated Geoff in naivety.

'Yeah, right,' added Barry. 'Take down a leader and another one fills the void – sharper, more political, level-headed and this time in finance not gambling.'

'That's called evolution,' added Paul.

Barry continued to talk openly. 'You stand in their way, they trip you up. Do it again, you feel pain. Continue to oppose them, and they kill you off.'

Martin continued, 'You mentioned the dead rat incident with your wife, Geoff. This is no doubt due to you sacking Abiola. Basically, he is Ricardo's man on the ground at the other end. In addition to our normal logistics operations and moving manufactured goods, they have started to move powder across the globe using our business as cover – a legitimate business. Some of our vehicles are being retrofitted with false panels at the bulkheads, each capable of carrying thirty kilos of their poison to profit from killing the next generation – our sons and daughters. That's why, Geoff, we will all go to prison if the FBI or any other local authority gets a sniff of this.'

Geoff thought about this for a few seconds. He took his glass and gulped the expensive wine. His brain quickly calculated that he had done nothing wrong; his innocence at this stage could not drag him down. He should use the corporate whistle-blower policy introduced into the legal system years before to protect him. He began wrestling this emotion against his newly confirmed loyalties for his new promotion. This was not as straightforward as he had hoped.

'With Peter Popov on the board shortly,' Barry said disrespectfully, 'we need the strength in numbers, Geoff. You were always destined for a board seat. Yes, the timing of your promotion helps me get a better balance, especially as François needed to go.'

Geoff knew that François was a straight-playing business leader. Corruption was abhorrent to him and he would sooner be sacked than support it. He could see that his dismissal was a kind gesture for the right reasons. 'Sure, Barry, I get it – and, as I say, I'm thankful for the opportunity.'

There was a pause across the table as Barry was the obvious choice to break the silence. 'That's why we need trust, Geoff. You see now why this shit is so sensitive, that we can only appoint a trustworthy person such as you. Otherwise, some fucking do-gooder would go to the FBI and put us in prison.'

Paul and Martin laughed as Barry's words hit Geoff hard between the ears. Thank goodness he was a body language expert or else he would surely give away his actions with the wrong look, yet he was in relative safety as Barry was by now a little sozzled to say the least. Geoff did not feel drunk. This news was having an instant sobering effect on his brain.

The natural pause in conversation prompted another bottle followed eventually by a cheese course, something to nibble on and soak up the next course of wine.

Geoff now felt guilty as Barry continued sharing. His thoughts of contacting the FBI were still on his mind. He knew it was the right step, but Barry was right about one thing: timing was everything.

As a parent, Geoff could relate to the impact of illegal drugs on the streets of Britain where his children were growing up. But how would he get out of it? The whole of his career had awaited this promotion. A mere five years and he could retire a rich man. What a dilemma. His judgement earlier on Barry's greed was now hitting him hard. It was like looking in a mirror and seeing the same greed, but with considerably less risks than the others – he had not invested any personal money or used his home as security.

What would his wife say? *Shit, yes, Nikki.* She would go crazy if he told her the newly discovered information. They were close and preferred no secrets. She was aware of Ricardo, or at least Geoff's thoughts on him, so how could he get around it? This was by far the most stressful promotion he had experienced, ever.

A part of him loved the thrill, the danger, which was probably from being married to a Gemini for all these years. Balancing two scenarios evenly and being indecisive like her was a characteristic he both loved and hated at the same time.

Alcohol, promotion, money, greed, or all of these, thought Geoff. All of the aforementioned could hang him. 'You can trust me.' The words were comforting to Barry and Martin, but he could tell that Paul was still on the fence from his body language, even though he'd had too many glasses of wine. Maybe this was just Paul being typically guarded as any lawyer would be.

He had to admit that they did make a formidable team. It would have been the dream team if François had not been axed. This new chap Dimitri the 'Russian' forcing himself in was less than positive, and Geoff felt like he was now on a rollercoaster unable to get off. It was not the way he liked to control things, nor was it what he had planned to do. Yet caught up in the moment of promotion, he was trapped until the ride was over. Five years perhaps. Could be longer, but it could be shorter if he went to the FBI.

This action, if he went through with it, would result in his new team of executives being arrested and banged up for a long time. Would there be death threats? Surely not – they could not know for sure that anyone would be dealt with in such a way. He recalled the number of times an angry soon-to-be ex-employee made the odd threat to him or the company. It was common; after all, people like to vent their anger towards such events. But, then again, people saying that they would kill you and actually doing it are two completely different things.

He had felt such emotions before when he was treated badly by an ex-CEO, who unnecessarily discarded him due to an episode of ill health. He recalled immediately the conversation all those years ago. In that instant he would have used a gun. Only lasting a moment, it was not an emotion that stayed with him; it was not calculated or predetermined. *Everyone has had these feelings*, he thought.

'Has anyone actually been killed?' Geoff asked.

Martin responded in a voice of panic. 'Not that we are aware of, but we don't know what these animals are capable of. These are criminals of the highest order. Have you never seen *The Godfather* films for heaven's sake?'

Geoff laughed briefly, but it was short-lived. As he looked at the others, he saw that they were serious.

'We are talking about a global empire of people funded by crime, laundering cash like it's going out of fashion, and I believe that anyone who threatens or disrupts this will get trodden on,' added Martin.

Barry turned quickly to Geoff and sincerely added his own thoughts. 'There is big money at stake for them. Goodness knows what they're into. All we know is that with this Peter chap and his crew in place, our distribution channels will soon increase from South America. For us that means an increase in turnover of exports to other parts of the globe, which will increase our product sales tenfold.'

'What do they do with the genuine products we make, Barry?' quizzed Geoff.

Barry responded almost enthusiastically, as if presenting to external clients or investors. 'We store them up for three months then ship to

Africa, Malaysia and back to South America at used stock value, and the cycle continues over. Okay, in five years' time things will change. There will be a glut of our products out there, and our sales will drop like a ship's anchor at sea, but by then we will be clear of this shit and it will be someone else's problem. Like fucking parasites, they move on; it's what they do. They have no problems making money, Geoff, just getting the product from A to B. So that's why they need a genuine business to work with – us, in other words.'

Geoff felt as if he had been a little naive in his earlier thinking. Maybe the compelling reason for keeping quiet was obvious. 'So, when I was in Atlanta, the FBI read my emails. Did Ricardo get hold of these through his "friends in high places"?' he asked.

'Are you kidding, Geoff?' added Paul. 'The FBI asked for them; we supplied them. We still have a business to run, and answering the FBI's request for disclosure is part of this. We thought it would help you.'

Barry added, 'Plus, we received a call from your lawyer friend telling us what to do. The email they sought was the one you wrote to Ricardo reinstating Abiola.'

'You bastard, Martin,' snapped Geoff. 'You told me to do that when we spoke.'

'I had my orders, Geoff, and so did you,' Martin replied.

Paul was keen to add some context. 'So basically, Geoff, you pointed the finger at Ricardo – the man we all know to be setting up distribution channels for his own goodies – then you got him off the hook by asking his homie to be reinstated. If ever the guy is arrested on his own merits, this will backfire on you. You do see this, don't you? You've retracted your statement to the FBI, so you're in this as well, my friend. It's important that you see this for yourself.'

Geoff felt a cold sensation move from his shoulders to his back, a realisation that Paul was right. Seeing Paul's wry smile as he delivered this message was disconcerting in itself. 'How did that Latin twat get my home address and know my wife's name? I suppose you gave him those as well?' Geoff demanded.

'No, no, not at all. They have this, somehow they know,' Martin confirmed. 'My wife, Sam, received a message also – a severed head of a pig, denoting in their strange manner for me not to be pig-headed. It was before Ricardo joined. The person who called me never gave his name, it was someone I had never spoken to before. It seemed I was being obstructive to the expansion of their operation.'

Barry added, 'It started off being a package from South America to the US, then it got out of control. I called the head of distribution to put a block on a few shipments that I was concerned about, then Adina, the current Mrs Isaacs, found our labradoodle drowned in the small lake in our garden. They had no trouble letting me know that I could be replaced if I was drowning in the process. They needed some extra help on a building site. I think I got the message. Don't tell Adina; she just thinks her beloved puppy was a bit too curious about the carp.'

'So, these people,' started Geoff, 'the private equity people, surely Interpol and FBI know of them?'

Barry shook his head in defiance. 'They are a legitimate business themselves, a proper global equity fund. It's just that their associates, no doubt the investors or people who put the money in and the companies they support, are some sort of crime set-up. Americans, South Americans and Russians, and no doubt one or two places in between. Paul checked out their portfolio. They only publish the largest companies they invest in, but from a glance we could see that they are into everything. From steel to soap powder, beverages to vitamins and even production of agricultural vehicles in Ukraine.'

Martin interjected, 'One thing we can see is that they push in capital at every opportunity and have seen good results in return. Okay, it's money laundering on an industrial scale. How else would you see a vitamin retail empire grow exponentially on an international scale from its humble beginnings.'

'So what's next for us?' asked Geoff.

'We welcome Peter Poppodopoulis to the board, give him some rope and hope he hangs himself,' Barry whispered in a drunken bleary-eyed manner.

'Hoping he keeps us away from the noose,' added Paul.

'Seriously though,' asked Geoff, 'how do we keep away from the trouble and these nasty guys? I for one want to stay out of prison and stay alive.'

'We have all agreed to carry on running our business as usual, staying out of the way of Dimitri and his merry men. So long as our goods get there on time, my head is happy up my own arse,' Barry humoured as he looked at Martin.

Martin was then prompted to add, 'We are here to make money and increase our shareholdings using the money from International Rescue. As far as we know it's legit funding and we use it to grow. Their growth channels pushes products for us, too, Geoff. What do we care if it's left on a heap and shipped back to South America as second-hand? We get reasonable residual value on the market, which shows consumers that it's a good purchase. Five years, Geoff, then we're out.'

They nibbled on the cheese, hungry from the copious amount of alcohol, while continuing their conversation on matters relating to the business as usual.

Then Barry focused on the soon-to-be operations leader. 'So, Geoff, can you meet up with Dimitri tonight and sort out his appointment?'

Tonight, thought Geoff. By now he was feeling rather weary on the grape juice. It was fine wine and more than drinkable. Hoping he could sober up enough by tonight, he agreed.

Paul sent a message from his smartphone, needing his glasses to do so, and showed the email to Martin. He probably did not trust his words in case of poor grammar or spelling caused by the light-headedness felt by all at this time. The invite was sent. Geoff was to meet Dimitri tonight at 7 p.m.

Geoff was pleased as always to do what he could, yet he felt completely compromised in making the appointment. Scapegoats are made from such things. Although, it was part of his job for goodness' sake, so how could this be misconstrued if investigated? The thought oscillated around the legal position for a few minutes while the others continued their dialogue.

Paul handed him the terms of Peter's appointment, which were essentially similar to those he had been offered. Barry then asked if Geoff could welcome him to the board that evening. Martin and Paul would be doing their bit with him in the morning, and then meeting Barry on Saturday at his home, which could be an awkward situation for him.

Geoff was limited in time as he flew out the next day to return home.

Barry handed the waiter his black American Express card, a card with no limits, the card of choice for the rich and famous, despite no request or bill being presented to him. Barry took the receipt without looking, not caring: expenses took care of it.

Geoff could not help thinking that the cost was into the thousands. A similar expense claimed by a VP in Italy whom he had to dismiss only last year, which was due to him abusing the expenses system through client entertaining. He was accompanied by his rather attractive marketing manager, whereby rumours had existed over an affair and was causing some embarrassment.

The four men walked slowly to the office to go back to work. Geoff was feeling the impact of the wine after inhaling the fresh air. No doubt the others did, too. Geoff wondered how the hell these guys were going to get any work done. He felt embarrassed going into the office in such a state breathing fumes over the staff. He felt he should tuck himself away somewhere, so he suggested this to Barry.

Barry called his secretary and told her the news of Geoff's appointment. Geoff could tell that she was pleased from listening in as he stood alongside. Barry then asked her to locate an office for him. Welcoming Geoff into the new world of riches and status, he added, 'Next week we will get you into the corner office on the sixteenth floor – you know, the small conference room used by sales.'

Geoff was clearly pleased with this, although Martin highlighted that it would still double as a conference room because he was not permanently based in New York.

He was rightly proud of his achievements and forgot momentarily about the sinister implications of his appointment. 'And what of Carolyn?' asked Geoff.

'Oh, that self-centred bitch had the fucking audacity to flirt with me while trying to milk your recent incident. She is just out for herself. Okay, she does a great job, but not someone who will progress until she can demonstrate putting other things before her own career. You will have the good fortune of being her line manager. Welcome to executive leadership,' said Barry.

Martin quickly said, 'I wouldn't have minded if she'd tried it on with me.'

The four men bonded as they laughed stewing in their alcohol-infused blood and inappropriate testosterone-fuelled banter.

No.4 Manhattan

Alone in the office, before reflecting on the conversations, Geoff did what any married man would do: call his wife with the good news of his promotion.

Nikki immediately answered the long-awaited call from her husband following the agreement for him to go to the FBI. She had been understandably concerned.

'Hi, darling, you are now talking to the *president*,' Geoff said glibly.

Nikki was in no mood for fun and games. 'What about the FBI?' she demanded.

'Calm down, it seems that the Ricardo thing was just a bit of high spirits and corporate politics, you know how it is,' he offered.

'You're pissed, aren't you?' Nikki reacted.

'Sounds like you are, too,' Geoff said playfully, insinuating that she was angry with him.

Nikki would not let it drop. The one-sided telephone call continued as she bombarded Geoff with demand after demand and accusations of him being a 'weak, pathetic knobhead', a phrase she often used. Nikki did not use strong bad language, which Geoff always found endearing and a good quality to nurture their children. Thomas and Alice were growing into fine young people each with their own talents and both showed love and kindness to others.

Geoff then discussed that he would be appointing a new board member to take charge of operations and hopefully nip Ricardo's bad boy behaviour into touch.

Nikki was confused. 'Was that not the French guy's job?'

Geoff told her that he had been sacked for something or other. She accepted this instantly as Geoff often came home with a similar story following his business trips. 'So, tonight I am appointing a new guy called Dimitri. I might not be able to talk until later,' he added.

Nikki trusted the views of her husband when it came to business matters, but she was not resting on the point about the FBI. It was clear to her that Ricardo needed locking up. For now, their attention turned to the promotion.

'Congratulations, my darling, this is really well deserved. I bet you're pleased?'

As Geoff told her about the terms being offered, her thoughts immediately turned to a house move. She always kept a watchful eye on the property market and had a good idea of what she wanted, but it needed to be within the same area as their friends and school.

Geoff had no doubt that during the coming week he would see a number of properties being promoted by her. He was happy in their current home. The mortgage was paid off and he had felt comfortable there for a number of years. With the children growing up fast, he felt no need to move. Maybe just downsize in a few years' time.

They had a good conversation. But after telling her that he did not want to move, the conversation turned back to the FBI. She was curious why Geoff was not going to discipline Ricardo. After all, that was part of his job. It was his expertise and a typical weekly activity for him.

In the end, the two decided that it was best to talk later or at the weekend. He was in no mood to justify himself having just delivered a potentially wealthy deal for them both, and he was still feeling light-headed despite this sobering call to his wife.

Geoff regretted the call as it ended. He wished that the conversation could have been happy. He was now feeling fed up. He just wanted her to be as excited about it all as he was. Sadly, it was not to be.

After a few resentful emails and reading the draft announcement regarding the main board restructure, which he tweaked a few times as it was going out to the press, he thought he would go to his hotel to freshen up, sober up and man up for the meeting with Dimitri.

The hotel that Veronica had booked was not his usual one; this one was much nicer. No.4 was a discrete place nestled only a few blocks away from his office. Not your typical Holiday Inn or Plaza-type establishment. Luckily, the cab driver knew of it.

There was no check-in desk, which was most unusual. Instead, there was a room similar to an executive office where he was welcomed and his card details taken. Geoff liked it very much. It was not like any other hotel as the lobby was not full of loitering business people sneaking a crafty wireless connection over a coffee. It was guests only. Such facilities were on the top floor with security to circumnavigate if you wanted to use them.

'Wow,' he mumbled out loud. He had no idea this place existed, and at *only* $1,300 per night per room. He felt a sense of guilt as he was escorted in the lift to his apartment by a hotel representative.

As he arrived at his room, he was shown around the two floors of his apartment with impressive views of the New York skyline. As the hotel employee was just leaving, there was a knock on the door still ajar.

'My name is Paoblo De Silva, and I am the general manager. I live here in the apartments. I am at your service. My card to you, sir.'

Geoff was impressed with the slick manner of his approach and was pleased to be treated in such a way. He confirmed he had a meeting that night and asked for a table.

'Ah yes, sir, with Mr Petrov. It is all taken care of. Mr Petrov is a familiar guest of ours, and we are happy to offer him a room this evening.'

Geoff thought nothing of this connection. After all, he would not have been shocked if the man was dressed in a 1970's gangster suit and white-ribboned trilby and carrying a cello case. Geoff smiled to himself at this thought as he pictured a character from *The Godfather* with a Russian accent.

As De Silva broke eye contact and closed the door in a confident yet subservient manner, Geoff felt the need for a doze. Although, he knew once he gave in to his sleepy desires that he would not be sharp for the meeting later. So he decided to sober up in the spa and pool. He often had the chance for travel recreation, but he felt that he should make full use of his spare time given the stunning facilities on offer tonight.

He was greeted at the reception when he arrived on the third floor. No room number needed as he was shown around by a member of staff. Geoff was impressed once more with the great facilities, which included a self-service swim-up bar. Geoff felt the need for a sauna, but he had a crafty swim and checked out the bottle of champagne already open with a beautifully crafted chrome stopper. After sweeping the water from his hair and gently rubbing his eyes, he poured himself a glass. It was delicious and at pleasant odds with the temperature of the heated pool. Geoff looked around as the cool wine was consumed. There were other guests in the pool and spa, but no one was looking. *Oh, what the hell*, he thought. *I'll have another glass.* It had been a tough week and the champagne was as refreshing as the swim itself.

As Geoff tilted back his head to consume the contents of the flute, his eyes glanced to the left where he saw a young lady heading towards the pool. As if casually looking around surveying the facilities, this was a polite distraction before observing the young lady again.

She elegantly walked down the steps into the pool, pausing for a moment as she acclimatised to the temperature.

Geoff could not help but look at her. He tried to be discrete, but it would have been obvious to others that he was staring intently.

The young woman was stunning. Geoff was embarrassed to be looking, yet he continued to absorb his surroundings, particularly her, with her long raven hair and magnificently slender shape. 'Geoff, you could be a dirty old man one day, my friend,' he muttered to himself, chuckling as he did so.

Geoff was never the kind of man to be distracted by a pretty face, even when away from home. He was always aware of such things, yet he never felt the need to initiate any kind of affair despite his marriage having the usual ups and downs. He had been divorced previously, as had his wife, and he did not want to jeopardise his marriage by a one-off moment of weakness. He branded others he had seen succumb to temptation as idiots.

That said, he always understood their reasons. With familiarity and children being the ultimate passion killers. Geoff, with needs and desires like any other person, would sometimes fantasise about meeting someone attractive, having meaningless sex and moving on without any emotional attachment. A fantasy that was merely human but never enacted.

As he moved on from his thoughts, he noticed that the young lady had disappeared under the water. He decided to move to the steam room, something he loved to do, the heat helping to remove any problems with every bead of sweat that disappeared down the drain.

The unbearable temperature and suffocating steam was a reminder of the entrapment of corporate life. Geoff especially enjoyed exiting the room and breathing in the normal air to fill his lungs with a feeling of freedom and survival. He always attempted to track his time, as though attempting the world record of breathing in hot steam, confident that he would be able to set a new time by going beyond his previous tolerance. In reality, he'd always had enough after around three minutes. He needed to emerge from the steam just like a person holding their breath under water.

The door opened as Geoff reached his limit and a waft of air entered the room. It was refreshing and offered an extension to his suffering. His nostrils tracked the cool air like a radar system following a fast-moving object. With his eyes half closed, he noticed the presence of two women. Almost voyeuristic, Geoff peered through the steam, clearly noticing the shape of two very beautiful women. The room was quite large compared to those Geoff had used in other hotels, so the visibility was impacted, but Geoff's senses were tuned in to their voices.

As a massive fan of the James Bond films, he was always alert to and turned on by an Eastern European accent. Geoff listened intently as the two women continued their conversation. He understood none of the dialogue, yet he remained focused on their words as if they were disclosing national secrets.

Geoff's eyes, once cool compared to the rest of his body, were now beginning to sting from the heat and steam. He was desperate to remain in the room, but he needed to leave. He headed next door to the sauna, which was occupied by three others.

He sat down on a towel near the smoked brown glass door. The others left after just a few minutes, leaving Geoff to stare out through the glass. As he did so, the two women from the steam room exited. They stood outside the door allowing Geoff to observe them up close whilst hearing them talking. One was the beautiful young woman from the pool earlier; Geoff was fixated by her. He estimated that she was in her mid-twenties and possibly Russian. Her subtle and sweet laughter filled him with excitement; her smile was completely enchanting and captivating.

The two women moved on after a few minutes, leaving him with his thoughts, desires and fantasies, which continued long after the women had left.

Geoff headed back to his room. He was dreading the meeting with Dimitri that evening, so the earlier remote encounter with the women was a great distraction – one he could not forget.

Showered and dressed, he sat looking at the stunning view out over the city. Geoff felt lonely wanting to share this experience, so he called his wife.

Nikki answered quickly and was keen to relay the events of her day. Not pausing for breath or asking about him, Geoff switched off mentally and drifted on to his own issues. Then Nikki turned her attention to his position with the FBI again.

The conversation was difficult, and Nikki was clear. 'The only course of action is for you to spill the beans to the FBI – to do the right thing.'

Deep down Geoff knew this was the right thing to do, but in the moment of his meetings with Martin, Paul and Barry it felt right to be one of the team, part of the new board structure. Geoff had waited so long for this; he would not want to throw it all away so quickly.

The telephone conversation ended badly. Nikki was understandably worried that her husband was being blinded by the temptations of his promotion. The trappings of success she desired so badly without wanting the risks.

Geoff was confused by her words. He knew that she wanted the advantages of the new role; on the other hand, he had to find a way of doing the right thing without compromising any of it. Cake and bloody eating it sprang to mind. Geoff was frustrated because she did not recognise that the promotion would end if he did the right thing. The company could even cease trading. Going from big job to no job, and without any time in the new role, he would not find it easy to find something comparable in terms of either salary or enjoyment.

Geoff looked at his smartphone and flicked through his unopened emails looking for something intangible. Not unlike his teenage son looking at a screen at any old information that may present itself. Zombie browsing, as Geoff referred to it. He was now a victim of it himself.

The compromising position he found himself in seemed to play a secondary importance to the promotion and rewards he faced under his new contract. He pondered the dilemma of finding a bag of money left behind from a security van – something that happened to him at college – and deciding whether to disclose it, pick it up and hand it in, or casually walk away with it. In an ideal world, with no one watching, most people would dream of what they could do with the cash. At the time, Geoff handed the bag back to the driver. Then, after being shoved by the security man in an attempt to compensate for his obvious incompetence, Geoff had instantly regretted it.

This time the rewards were given to him as a remuneration for the responsibility he held. After a few years, his shares would be worth a great deal of money. He could then enjoy early retirement or a very comfortable semi-retirement with the security he deserved and had waited for years to achieve. A dream come true.

A Fallen Hero

Meanwhile, back at the office, Martin, Paul and Barry were deep in discussion. They were worried about Geoff's meeting with Dimitri. Connecting a man of principle and a man from a corrupt society was a recipe for confrontation.

Barry knew deep down that Geoff would need to fend for himself, especially now he was part of the board. In any event, they were both new to the company and both board directors. Barry feared his intervention would see Geoff acting in a subservient capacity alongside him. That he would hide behind Barry's title.

Martin and Paul had opposing views. 'What happens if Geoff meets Dimitri and he doesn't stay the course?' Paul suggested. 'We will all be in the shit if he stands up for his principles.'

'Remember, he has waited years for this opportunity, always been loyal and this opportunity ticks all of his boxes,' Martin added. 'I think he will stay aligned with us.'

'Geoff on form is a good addition to the board. He may be just what we need in keeping Dimitri and his cronies contained in their activities. Okay, we're stuck with them. We need their money; they need our distribution resources. Our job is to make sure their greed does not get us all compromised and put in the slammer. With Geoff on our side, we stand a better chance,' said Barry.

'And if things go wrong?' asked Paul.

'Then we have someone to hang it on,' added Martin.

The three men continued their discussion over a few glasses of wine. Barry always had a few bottles in his office for entertainment purposes, although this meeting was more like a board discussion than a social event. The men always favoured airing their opinions, concerns and plans over enjoying the finely chosen labels in Barry's drinks cabinet.

Geoff's promotion was indeed well planned by the board. An extra and super loyal head on their side would help retain some controlling balance of decision-making over the investors' appointing Dimitri. Yet, in the back of their minds, the motive to appoint Geoff rather than any other vice president was to do with his involvement in certain situations.

Geoff had already compromised himself in reversing the redundancy of Abiola in France, someone deemed to be a key operational contact for the 'investors' side operations'. Geoff had also compromised himself over Ricardo. The only recommendation in writing was formally proposed by Geoff – something that could come back to haunt him if he decided to talk.

Paul was keen to recall Geoff's interaction with the FBI, when he retracted his statement about Ricardo. This single act was enough to hang him if things ever went south. Although, Paul as a lawyer, and a corporate bastard at that, was keen for further links to be established just to add further weighty reminders of his involvement.

Barry interjected, 'Chaps, can I remind you that we are not here to burn him, just have some insurance. If Geoff gets burnt, it means we have run out of options – and, frankly, I am keen to avoid that. Put your sword away, Paul, for fuck's sake. You sound like the executioner during the French revolution.'

Paul recognised his comments had been somewhat aggressive, even though they were true.

Barry had a knack of getting to the point quickly. A trait he recognised was needed in most CEOs. Barry had the ability to make people feel a million dollars or like a steaming pile of excrement. Often, the path was difficult to determine in advance.

Paul actually liked his directness and leadership style, which was open and inclusive, and the potential of extreme wealth that had been shared with him, for selfish reasons. Something Paul constantly reminded himself about.

In truth, Paul was jealous of Geoff. Paul had once been a politically correct legal brain in other corporations. Whiter than white and uncompromising in his approach.

He was once caught up in a dilemma of whistle-blowing that saw his boss, a CFO in a large firm, being arrested based on his evidence. Don was the chap. The then CFO was the man who had brought Paul through the ranks of corporate life from legal adviser in the contracts team to the head of legal services. Essentially Paul's sponsor in life, creating a masterpiece from basic ingredients.

It was a sad tale. The credit control team were at head office for a series of meetings with Paul and others. The usual things relating to taking legal action over unpaid contracts; typically productive and collaborative with successful planned outcomes.

On one particular occasion, there was a new recruit named Julia who was in her early twenties. She was incredibly attractive, not necessarily in looks but as a person, and someone you could not help but like instantly. Paul was the meeting sponsor and responsible for taking them for dinner at the hotel where they were staying.

He had been uncomfortable in noticing some unwanted attention towards Julia from Don, which seemed both inappropriate and overstepping the boundaries of sexual harassment. Julia was sweet to everyone, not at all flirtatious but friendly, considerate and a good listener. She was clearly uncomfortable to be in the presence of the big boss CFO and unsure how to react to his attention, as did Paul and others.

After a good meal, much drinking and laughter, Julia and others retired to their respective rooms, with Paul and Don downstairs continuing their conversation with the head of credit control.

Don had not held back on his drinking. Eventually he made his excuses and left the table to use the men's room. Paul was concerned after some time had passed, so he walked towards reception on the way to the men's room to check if he was okay. As he walked back to the restaurant, he saw Don coming down the staircase that led from the rooms. Paul noticed his unusually flushed complexion and that he was looking decidedly worried against the backdrop of the red and cream wallpaper. As Don approached, he noticed scratches on his face. He left for the exit without stopping to talk to him, presumably heading towards his car.

Typically, Paul would have followed him to prevent Don from getting behind the wheel given his alcohol consumption, yet on this occasion his concern was how he came by the scratches.

As he stood by the staircase looking at the night manager sitting behind the reception desk, both of them noticed Don's scratches. Then the reception phone rang. It was Julia in room eleven. She was in tears reporting an attempted rape by Don.

Paul flew up the stairs with the night manager. They found the door open and a young lady sitting on the floor clutching her knees for comfort and support.

Paul instantly knew what had happened, despite never needing to question Don's behaviours previously. He could not deny what he saw.

He was asked to give evidence to the police, whereby Don was suspended from his work and dismissed based on Paul's statement. Don was arrested, but then released due to lack of evidence. In any case, his career was in ruins. It was a tough call to make at the time, but Paul's integrity was strong and unwavering on such things. He had lost many nights' sleep over his actions: bringing ruin upon his friend, mentor and career champion.

Geoff reminded Paul of the person he once was. Something that Paul resented. He was in one way pleased to involve Geoff in a dilemma that would compromise his strong values in the same way that had happened to him some time ago.

Paul recalled the turning point in his own life when he faced a challenge on his values. It was not so long ago.

He had reached the dizzy heights as president of legal and risk, reporting to Barry. Barry had presented a business case to buy out the previous owners. Meaning that he would need to use his home as security against a business loan; something shared by others on the board.

It was an exciting and stressful event lasting several months. As a lawyer, his involvement was intense as both a shareholder and corporate lawyer.

Shortly after raising the capital to fund the management buyout, an event happened in one of the manufacturing facilities in Asia. The death of an employee. Understandably, an investigation was carried out by the country's safety committee. Beyond this, big companies are subject to the press making a meal of it. The bad press alone was the reason for the investor withdrawing.

Given the way the ownership transfer was constructed, Paul and others were committed to buying the company – but without the funds to match. Which meant they would be broke after a few months.

Barry had been the saviour by introducing an investor at the eleventh hour to keep them afloat and in jobs. Paul had at this point made the decision to preserve his assets, his job and his life by getting into bed with investors who would demand more than an appropriate portion of shares. Something that Paul would never have envisaged doing two years previously. He had been loyal to Barry, trusted him and recognised the limited options that lay in front of them.

Paul's involvement with the new investors was constant and intense throughout the purchase phase. He could never have claimed ignorance to their demands, their corruption; he feared the consequences from declining their requests.

To make sure of his commitment, Paul had encountered their actions directly. Something that would remain with him like a stain on his favourite garment. The investors' way of reminding him of their reach, power and lack of moral behaviour.

He remembered the October morning waking up at the local hotel No.4 in Manhattan, where he had met the lawyer representing the investor Carlos Ferreira in an attempt to agree a few points. Not the kind that lawyers put in writing, but those based on unofficial demands that were far from legal. Those that needed to protect the investors and offered rewards in return.

Paul had awoken that morning with limited recollection of exactly how he got to his room that evening. He remembered the confusion that he faced: the evidence in his room of a drunken party, bottles scattered, furniture broken and a bag of what looked like flour on the coffee table. The white powder was distributed randomly over the glass surface, the chromium edging and the carpet.

Pausing to make some sense of his surroundings, there was a sudden knock at the door. Mr De Silva, who was and still is the hotel manager, stood with two men wearing dark blue jackets with yellow lettering highlighting that they were the FBI.

As Paul stuttered his way through the limited options to explain the mess in the room, the door closed and one of the FBI team moved towards the table. He was interested in the white substance decorating the piece of modern furniture.

Paul was speechless at the sound of the agent's confirmation that it was cocaine, and a shit load of it.

The agent told another who was standing inside the doorway with De Silva that the bag had a street value of $30,000. Enough to convict him for a long time.

Paul sank to the floor on his knees, his head in his hands. He had no concept of the events leading to this situation and was unable to piece together any sort of explanation.

Rather than arrest him, Paul was thankful that the three men sat down and talked to him.

De Silva said that he did not want any form of scandal in his establishment. It was a rather expensive, exclusive and discrete hotel – not for the mass travellers – more of an invitation-only club. De Silva took the FBI agents to the other side of the massive suite and continued his private discussion away from Paul's curious ears.

De Silva returned after a few minutes to see a confused, broken man with a grey complexion fearing for his life. 'I have managed to reason with these people, Paul, and for now they are happy to bury the photos of the event on the basis that you do something for them,' De Silva stated.

Paul confirmed that he would do anything to help. An unusual response from a lawyer, but totally understandable given his predicament – if not a little naive.

Standing together without speaking, the FBI agents relinquished control of the conversation with De Silva. Something Paul did not understand and thought highly irregular upon later reflection.

De Silva went on to highlight the details of the request: to put a series of bugs in Barry's house. His boss, as he was then, being monitored by the FBI.

'If I won't do it?' asked Paul in a defiant tone. After all, Barry was his boss, friend and trusted business partner.

The two agents walked rapidly towards Paul. They grabbed him by the arm and performed a move on him like something from a film. He was forced to his knees once again and handcuffed.

'Okay, for fuck's sake. I'll do it. But all this stuff, the cocaine and whatever this is, I need to be released without charge and not compromised,' Paul quickly responded, this time in lawyer mode again.

Turning to each other, the two agents confirmed that Paul must visit Barry at his home in the next forty-eight hours and place five separate bugs in the places they requested.

Paul knew nothing of how to place these devices. He was not a resourceful man with a toolkit. He was a lawyer, for goodness' sake, and it was his boss. However, the men explained that the devices needed no tools or knowledge.

Highly uncomfortable, Paul agreed to do the deed. And, more importantly, to never divulge the events or demands to anyone. He agreed just to keep his sorry arse out of jail.

The FBI agents took photos of the room and Paul. They took away the bag of drugs that lay in front of him, confirming that his prints were all over it like a bad rash as they did so.

He had just two days to plant the bugs or face prosecution. By now, he had sobered up somewhat. He recognised that he was not capable of taking drugs, had no idea where they came from or how the stuff came to be in his room. Although, looking at De Silva, his shady smile and piercing eyes, it was clear that it was a set-up of big proportions.

As the FBI left the room, De Silva remained and closed the door behind them. 'I hope you understand your situation, Mr Newark?' he said. 'Either you do what we need or you will...how you say...will be completely fucked.'

'What do you mean by "we"?' demanded Paul.

'I represent the interests of our mutual friends. The same people who are funding you and own this hotel, so it would be in your best interests to help them. That way, they will be keen to help you fund your management buyout. Besides, I don't think you have a choice,' De Silva responded.

Paul thought for a moment before saying, 'And the FBI people, are they...you know...on your payroll?'

De Silva paused for a second or two and developed a supercilious smile. 'Let's just say that our mutual friends are well connected and your supportive actions can make anything seem less threatening for you or can make things disappear. Forty-eight hours, Mr Newark. We look forward to welcoming you for dinner with Mr Carlos Ferreira to tie up your loose ends.'

With that, De Silva slid away, like a snake evading capture. *The slimy little shit. Who the hell were these people?* One thing for sure was that he had to comply with their demands. Paul stared at the five bugging devices looking for inspiration on how to do what was needed.

The same day, and once in the office, Paul manufactured a reason to bump into Barry. They typically saw each other every day, but Barry's secretary, Veronica, confirmed that he was not to be disturbed. This was unlike him, especially as they were in the middle of the funding deal.

Paul sent Barry an email asking to meet him that evening and suggesting, for obvious reasons, he would drive to his house.

Barry responded after thirty minutes that they meet at No.4 for a drink. He was untypically evasive, which was a problem for Paul, especially as he had genuine reasons to talk to Barry about the deal along with the unofficial and contractual terms proposed.

After some email tennis, Barry agreed for Paul to come to his house. A decision that was both disturbing and exciting for Paul.

The two men had no further interaction until eight o'clock when Paul arrived at Barry's house. Barry was clinical in his approach to Paul, which was very unusual indeed. Surely Barry could not be aware of Paul's hidden agenda and his brush with the FBI?

Paul broke the discomfort. 'Are you going to open a bottle of red, or am I to die of thirst?'

The two men smiled at each other; Barry needed no excuse to open a bottle. Within minutes, the awkwardness had given way to one of their normal open conversations.

'You seem unhappy today, mate,' said Paul.

'Just some personal stuff. Nothing for you...er... Tell me, where are we with the deal?' asked Barry.

Paul explained the terms, but Barry gave no reaction to Paul's comments. It was as if he knew them intimately already and was merely taking the time to reflect and chew over the uncomfortable terms that were on offer, as if they could affect them somehow.

All the terms were discussed, with Barry confirming his acceptance of the deal. He was basically conceding, given that the choices were to either accept the terms or lose his house, his job and no doubt the jobs of many more otherwise the company may cease trading. At least Barry gave the impression that he was still in control – something that was only convincing himself.

The two men continued the conversation into the late evening, with Paul deliberately consuming more than the legal limit of alcohol.

At midnight, Barry needed to sleep and offered a spare room to Paul. He readily accepted as this gave him the opportunity to secure the devices for the FBI.

By one o'clock in the morning, Paul had achieved his goal. The listening bugs were planted as requested, hidden like submarines during the Cold War; dormant until activated by the corrupt men who were supposedly beyond such things, the men appointed to protect and serve.

One device was hidden underneath the kitchen hob, between the surface and the drawer. Another in his office, in the top drawer of his desk nearest to his phone. Another in his library, which was where Barry had his cinema system with more DVDs than books. One in his car under the driver's seat, which was more complicated as it took a while to locate his keys and he was conscious of the lights flashing on in an otherwise pitch-black driveway. The final device was to be placed under a ceiling light in the living room, the type of light that is countersunk into the ceiling itself, but it was just a quick movement downwards and the bug popped into the hole that the light sits in.

The job was done; there was no turning back. Paul felt instantly sober. The sensation of sickness filled him as he felt both regret and relief.

Despite his physical and emotional exhaustion, Paul was unable to sleep. Riddled with extreme guilt, planting monitoring devices on his boss was torture, divisive and morally incorrect.

The Alpha Male

Barry started his career with the company seventeen years ago. Eleven years ago, he divorced and remarried. He always described that period of his life as disastrous: he was on the brink of failure, financial ruin and depression.

His ex-wife had all but taken his soul, and drained him of his money, rights and dignity. It would be hard to recognise Barry as he is today from this description. Rising from the ashes of such a disaster, Barry had made a successful return to happiness and wealth over the last six years. He had remarried and benefitted from taking two businesses from failure to success. Each time he took a percentage of the share options, which amounted to a good level of excess and enabled him to heavily reinvest in the company. Having experienced riches to rags and then back to riches, Barry would not survive a return to being broke again. Therefore, the deal being offered by the investors was a better alternative to losing everything once more.

Barry was unlike Paul and Geoff: he was much more focused, hungrier, from a poor background and completely insecure. Not that he offered this vulnerability to those around him, of course.

At the point of agreeing the management buyout of the previous major shareholders, Barry was fearful of them selling to another corporation. This could have resulted in a new CEO being appointed.

Given his obvious insecurity, he acted with some desperation in seeking funding even though at the time everything was looking great.

The death of a colleague was sad. Barry was a man of the people, and he always believed that people were the most important ingredient.

The colleague in question, Jaypee from Manila, was found dead at work. Jaypee was a long-term manager whom Barry had met many times. A stickler for safety, he was responsible for the production of white goods at the plant in the Philippines. When Jaypee's death was announced, Barry failed to accept that he had fallen into the steel press on the night shift. His death came at a crucial time in the refinancing of the management buyout, which ruined any hope of the investors continuing to sign contracts because of possible legal action and ultimate bad press.

Shortly after the incident and while on-site in Manila, Barry was approached in his hotel by Carlos Ferreira, a lawyer acting for a private equity business called International Rescue. He offered him a funding solution for his management buyout.

Barry was not naive; he was aware that the death was well-timed to cause negative impact to his funding. At the last minute, Barry had few options other than bankruptcy. He was convinced that this was no coincidence, particularly as one of the contract terms was assigning their own new production manager to replace Jaypee.

Time was running out for Barry. The meeting with Carlos *the dodgy lawyer* was pretty much one-way traffic.

Essentially, they were offering $100 million in return for seventy-eight per cent ownership. An identical deal to the previous offer, which was suspicious in itself.

The main differences were that after five years progressive profit making, Barry could take his fourteen per cent shareholding to forty per cent, some of which would be offered to his team. He would need to increase profits by twenty-five per cent, which he believed was achievable over five years. In return, Barry would oversee and facilitate the distribution of cocaine using the company's channels for their white goods from the Far East and those same unregulated chemicals from Europe and Africa.

Transport of goods would supposedly only happen once every three months, but this would be a mass transaction. To ensure the company could operate normally most of the time, International Rescue would insist on the company appointing their own team to run operations alongside normal employees. The corrupt ones would still take a normal salary most of the month, with a corrupt process in between for good measure.

Barry was always conscious that the private equity firm could make life difficult for him at any time. He had taken professional advice on working with International Rescue; to his surprise, they checked out well.

The private equity firm was pretty much that, a genuine investment fund offering cash for a share and often a form of control in the company. Just like any of their competitors.

Barry knew it was corrupt – a front for someone else. The Russian Mafia was his belief. Barry's previous attempts of negotiating had backfired; they clearly knew of his predicament. The coincidence of events he initially believed were nothing of the sort.

Looking back, Carlos Ferreira's comments were painful to listen to. Barry would remember them forever. At the time of meeting Carlos, Jaypee had just been buried. Barry was apologetic to Carlos for his less than usual upbeat self when the offer was made to fund his transaction. Carlos had offered his condolences, which Barry recalled as completely insincere, but he did not place too much emphasis on the moment recognising that he was merely a corporate lawyer with a job to do.

'I recognise the timing of your colleague's tragic death has caused your investor to withdraw,' said Carlos, 'but this clearly represents an opportunity for the people I represent.'

Barry thought that Carlos was an opportunistic bastard, but he was thankful for this opportunity for obvious reasons. Then, Barry smelt the rat that had crawled stealthily into the room. The rat called Carlos, that is.

'Firstly, Barry, we need you to do something for us: appoint a friend to replace Jaypee. His details are in the attached envelope.' Carlos handed a brown A4-sized package to Barry.

As Barry looked inside, the details of the new recruit stared at him. He already knew that his local country director had replaced Jaypee. Not wishing to be insensitive to Jaypee's passing, but it was just business as usual. 'I am always happy to welcome new talent, Mr Ferreira, but I believe we already have a new head of production. Sorry I may not be able to help you.'

'I don't think you quite understand, Mr Isaacs, we are asking politely. You could say that this job was made for our friend…literally,' replied Carlos, smirking.

'Okay, I recognise that he may be a good fit and I'm sure he is a talented chap, but I—'

'It would be a shame to kill anyone else, Mr Isaacs,' interrupted Carlos, quickly shooting him down. 'We thought that one example of our ability would be enough to alert you to our way of working.'

Barry paused for a few seconds before saying, 'How did you…? I mean…'

'Kill him?' asked Carlos. 'We have people everywhere. Your man seemed the sort of guy who was a stickler for honesty; not someone we could rely on. He was called in one night to sort out an issue, and it seemed that the issue sorted him instead. We decided that your company would be helpful to our distribution requirements, so we needed a reason for your investor to withdraw. A suspicious death relating to corporate safety is usually a good way of getting the balance in our favour.'

Barry's face filled with rage, his complexion looked like it did after too much red wine, without the benefit of enjoyment. The humidity of the surroundings were making him sweat at an accelerated rate. 'I'll have you arrested, you fucking murderer!' he exclaimed.

'Is that before you're arrested for corporate manslaughter?' asked Carlos in a playful tone. 'We have a witness to Jaypee's unilateral act of stupidity and another who will state that the safety guard has been missing for months. Naturally, with photographic evidence and some unanswered letters to yourself – fabricated, of course. Something that will fuck you up in terms of a safety lawsuit and make sure investors avoid you like a plague-ridden sewer rat. You decide, my friend. You are the CEO, after all.'

Barry sat down on the nearest stool almost collapsing with exasperation. He was sweating, stressed and feeling the adrenaline racing through his body whilst suppressing his need to fight. He felt sickened by this person in front of him. Good-looking, Mediterranean or South American, sweaty and quintessentially confident.

He knew that Carlos held the cards. Barry was trapped by an event that had been manufactured against him. He would either be ruined or maintained in some sort of executive lifestyle he had fought hard to attain and preserve.

'Who are you, really, I mean? Who are these people you work for? Surely I should know.

I mean, if I am to support this, this circus or whatever it is we're doing, I have a right to know what I'm getting into and with who.' Barry knew he had no right to demand, yet now was the time if he was to ask.

'Very well,' said Carlos. 'I will tell you what you need to know, but please remember that this is no game show. We make all the rules, we make things happen and we play for high stakes. And when so much is at stake, we will always protect ourselves by doing whatever is needed.'

Barry just nodded. He recognised that anyone who would kill to force themselves into a deal and get what they wanted were not the kind of people to cross or challenge too wildly.

Carlos went on to explain. 'International Rescue is a genuine private equity business helping companies such as yours with funding growth plans, rescue plans or buyouts. You may have wondered about this, but there is nothing illegal about it at all. This is business, nothing more.

'The seventy or so companies that are owned in part or in full by International Rescue are extremely profitable. Each one of these companies has a connection with the Ivanov family in the Ukraine.

'The family's representatives sit on the board of investors at International Rescue, with other representatives sitting on the boards of each of the investments or companies we own. The extraordinary profits are our way of channelling monies earned, with reinvestment of this into other businesses. Those who collaborate with us earn well, very well indeed. We keep the money moving, growing, and the businesses have, in the main, a normal operation.

'Once every few months, each business helps with the movement of goods that the family requires, this results in a seasonal boost in profits and the investors take massive dividends.

'The distribution of your white goods, for example, will result in us creating a false need for your products in some far-flung country. The cost of the goods we absorb via another partner organisation is a small price to pay for the value of the goods that are moved, sold and payments made directly to the family.

'It is simple, my friend, all we ask is that you keep your head down, make space for our own representatives to sit on your board, help us place our people in your distribution depots and ensure that you are well versed in how to account for the transactions we ask you to make.'

Barry was daring in asking, 'So, the goods you need us to move are what, exactly?'

'We move white goods too, Mr Isaacs, ours being smaller but more profitable than domestic appliances, shall we say.' Carlos laughed insincerely.

Barry's internal rage continued. He needed to keep his temper in check whilst using a handkerchief to mop his forehead and neck. He felt that he was melting in the warmth of his surroundings, even though he recognised that the air conditioning was still operating as normal. He knew he must be exhibiting stress and felt his heart pounding beyond any workout he was capable of attempting on his treadmill at home. 'Drugs, illegal drugs,' Barry stated with indignation. 'You want me to head up your fucking distribution channel and become a criminal.'

Carlos continued in his confident delivery. 'You're already a guilty man, Mr Isaacs. You have blood on your hands, at least that's how the authorities will see it. As the CEO, you and your friends will face an investigation, and we can make this go the way we want. You flatter yourself. We are not asking you to head up our distribution, just be the CEO of your company and play your part, as others do around the world.'

'I will need to get my CFO and COO on board. We are a team and they do hold some shares. This will not be easy,' added Barry. 'What if I cannot convince them? I am only one person; they may not like where this is going.'

'I have every faith you will do what is necessary. And if you cannot, we will help you remove the problem, just as we facilitated the change by appointing a new head of production,' said Carlos.

'Please no more fucking killing. There is no need for this, please promise me,' Barry pleaded.

'You are in no place to demand,' Carlos replied. 'No one wants this course of action. Just get the job done, then I'm sure this will be unnecessary.'

Barry once again acknowledged his position with a nod of the head as he held his chin. He was concerned about being found out; it was natural for a man with a lot to lose. 'What happens if I get caught? Or one of my team is caught?' asked Barry genuinely concerned, having never been a criminal despite being rather sharp and aggressive at times.

'Then you go down, that's obvious. If you compromise us, your family will help our construction business to make new ground structures – make no mistake,' said Carlos in a stern tone.

Barry wanted to punch the slick-haired, tanned chap in the face, although he knew this would not be a good idea at all. He believed his words. Barry knew that he referred to killing his family and putting their bodies in the cement structures holding up bridges and roads, no doubt in some Third World shitty country where they could easily control it. 'A serious question… How have you never been found out?'

Carlos was happy to oblige. 'We typically follow the same profile as any other private equity business. We hold on to companies for five to ten years, gradually giving back more of the ownership to their management team. We then eventually sell and move on to the next, in turn making a profit as any other by selling shares.'

Barry instantly had the image of a large, tanned, smooth-talking parasite in his mind, which gave some short-lived entertainment as he imagined himself swatting it with a rolled-up newspaper.

Carlos went on to explain that at some point between five and ten years, providing the company continued to grow its profits, he would be given a bigger share of the company until one day, when the investors deemed it necessary, they would sell their remaining shares, leaving the company to its core activities once more.

Barry lost sight of his original question; he was now focused on the wealth that could await him. This was suddenly worth a risk. Besides, he had no option but to comply. In real terms, he convinced himself that this was actually rather generous.

His anger about Jaypee's death soon gave way to fear. The fear of losing everything, being charged with corporate manslaughter, the fear of more people dying – including his family – and the fear that he may not actually be rid of such concerns after five years as discussed. Things had gone too far to walk away now. He knew too much and needed them as much as they needed the company.

Barry turned his focus on how to convince other members of the board. How to build a solid framework that would spread the risk and help him deal with the new investors while also sharing the wealth opportunity in return, naturally.

He was sure that Martin Brinstein and Paul Newark would understand and support him as they, too, held a small shareholding, which their homes were secured against, but he recognised that it would not be an easy conversation at all.

The sales and marketing president, Bernard Urkhart, was typically an insecure salesperson. Good at his job but selfish and overconfident. Barry knew that he would not be able to trust him with something so sensitive. He was not a close friend as the other board members were to him.

The president of operations, François Bertrand, a close friend of Barry's, was not someone who took risks. He was whiter than white and a super loyal chap to the company. Barry knew instantly that while he would do anything to support him, François would never entertain the concept of what was expected. Particularly in operations where they would have to place the drugs in their manufactured shipments to then transport around the globe.

Barry continued to ponder this dilemma and attempted to talk to Carlos about getting the best outcomes for all.

Carlos knew that he held all the cards, super confident as usual. He made a suggestion based on Barry's clear loyalty concerns about both Bernard and François. 'Let me be clear, this is your issue. We are not here to wipe your nose every five minutes, otherwise we will need a new CEO – and believe me when I say it would not be difficult.

'That said, we like what you have done and stability with you at the helm is not a bad thing at all. So, I will help you. You will find a way to dismiss your operations president. You know him; you get rid of him. But we do not expect any enhanced payoffs to impact us after the sale, so do it quickly. You will be asked to appoint one of our people to replace him. Dimitri Petrov, but he calls himself Peter on his emails.

'The sales and marketing president will be replaced by one of our people, too. Although, to reduce the sensitivity of change, I have been told that this will not happen immediately. More that a new position will be created as VP of emerging markets reporting to you. When the time is right, say six months, he will take over from your man by merging roles.'

'Sounds like you have it all sorted out,' confirmed Barry. 'When you say you've been told, who may I ask is doing the telling?'

'Our investment board consists of people close to the family. It is from them that I take instruction. I advise you to follow my example,' Carlos added sternly.

A Man of Principle

François Bertrand was a hard-working and loyal man. He was formally recognised for his great work by his promotion to president of operations. Barry had been his champion since he took over as CEO. They had instantly clicked as friends and great trust had been generated. He had been in the company for many years, earning the right to be there through personal sacrifice. Although, when the time came to invest and become a minor shareholder, as Barry, Paul and Martin did, the shock announcement was delivered that he would not do this.

Given François' risk-averse mindset, he was not happy to risk his home by securing it against a twenty-five year loan to buy shares. He had just become free from debt and owned his home, which he bought with his wife using an inheritance payment she had received after her parents passed away.

His house was quite magnificent. It was a reflection of his in-laws' hard work and wealth passed on to them. Regardless of his attitude to risk, there was no way that his wife, Amily, would entertain such a thing, even though in time the transaction could make them wealthier.

Barry understood that he was not happy, so this meant he needed to absorb his share and further increase his own borrowing. Despite this, they remained close.

Barry's daily calls to François made life awkward; he knew that he would need to protect his friend from the actions of the Ivanov family. He could not risk spooking him with anything like the truth because he would take matters to Interpol, which would be an easy target for supporting an investigation if the FBI leant on him.

Barry knew what he needed to do, yet this made the task no easier for him. Time had elapsed, and he needed to take action.

He asked his PA, Veronica, to invite him to a meeting at the local hotel No.4 in Manhattan, which was arranged for the following week. By this time, the funding for the share purchase had been arranged and was ready to be released. It was a condition of the contract for Barry to move the pieces around at top-level management before the cash was transferred by corporate lawyers.

At the same time, Barry was aware of Geoff's interaction with Ricardo and his recent appointment. He was anxious to see what his influence would bring to the table, other than the anticipated corruption, threats and attempt of control. Like an unwanted backseat driver on any long journey: interfering, annoying and attempting to criticise at every opportunity.

Barry waited in his office until a few minutes before his dinner meeting with François. It was a meeting he dreaded as he knew it would not go well, yet he knew it was the right course of action even if François would hate him for it.

François waited eagerly for his boss to turn up, just as he had many times before. He had checked into No.4 and admired its glamorous and plush surroundings. Not a hotel he was used to staying at and seemingly unlike any other. Gaining entry to the bar was not like walking into a hotel lobby and taking a chai. His name was taken by the hotel staff and checked off a register. Thankfully, his name was there listed as a guest of Barry Isaacs, like a five-star golf club eager to reject the riffraff or anyone who could not afford it.

He did not suspect any agenda other than Barry's typical open and engaging dialogue, this time to update him on the position of the new owners, the obstacles and hopefully a taste of things to come.

François had always respected Barry, particularly the mountainous amount of stress in running this large company. He was happy to be second to Barry's alpha status, as were the other executives, something he detected during many boardroom discussions.

François sipped his iced water as if to make it last for some time. Barry was typically twenty minutes late. The attentive barman was aware of François constantly staring at his Swiss gold wristwatch whilst attempting to connect with him through polite acknowledging stares and smiles.

At last, Barry arrived. Both men were dressed in suits and open-necked dress shirts, which reflected their familiarity as they greeted each other with a handshake and man hug. Although Barry's demeanour was understandably a little deflated, he masked it well. A reflection of him being a corporate CEO and needing to step up to challenges.

Having known each other for some time, François immediately picked up on the acute change in atmosphere upon Barry's arrival, despite his obvious attempts to cover it up.

François looked up at the barman who was already awaiting his order. Barry looked at François' iced water, yet proceeded to order an expensive glass of red. Something François was both used to and not offended by, given that he did not drink alcohol.

François listened intently as his boss went into download mode, sharing his last few days of problems, issues and all the frustrations relating to the refinancing of the company. It was a typical meeting with the boss, and François liked being in the know.

François noted a difference in Barry that evening. Typically, the conversation would involve Barry asking François probing questions about operations, something that François was always well prepared for.

Barry continued providing a general update, undeterred even when his wine was poured in front of him. He paused only to say thank you and to toast his dinner guest.

François was unusually cautious as he interrupted Barry. 'Something is wrong? Can you tell me?'

Barry looked up from his flow of words, recognising that his rambling had caused concern. He was almost thankful for François' intelligence in prompting a change of conversation. Barry could see the concern on his friend's face. He looked at his eyes from left to right, buying a few moments to gather his opening response. 'Things are not going to plan,' he stated. 'The people we will shortly be owned by are making life difficult for us... I am being pushed to make some changes before the deal goes through in order for the finance to be confirmed.'

'So, what are you being asked to do exactly?' François asked, almost certain that the look on Barry's face was a sign of his pain in delivering bad news to him personally, yet he needed to hear this directly.

Barry was less than honest by saying that he was being asked to reduce costs in terms of large salaries.

François knew that the company was not struggling with excess headcount and he was not convinced that his friend, his boss, was telling the truth.

A simple and humble conversation quickly turned into an aggressive debate between boss and employee. The years of friendship and loyalty now a distant thought as the two continued to push each other around the subject of whether François' job was at risk.

François' level-headedness eventually drew a line under the argument. 'Unless you start to be open with me, I will raise a formal grievance and drag this fucking thing out. Something that will mess up the funding from International Rescue,' he stated in clinical defiance.

Barry stared into his wine glass, which was relatively untouched. He took a large gulp and held the liquid in his mouth for a number of seconds before swallowing, leaving Barry with a facial expression reflecting the immediate impact of the alcohol on his taste buds.

It was clear to Barry that François could indeed scupper the plans of immediate financing by dragging out a formal grievance over his position. The buyers would not proceed with a legal case on their hands.

Barry leant towards François and began to share his knowledge of the new owners, their needs and touched on the concerns surrounding their methods and demands.

François recognised that his friend was back in the room being open once again, whereby a sense of reality hit him. 'So, I am a sacrifice to allow my job to be taken over by some fucking Mafia person?' he summarised.

'Basically, yes, and it doesn't stop there. Yours is not the only job affected,' Barry added.

François flippantly attempted to question the legitimacy of the transaction and the morality of his friend's request. He saw this as an opportunity to negotiate with Barry showing no concern towards others affected.

Barry put an offer to François. It was typically generous attempting to achieve unquestioned compliance, but he was not factoring in François keeping his mouth shut. He knew that the only job François could do was the one he was performing currently, with the only option for him to go quickly and quietly.

François continued in his attempt to negotiate, as it was expected that he would simply roll over and resign from his position with immediate effect.

Barry was becoming frustrated. He knew that his position would be vacant regardless of agreement, that the Ivanov family connections would ensure it would be so, with their negotiation tactics involving death rather than payment. His frustrations eventually pushed him too far in disclosing the events leading to Jaypee's death. Something that on reflection seemed unbelievable, yet he knew the truth – they had murdered him.

François laughed at the idea that in modern corporations such a thing was not possible without detection or prosecution, yet looking at Barry's face he knew that he believed it.

The conversation continued on a more subdued tone, with Barry sharing his concern for the well-being and survival of François.

'So are you saying that if I do not accept the deal someone will turn up on my doorstep and put me in a metal press?' François asked jokingly.

Barry continued, 'I know it sounds farfetched, but I have met these people, the people behind the investment company, and they cannot be trusted. They are into things that are highly illegal and will stop at nothing to get what they want. There have been death threats made to others, and I can confirm that I am trying to protect you and do what I can to help.'

François agreed to accept the financial deal. He was disgusted at the thought of him falling on his sword and believed that he was selected because he had refused to buy shares previously. However, he did not agree to sign the terms to waive his rights in taking legal action against the company or its new owners.

Barry was compromised in all directions. The resignation was an essential step, but the company was open to future legal action if the settlement agreement was not signed.

He had no choice but to accept François' resignation on this basis. At least it would tick the box for the finance to complete, and at this point

François would not have had the opportunity to lodge a legal claim.

The planned dinner did not continue. Neither of them with an appetite for each other's company, despite feeling as hungry as any other evening. Racing heartbeats had overtaken the hunger pangs.

François returned to his room on the fourth floor disgusted that he needed to resign. He was eager to send Barry a note to reflect their agreement accepting the payment but not the terms. There was no way he was backing down on this. Signing the settlement agreement as presented would prevent him from seeking unfair dismissal claims under European Law, which was the basis of his contract, or so he believed.

François was not a vindictive person, far from it. He always tried hard to act fairly, doing the right thing at all times like an overzealous police officer. François knew that his forced resignation was wrong. He had performed well, been loyal to a fault, and this injustice forced upon him should be pursued legally as a principle regardless of financial gain. It was clear to him that his friendship with Barry could not continue. It was to be replaced by a legal claim to right the wrong done unto him that day.

François knew that Barry would have no choice but to pay him the money offered without signing the terms of departure given his explanation of the current culture. If Barry failed to accept this, the deal would not proceed. At least that was the understanding, and François would use this to his advantage.

Barry's attempt to be open and honest had backfired on him, and he had wrongly underestimated François' passion and sense of correctness. His attempts to protect his friend were not recognised as the right thing to do.

François did not believe for one minute that he would be killed if he put up a fight. This was not New York in the 1970s with gangs fighting the cops and getting away with corruption and murder. Did Barry take him for some kind of idiot?

Barry received the email from François minutes after switching on his laptop in his twelfth-floor suite. Looking out over the Manhattan skyline, Barry reflected that his position had become untenable due to a total breakdown in trust between the two directors, and had resulted in an agreement to resign with immediate effect subject to his payment being agreed.

Barry knew that he would need to report this to the legal teams representing each party. This was not the terms of the refinancing from International Rescue and it would certainly not be accepted by those representing the Ivanov family's interests.

Barry simply stared at the flow of moving taillights in the distance below. An hour had passed with him not knowing how or what he had done during that time. His tummy rumbled. As he reached for the phone to order room service, he glanced at the bar in his room and favoured to help himself to a drink instead. He poured a glass of scotch, the golden liquid splashing over the ice cubes, but paused after dispensing a good measure or two. He then continued to fill the glass to three quarters. He needed this more than usual, and more than food.

He returned to his laptop after reading the message from François once more, and then proceeded to read other emails before attempting to respond. His mind was firmly focused on two things: He knew that François would go to a lawyer the next day. Also, and more concerning, his message to the new owners would need to highlight the pending legal action that would follow. He was personally responsible for disclosure, so he had no other choice open to him.

After several edits, he sent the response to François. It was not aggressive or forceful, which was most unlike his usual style of writing. He expressed sadness that they had reached this point in their relationship and suggested that the payment was in lieu of salary, benefits and bonuses whilst highlighting that François had refused to accept the settlement terms. Barry hoped this would be useful if it went to court; although, he was more concerned that he would compromise himself instead.

Both men acknowledged and agreed the points in each other's emails via curt and swift responses. Barry missed his friend already. No longer would he rely on his unwavering loyalty and friendship.

François texted his wife to discuss the evening's events, and then commenced a rather difficult conversation that continued by telephone despite the time differences. Both never reached the truth in the reasoning, yet François had the support from his loving wife.

Barry, on the other hand, was alone. He had cc'd Paul, his legal director, to advise on the situation, with the main recipient being Carlos, the lawyer representing International Rescue.

Barry hoped that he would retire to his bed that evening without a response from Carlos, yet the reply was immediate.

> *Barry*
>
> *This will be viewed as disappointing. We clearly need to recognise the sensitivity of François' position, as it is sad that he does not want to be part of our journey together. We will need to discuss the implications of any such legal claim on the deal while looking at options to limit our exposure on this.*
>
> *Yours,*
> *Carlos*

Barry was pleasantly surprised by the tone of the email. It was clear that the deal was still going through; after all, they wanted to buy the company as much as Barry needed the funding.

With a sense of warmth, Barry wandered out onto his balcony once again to take in his surroundings. He felt better now than an hour previously as he swirled the remaining ice cubes around his glass. Whilst contemplating a little more scotch before getting into bed, the hotel room phone rang.

It was a strange call from a man who gave no name. He said he was representing the new investors.

Barry's tired eyes recovered instantly, just like taking a cold shower in the morning.

'We are concerned that you have failed to contain the situation regarding your operations colleague. You are aware that the organisation, whose interests I represent, cannot afford any loose ends and legal claims. We are aware that you met with him this evening and said more than you should about the organisation and our affairs – which is, shall we say, potentially dangerous.'

Barry was horrified. Had they been listening to his conversation with François? Frightened, Barry attempted to reason with the man, explaining, quite successfully as a seasoned business leader can, the reasons for him discussing the facts with François and how this had not gone to plan.

The man calmly highlighted to Barry that he was concerned François may go to the FBI, given that Barry had disclosed such detail in his conversation.

Barry attempted to convince the man that François was not the type to do this, yet instantly the man cut him short.

'We will determine the situation for ourselves. The outcome will be on your head, Mr Isaacs.' The phone call ended.

Barry was alert and concerned that he was being monitored. His mind was working like crazy as he retraced his surroundings at the bar… *The barman is our spy?* He must have been listening and reported back like a sewer rat finding a juicy meal and rushing to the lair to share it in a fit of excitement. *Bastard*, he thought to himself, having tipped the chap on several occasions.

He was keen to call François. As he lifted the telephone handset, he paused and looked around. Not that there was anyone there. He reminded himself that the people he was dealing with would definitely be tapping his phone. He was an insecure wreck. He placed the handset down with gentle caution trying not to make a noise as it rested back in its place.

Should he warn François not to go to the FBI? He had never mentioned it, so this could provoke him to do so. Barry considered the options. He still regarded François a friend regardless of their last conversation. What to do?

Instead, he decided to leave things as they were. There was far too much at stake for him. He turned his attention to the man who was calm and in control. As an alpha character, Barry was rarely intimidated, yet tonight that is how he felt. It was a strange emotion and something that reminded him of his past before achieving the dizzy heights of his leadership status.

Meanwhile, François received a knock at the door. It was eleven o clock, but he was not concerned as he was expecting Barry to pop down and apologise for the conversation. *It was about bloody time*, he thought to himself as he opened the door eagerly with a sense of satisfaction. François was ready to confront

Barry, but instead he saw a stranger smiling at him.

In a calm and quiet voice, the man introduced himself as the hotel manager and asked if he could enter the room to discuss something with a little more discretion.

François turned on the man stating that the time was past eleven o'clock, but the man once again insisted that it was better to talk in private.

Looking at his name badge, he gestured for him to enter.

The manager walked towards the windows, where there was much more space around the sofa where he asked to sit.

François gestured once again as the manager took his seat and joined him shortly afterwards.

'I have been made aware of a disturbance earlier at the bar involving you and another guest,' he said.

François apologised and defended the discussion firmly; he believed it was not disruptive or intrusive on any other guest.

The man continued, 'I am aware of your resignation and that Mr Isaacs has shared certain pieces of information regarding your new owners. It concerns us that—'

'Who the hell are you again?' François demanded. 'You said you're the hotel manager, but…this does not add up at all.'

'I am indeed the manager of this hotel. Similarly, your new owners have an interest in this establishment, so you could say I work for them, too.'

'This is just disturbing,' François added. 'I am going to call the police and see what they make of this.' He attempted to usher the manager out of the room, but the man stood firm as he walked towards the door and turned around to face François.

'Of course, if you wish to report this, then it's clear that we cannot rely on your discretion about your resignation or your conversation with Mr Isaacs. I would urge you to reconsider, as I hoped Mr Isaacs had been clear on our need for trust, discretion and loyalty. Attempts to disrupt this are not appreciated by the organisation,' the manager concluded with a smile of the mouth but with insincere and cold eyes.

'Please leave my bloody room. I do not want you here, or your weak threats. Take them back to wherever you came from and shove them up your arse.' François was firm and felt in his rights to be rude and insulting given this visit at such an hour, attempting to intimidate and confront him.

François' immediate text to Barry was full of emotional ramblings about the intrusion, further highlighting that he would go to the police in the morning.

Barry did not respond.

It was in the early hours of the morning when François finally fell asleep.

A short while later, the door of François' hotel room was opened with a key. Three men entered casually dressed in housekeeping attire.

One of the men followed the other two with the laundry trolley. They stood over François as he lay there oblivious to the fate that awaited him.

In an instant, a drug was injected into François' neck.

He woke with a shock whilst his mouth was covered to muffle any screams or shouts. The look of fear, panic and desperation in his eyes was clear as he fought bravely against the men for less than three seconds, after which his body became limp and lifeless under the assailants' strong hands covering his mouth with their gloved hands.

Waiting for a few more seconds to check for signs of life, the men casually tossed his dead, half-naked body into the laundry trolley. After covering him with used towels, they once again casually exited the room and made their way to the basement where they awaited a laundry vehicle sent to take care of the disposal.

The vehicle left the premises, driven by the same man who operated the laundry trolley and accompanied by the other two. They embarked on their one-hour journey to New York State. The body was then transferred to a building site. A bulldozer-type vehicle prepared to cover the cadaver with new sand and gravel in a purpose-made hole ready for the concrete mix to be poured on top – to be sealed for many years to come with no trace.

The men showed no emotion throughout the process, no different to cutting the grass or sweeping the driveway. Clearly this was not their first venture into this type of work, nor would it be their last.

As the dead body turned from warm to cold under the pressure of the building materials,

Barry awoke in his plush surroundings unaware of the events in the early hours several floors beneath him.

Barry was hungrier than ever. He headed to the restaurant for breakfast looking around as he sat alone expecting to see François, yet clearly he was not there. He had received his text from the previous evening and hoped that his anger had calmed.

He called François at 7:33 a.m. but received an unobtainable message. He tried again a few minutes later. A Groundhog Day moment indeed. Barry hurried to a waiting member of staff asking that they contact Mr Bertrand in his room.

The hotel representative came back a few minutes later with a response that Barry did not want to hear. 'I am sorry, sir. Mr Bertrand checked out early this morning, very early it seems. Is there anything else I can do for you?'

Barry was not shocked that François had departed early. No doubt he needed to return home on an early flight. Perhaps his mobile was not connecting due to being over the Atlantic at 37,000 feet. *Yes*, he thought, *that would easily explain things.* He remained hopeful that his friend was safe and on his way home, unaware of the reality.

Celebration and Concern

The next few days passed slowly for Barry. He had ordered the money to be transferred to François, so he would have had this by now, yet there was still no contact.

Veronica knocked on Barry's door. She looked concerned as François' wife was on the phone.

He took the call immediately without asking why.

She was going crazy with worry as to why François had not been contactable, not come home and there was no response from the messages she'd left on his office voicemail. She was demanding answers.

Barry had none other than to explain that François had resigned and they had agreed an immediate settlement now transferred into his account.

She was shocked that he would resign. He loved his job and loved working with Barry. She demanded to know what had happened, as clearly she had been aware of the events as described to her by her husband, even if they lacked the truth. More importantly, she was worried about where François was since this had happened.

Barry was unwilling to go into too much detail, so naturally his wife was not a happy woman and took her anger out on him. He merely sat there and took it on the chin as he listened intently whilst rocking from side to side in his wide leather chair. François' wife had immediately filed a missing person's report with the local police in France. Barry knew to expect a knock on the door from the Manhattan police in due course. He emailed Carlos to discuss François, but there was no response on this specific point as all details were handled by the brokers lawyers representing each party.

After forty-eight hours, the deal was completed. At long last, Barry's hopes of long-term funding had concluded. The company was fluid and secure once again.

A meal was arranged to meet the company board and International Rescue partners. It was to be held at No.4 to celebrate the share sale.

Barry was less stressed than usual as the event commenced. The events leading up to the transaction had placed a mountain of stress upon him. He had been hell to live with, even his typically tolerant wife had told him to live at a hotel until the deal was completed, which was her way of saying let's have some space until you can become a normal human being again.

Barry was a great host in welcoming the three new partners. Carlos was the first to greet him and reintroduced his fellow partner Simon Ray, a quintessential businessman, everything you would expect from a major private equity firm. The other partner in attendance was a Ukrainian chap called Alexandre Sokolov, someone Barry had neither met nor heard of previously.

Carlos highlighted that Alexandre had just been appointed as a partner and would be allocated to oversee performance in regular board meetings.

Barry's veneer was well polished in entertaining the group, which included his main colleagues Paul Newark, Martin Brinstein and Bernard Urkhart, the president of sales and marketing, along with the new recruit to the board, Geoff.

Under the veneer was a man desperate to talk about the whereabouts of his ex-colleague François, as he believed that there was a sinister reason for his disappearance.

During the pre-dinner drinks, Alexandre Sokolov monopolised Barry's attention. It was understandable given Barry's position as CEO. Alexandre was suitably eloquent, very focused and wanted to talk business. Barry would have seemed distracted at times, yet he maintained engagement as only a seasoned CEO could.

Barry spotted the opportunity to introduce Martin into the main theme of this conversation. He executed the move with precision timing, and then edged away to grab the attention of Carlos as the two men commenced their detailed financial conversation without noticing his discrete departure.

With the group maintaining a good level of humour and involvement, Barry gently squeezed Carlos's elbow as he attempted to move from earshot of the group. 'Carlos, please, I must know what happened to François. He is missing and his wife has filed a missing person's report. It's just a matter of—'

'I think you need to stay composed, Barry,' cut in Carlos. 'We have no need for a flaky CEO, and we need business as usual, so keep it together. Why do you burden yourself with his issues? You have done what is needed, to hire his replacement. In a week's time, Dimitri will have filled the role and you move on, so move on.'

'Did you...you know, get rid of him...?' Barry questioned Carlos softly.

'No, Barry, you got rid of him. We just tidy up your loose ends when you fail to get your team onside,' Carlos responded in a defiant tone.

'So, you did. Is he alive? Just give me that, Carlos. I just need to know,' Barry insisted, starting to draw the attention of others as he did so.

'Barry, let me be clear, you know that we protect ourselves at all costs. Your man was creating a liability for us all. The family become concerned when this is the case, so we remove the problem. That's what we do. It's best you don't push this, Barry. You have more value to us than becoming another ingredient in our concrete mix.'

Barry went cold with anger and fear. He knew that his words, which were chosen carefully, confirmed his worse fears: François had been needlessly killed.

Barry needed a moment. He made his polite excuses to visit the bathroom as he rushed into a cubicle to throw up, his eyes stinging as he wept over the once immaculately clean toilet basin. He knew that he had tried to warn him off, tried to help his friend and avoid this outcome. *These bastards, the murderers.* He knew that he needed to prevent anymore killing.

He had two options: to use his persuasive talents to guide his teams through these turbulent, dangerous times or to go to the FBI. The latter would definitely lead to his own unpleasant death. What of his family? He could not risk placing them in danger, but the FBI was not an option despite knowing it was the right thing to do.

How the hell could he look at himself in the mirror each day knowing that he had put his team, himself and ultimately his family at risk? How could he talk to the local police about François and keep up the pretence?

His only conclusion was that he must return to the charade that was the completion dinner to celebrate the coming together of two like-minded businesses to help each other prosper. He knew it was all bullshit, yet he had secured the financial security of the company. This meant jobs for many people, preservation of their lifestyles and security for them individually.

Once again, as Barry entered the room with his guests, he was focused on the success the funding had created and felt on top of his game once more. His jolly demeanour returned to entertain, engage and create the vehicle for positive relations. So much so that none of his team noticed his absence as anything more than a natural break after a drink or two.

Geoff noticed Alexandre a few feet away from him, his dark deep-set eyes glaring at him whilst in a two-way conversation with Martin. Geoff knew that this was his cue to join the two men, to add a fresh injection of dialogue and humour to prevent Martin from boring this guy's legs off as only an accountant could have perfected.

As Geoff approached moving only a few steps from where he was standing, Alexandre welcomed him quickly, just as Geoff had predicted. He was great at reading others, and tonight was no different as the man with the wolf-like stare engaged him with a grasp of his lower arm.

Bernard Urkhart tagged along behind Geoff like a dog following its master, and looking uncomfortable in the process. His discomfort was borne out of his natural insecurity as a sales person, believing that profit and growth were the drivers for their new owners. He was unaware of their motives, the 'real' private equity company that was with him that evening and he certainly had no idea of the driving forces behind them.

Geoff was surprised to see his more experienced board director looking so sheepish. After all, someone in a senior sales and marketing role would typically be good at entertaining and networking, yet Geoff did not empathise with Bernard. He had his own agenda with Alexandre.

As Alexandre greeted the two men more formally, he seemed strangely uninterested in Bernard. Instead, he focused his intensity and curiosity solely on Geoff.

Bernard became even more insecure as he listened to the conversation, which seemed like a job interview and more favourable towards Geoff. Bernard turned to Martin and whispered through a smile, 'Hope he gets the job.'

Martin's light-hearted response helped to alleviate his insecurity. 'He is curious why Barry has appointed him to the board just before the deal went through, having not disclosed his intentions to the new owners previously.'

Bernard smiled in a way that reflected his selfishness. As a long-termer, he was pleased that Geoff was being given a damn good grilling. At least it took some of the pressure from himself.

He had been part of a takeover before, where sales targets were raised, customer contracts required renegotiating and profit levels were unacceptable despite his best efforts. It was not a pleasant position for him. He constantly reminded himself of that point in his career when he was forced out of his job to make way for the next generation. Not his best career memories.

Although it was many years ago, his recollection focused on a dinner with a newly appointed CEO at the time, an Italian chap, the godson of the global chairman, although this fact was never referred to openly. The new CEO had asked Bernard his views on taking the company from five per cent market share to ten per cent in two years with no money for acquisitions. It was all to be organic growth.

Bernard, being a hard-working yet incredibly direct German, announced that the company only had two and a half per cent of the market and that achieving such growth to ten per cent would be impossible through increasing sales alone.

He was branded lazy and unambitious by the ill-informed CEO in front of others at the table. This caused huge embarrassment for him and made him feel both isolated and insecure. Something that was to be his downfall at this point in his career.

Bernard was never known as a yes-man, but it seemed that this CEO just lapped up the attention from the others at the dinner table who were, in his opinion, just agreeing with him, sucking up to him, despite thinking he was an over-promoted brat who had no clue how to run the company.

Bernard felt that he had done the right thing in being honest, but later he regretted it after being under exceptional pressure to quit his job and leave. He had led his sales team well to this point. The results were accepted as hitting budget, yet the chemistry with the new CEO was just not there at all.

Bernard knew that he was being forced out, but he had no other job offer. Otherwise, he would have left with a two-fingered salute to the Italian brat and smiling like the proverbial Cheshire cat on the way out.

Yet, he was trapped in his unhappy work environment. Highly paid but constrained to doing what he was told to do, like a jack-in-the-box jumping every time the lid was opened. This pain continued for several months, until the day finally arrived.

The new CEO had no real reason to dismiss him. He did so based on manufacturing a story that placed Bernard directly at the heart of a price-fixing scandal. He was offered the chance to resign before the investigation could commence.

Bernard knew that he was free of corruption, but the CEO indicated that this would stain his career. The story would be hard to disprove and would put off potential employers in an otherwise incestuous industry.

Bernard wasn't given much time to think it through as he was invited to a meeting that he knew would lead to his immediate suspension.

Sick to the stomach, he sent his resignation letter. He left without serving his notice not realising that he would be unemployed for seven months with no compensation for his legal entitlements. It was a breach of contract to leave without serving his notice. The CEO had really fucked him up.

Back in the present, Bernard was now talking business with Martin while Barry was still locked in conversation with Carlos nearby but purposefully out of earshot.

Picking up on Alexandre's comments to Geoff, Bernard questioned Martin about the reasons why Geoff had been appointed to the board, attempting to stir the corporate political cauldron with yet more snipes about Geoff. He believed that Martin would be an ally in the debate. To his surprise, Martin was hugely supportive of Geoff's appointment, which served Bernard a crushing blow in the process.

'If I were you, Bernard, I would keep my head down and view Geoff as on our side. He is a fish out of water at the moment, but given time he will be vital to our survival,' Martin confirmed, having chosen his words carefully.

Bernard's verbal attack was at a standstill while Martin continued discussing how they should be prepared for a rough ride regarding the changes and an increased demand for facts and figures. Some of which would be up to Bernard to lead and deliver. After all, the company needed to present a success story to the external world.

In the back of Martin's mind, he truly believed that Geoff would be key to the survival of the team. Although realistically he knew that Geoff would be the fall guy in the event of any FBI investigation, the man making the appointments of the very people who would be deemed criminals in their so-called unsavoury behaviours. Whereas, Martin, Paul and Barry would continue unscathed. At least that was his contingency plan for self-preservation. This is what he meant by Geoff being key to their survival.

Paul and Carlos somehow seemed to find themselves together as the waiter came around with more drinks near the bar.

Bernard was joined by Geoff and Alexandre. Geoff was pleased as he was beginning to get fed up with being the centre of attention. Alexandre was an intense man, pretentious and lacking any sort of empathy for people as humans. He believed that people had a limited shelf life and were there just to get results. He was not on the same planet as Geoff, or most decent humans for that matter.

Wishing to score points as he sank his half glass of wine in one gulp, Bernard was feeding off Geoff's discomfort having been grilled, baked and fried by the 'wolf man' known as Alexandre. It was Bernard's way of dealing with adversity by ridiculing others for their imperfections, like an artist accentuating features in a caricature. 'So, the offer made to Ricardo?' Bernard began. 'I hear he's going to report to Barry. Geoff, this is an outrage. This role should be in my team, and I hear you negotiated this directly between Barry and Ricardo,' he asserted in a confident and loud tone. He wanted to ensure that others would hear him in what he felt would be viewed as a strong leadership tone.

Clearly out of his depth, Bernard was unaware that Ricardo had been appointed at the request of Barry and the new owner's pet recruit, who was set to take over from Bernard when the time was right.

Geoff took it on the chin and did not react as Bernard expected. Now being overheard by the others, it was crucial that Geoff remained loyal to Barry and did not divulge the details of the appointment.

Similarly, Geoff needed to respond. He had to deal with Bernard who was clearly working an agenda in front of Carlos and his fellow investment colleagues. Geoff, being a master of behavioural psychology at work, played to Bernard's weakness, attempting to sever his legs before he gained political pace at his own expense. 'With the new owners' expectations being so high regarding sales, Bernard, we felt that you would be under enormous strain just keeping up with expectations,' Geoff replied, holding back the smile whilst delivering his words sincerely. He caught a glimpse of Barry's smile from the corner of his eye.

Bernard once again demonstrated his inadequacy in boardroom politics, crashing and burning like a World War II bomber over the channel. The group watched him sink into deep unchartered waters, unable to return to the fight as the conversation and banter continued long after sitting down to dinner.

As the main course was being devoured, Barry looked at Paul and held his stare for several seconds. Paul noticed this, as did Carlos.

'Any news on your colleague? François, I believe?' Carlos asked as if to antagonise Barry and remind him of where his loyalties should lie.

Barry maintained eye contact with Paul for another second before looking around the table and responding. 'It seems that he disappeared, which is deeply saddening for his wife who is reporting it to the police as we speak. She believes something nasty has happened to him,' he added, hoping to spook Carlos just a little. Not that Carlos reacted or appeared interested other than to make his point.

Barry's colleagues, aware that François had been forced out, did not attempt to push Barry for details. They trusted his judgement and knew that he had good relationships with them all.

Geoff interjected, 'We will shortly have Dimitri joining us, though. Something we are really excited about.' The conversation stagnated at this point. Geoff attempted to deflect the attention from Barry's pain over his friend and colleague, but he had created a conversation hurdle instead.

Given the uncomfortable silence, Barry felt he should continue. 'Yes, Geoff, it is good that Dimitri will be joining us. It was sad that I had to part company with François, but I'm hopeful that Dimitri will bring much-needed fresh eyes and skills to the operational teams.'

Bernard was dying to ask about Dimitri. He could not wait to find a new weak link in the board structure to preserve himself a little longer. He recognised that any team needed to be strong, and it makes the others more desirable when there was a weak link, hence his reaction.

Paul made his excuses when Alexandre put down his cutlery. He bought some time away from the group by suggesting that he had to call home and get some fresh air. He headed for the balcony a few hundred yards from the dining table. As he did so, he glanced at Barry. The two of them had known each other for years; their trust was established almost instantly when they began working together.

The two men were unable to talk as their guests were rather attentive, which left little room for private dialogue at the table. Barry saw this as his cue to talk to him. He was in pain, mental pain, holding on to the fate of François was not healthy, and he needed to share it.

Alexandre gave a final toast as Paul returned to the table. 'I am looking forward to working with you, to realise the potential of this company and to seeing us all get a little richer in the process.'

Carlos echoed his colleague's comments before the two set off for their own conversation, leaving the four executives to their cheese and biscuits with coffee.

Paul challenged Barry to determine if he was okay following the prolonged eye contact earlier, as he hoped to talk before now.

Barry was keen to talk with Paul alone, yet alone was how he felt, so he decided to share his feelings. 'François is dead, I just know it.'

Martin attempted to console him. 'We don't know this, Barry. Perhaps he's had a breakdown, or gone off with some young lady and living the dream.'

The others joined in the banter and attempted to lift the conversation with happier yet inappropriate sexual references.

'They have fucking killed him, I know they have!' exclaimed Barry trying to maintain a soft voice, once more bringing the humour to ground zero again. He went on to explain his conversation with Carlos while the others just sat listening looking down at their coffee cups sombre and somewhat disbelieving. Could their leader be heading for a mental breakdown himself?

Geoff felt it was his place to highlight his own experiences, citing the example of Ricardo and his merry men. Martin and Paul fell silent.

There was no mention of the Russian connections or drug smuggling.

Bernard decided to inflame the situation. 'So, Geoff, tell us about your little rendezvous with the FBI. Why were you arrested again?' He continued to insinuate that Geoff was involved with the killers, believing Barry's story however farfetched it may have seemed. He had been drinking non-stop at this point.

'Wind it in, Bernard. That was all a misunderstanding, and you fucking know it!' Geoff was truly disappointed that this was being used to incriminate him. He remained convinced that he knew more about the drugs and the Ivanov family business than Bernard, and was rather surprised by the attack.

The two men went into battle hurling abuse and comments at each other. Nothing personal, just healthy aggression between two opposing forces.

Bernard viewed Geoff as unnecessary on the board. A fluffy HR-type and people person.

Whereas, Geoff viewed Bernard as a selfish person, not a team player and lacking the people skills to lead his teams in line with the rest of the company, the way that François and Martin did for example.

Barry let it play out. The others followed suit.

Paul was not going to let on that he was arrested in his hotel room surrounded by cocaine and FBI agents, and he certainly was not going to let on that he had planted bugs in Barry's house.

Geoff continued to spill the beans and disclose his knowledge of Ricardo's behaviour. He hoped that he may prompt the others to disclose their experiences, but he was alone in his comments and feeling rather compromised.

Being drunk, Bernard was full of advice and suggestions on how to deal with the investors. It was clear to Barry that he needed to share the whole story with him.

As Barry commenced his journey of events for the sake of clarity, openness and his own sanity, Bernard seemed to quickly sober. Common sense replaced the alcohol like a drug, fast acting on the problem area, allowing Bernard to return to his former self.

'How the fuck could you do this to us, Barry?' Bernard complained. 'You've got into bed with the Russian Mafia for Christ's sake, and now we're all in danger. They have already killed off François!'

'Have you not listened to me, you arsehole! Without this funding we would not be able to pay the bills, your overinflated bonuses – and we would be in receivership within the year. So, everything we've worked for, put our homes on the line for, would be all gone,' Barry quickly responded.

Bernard looked disorientated as if he had been slapped around the face with a cricket bat. As he sank with his head into his hands, Martin wanted to make a confession.

He offered a parallel to Geoff regarding the rat incident by recalling the pig's head event in an attempt to lead into the bigger story. Treading carefully as he did so, he looked at the others uncertain of his path of delivery.

Martin had a daughter aged eighteen, his youngest child. She was just commencing her chosen path in life and making the break from home to study law at university. A proud moment for Martin and his wife. She was a determined young lady who was clever, pretty and just all-round lovely. He told the story again when he was given a pig's head, highlighting that he had refused to support the funding when Barry told him what was behind it.

'Yes, we know, you told us just now,' Bernard said arrogantly.

Martin continued, 'What I didn't tell you was that last week I had a broken window on the car while it was parked at the mall. A traffic cop was hanging around, so I called him over. He was no cop. If he was, then we have bigger problems than I first thought. Whilst empathising with me, he began talking about the things that cause us pain, bringing up the subject of family, and daughters in particular. I was confused how a smashed car window related, but he continued. He referred to my daughter's university campus and knew her name and class, everything. He even had a fucking picture on him. I wanted to hit him, but he was dressed as a cop – a proper cop, not some mall security off-cast – the real deal. I stopped my anger as his other hand rested on his firearm, his helmet and glasses marginally disguising his identity, and all I could think about was the safety of my daughter. He said he was friends with a certain family who needed our cooperation, and any concerns around not helping them with their distribution of product would result in my self-induced unhappiness. Oh, he continued… He went into details saying that my daughter would be paralysed as a result of a drug-fuelled car accident or something similar, or worse. These are not people we need to cross, guys. I cannot compromise my family.'

Paul kept quiet as Barry said, 'François' death is my fault. I was asked to get rid of him to make way for the new guy, Dimitri, which I did. Knowing François, he would never support us transporting anything illegal, so I attempted to reason with him and paid him very well. I did divulge the reasons why I was doing it. I had to because he wasn't accepting the idea of resigning without reason, which I can understand. After telling him, he went crazy. I contacted International Rescue as François' immediate resignation was a condition of the funding. François refused to accept the non-disclosure terms. Carlos, the slippery shit, knew this…and I never saw François again. Carlos acknowledged his death in not so many words tonight. It's my fault, now I have to lie to the police.'

Martin turned on Paul. 'What's your story? You've had more involvement than me, so you must have had them turn on you, too.'

Paul was hesitant. He was a lawyer and not accustomed to lies, certainly not to his colleagues.

Barry could tell something had happened and pushed him hard for him to divulge his story.

Paul verbally danced around disclosure like a cat on a hot tin roof until Barry stood up and confronted him in a tone that Paul would not want to hear too often. He reluctantly and hesitantly began his cocaine and FBI story in the very same hotel. Something that would put him in jail for a long time.

'But they let you off?' asked Martin.

'Yes, they did. But if I snitch on them, they would use the evidence.'

'Come on, Paul, you're a lawyer, they cannot bury evidence then use it again to suit them. They would get into trouble. If they let you off, they let you off. Something doesn't add up here,' said Barry. He was convinced that Paul was holding back, but he could not find out what. Instead, he turned to Geoff. 'So, if you go to the FBI, you're right in it up to your neck, my friend, and they know it.'

Geoff acknowledged that he had appointed Ricardo, reinstated Ricardo's operations man in France, despite mass redundancies, and had retracted a statement to the FBI after meeting with Carlos.

Paul thought he was off the hook, but Barry had not forgotten and continued to pursue his hidden story. Eventually, Paul buckled under the pressure from all his peers. He began to divulge that he had placed bugs in Barry's home.

The confession left Barry cold and weakened. He was disappointed that Paul had actually done this. He would never have believed this was the reason he was let off by the FBI. He was also hurt that the Ivanov family were monitoring him and his family. He knew deep down that his position would terminate before he retired, but he thought this was a few years away. Barry slumped into his chair defeated and punch-drunk, like a boxer returning to his corner needing time out to recover from the beating he had just endured by those he least expected to hurt him.

The others were speechless, but Paul compensated for his embarrassment by turning on Bernard. He was not convinced that Bernard had been left alone, yet he continued to plead innocence throughout the barrage of intense and emotional questioning, which by now seemed like a political fight for the US presidency.

As Paul continued to beat up Bernard verbally, Geoff was now happily joining in. All men believing that either Bernard was lying or somehow linked to the Ivanov family. Even if he now admitted to something similar happening, would they believe him?

Under stress, Bernard shouted for a timeout. The others stopped to listen to him. Bernard paused for ages as the others watched his eyes fill with pain and tears before hitting them with a story that silenced them all instantly.

Whilst on business in Indonesia recently, Bernard was out entertaining as usual and admitted to a rather large drinks bill, even at local rates, and being 'hammered'. He was embarrassed to divulge that he and his potential client, Mo, decided to take a little company in the form of some young prostitutes. 'It was just some fun,' Bernard added, 'don't you guys fucking judge me. I recall the two girls being beautiful and I knew they were on drugs, but I swear I don't do drugs.

I just wouldn't. I was drunk, that's all. Okay, I was having sex with one of the girls while my client was in the room next door. I noticed the girl's nose bleeding and her body went limp. It was the drugs that killed her, not me. I rushed next door and asked for help straight away. Mo was a local man and knew what to do. He called his friend in the local vice squad who dealt with the whole thing. Mo and I went our separate ways after the police reported that the killer had fled the scene despite DNA evidence being gathered.'

'You lying shit,' said Barry. 'You told me that deal went cold due to them wanting too much discount. I was there in Indonesia with you. I was dealing with an employee death while you were filling your boots with the local call girls.'

Bernard looked sheepish as he continued, 'The policeman told me that this would be reported as unsolved, but I must stay out of Indonesia as my DNA was all over the dead girl – something I could be arrested for. He told me that one day one of his colleagues would ask a favour of me, and that I should comply. I had no choice but to agree.'

'And the favour?' Paul asked.

'To supply Barry's hair sample and fingerprints,' confirmed Bernard.

'My fucking DNA so they can incriminate me as well despite not being there!'

The conversation was generating more heat. The pushing and shoving continued towards Bernard when the hotel manager, Paoblo De Silva, approached them.

'Gentlemen, please, this is getting out of hand. My staff alerted me to a situation. Let's settle this down.'

The men sat down to fresh coffee while they looked at each other in silence.

De Silva continued, 'My friends, the Ivanov family have a vested interest in this lovely establishment and they have sent a message to you via me. These problems should bind you together, not to separate you by dividing friendships and loyalties. The family are well connected and can either make you incredibly rich or destroy you. I know which I would prefer. Make your decisions quickly. This evening should allow you to celebrate, and all the family ask for in return is that they use your domestic appliances to ship certain goods.'

'What happened to our colleague François?' Barry asked defiantly.

'He was going to the FBI to tell them what he knew. I can confirm that your friend is dead and that he was killed in, well, the same room you're in, Mr Urkhart.'

Bernard was cold with fear. Sleeping in a dead man's bed tonight was not what he expected at all.

De Silva was pleased to have delivered his powerful and fearful message. He politely excused himself from the table, slithering away like a snake retreating from unwanted conflict.

The executive team looked on in amazement at the clinical way he breezed in and out like he was upgrading someone to a better room. The five men sat sipping their coffee looking at each other in silence, just thinking.

Paul was the first to speak. 'That man De Silva is just corrupt. He's the worst of them.'

'I doubt it, Paul,' said Barry. 'He's just an employee, not one of the Russians. Although, I agree we must be careful around him, he cannot be trusted, and choosing a different hotel may not be as prudent as it might first seem.'

'Is it safe to assume that our offices are also bugged?' asked Geoff. 'No doubt they've asked someone in the company to place a few listening devices here and there.'

'I doubt it,' said Paul. 'They didn't seem aware of our stance on some of the legal points during the negotiation to resolve the funding. Barry and I had talked in the boardroom at length on how we could push back and move them on a number of items. If they were prepared for this, I think it would have been obvious.'

Barry suggested everyone act as normal and that perhaps De Silva was right about this adversity should bind them in making it work, making money and keeping the wheels turning.

'It's all right for you, Barry, some of us have a prison sentence hanging over our heads,' snapped Bernard as if his situation was somehow not borne out of his own selfishness and stupidity.

'You selfish bastard, Bernard,' Barry responded. 'I have the death of my good friend, your good friend, on my conscience, or have you suddenly forgotten the last thirty minutes. I have to keep up appearances to the bloody cops, François' wife and everyone else in between. All

I ever tried to do was keep this bloody company going, keep us all in jobs so you can go on fucking prostitutes on expenses and offering my head on the block to save your own!'

Paul was the voice of reason. He interjected using his negotiation techniques as a lawyer to position both sides and lay the foundation for them all to stand on, especially as each were implicated in some way. The only way to prevent them all ending up in jail was to continue running the company and allow the Russians and their countless international relatives the opportunity to piggyback on their distribution channels, turning a blind eye to the corruptness and making sure nothing stuck to them in the process.

The men agreed that their involvement in this illegal drug distribution would stay secret from their friends and families, and that now they understood each other's connections in this. They would need to protect and preserve their lives by working as a team, more than ever before.

As much as they disliked De Silva, his words echoed into the night and beyond.

Dimitri and the Ballet Dancer

A few days later, Barry was due to meet Alexandre for their first formal review meeting. He was conscious that he also needed to spend time with Dimitri who had just arrived in Manhattan. Understandably, Barry was not keen to spend time with Dimitri or Ricardo for numerous reasons. One being that in an ideal world without corruption Ricardo would report to Bernard, given that his role was to develop new markets; whereas, sales and partnerships were Bernard's baby. Barry resented the extra reporting line, but he knew that Bernard would open his big mouth and cause trouble. The recent dinner did little to settle this concern, and it made sense to create the reporting structure this way from day one knowing that a merge of roles was to be forced by the owners.

Similarly, Dimitri reminded Barry that he would be conducting a parallel operation despite his position in running the company, which scared him shitless. He worried about how far he could push essential things like being able to manage him seeing as he had strong connections with the Ivanov family.

Barry asked Veronica to set up the induction meetings for Dimitri and substituted himself for Geoff, which Veronica needed to arrange. Geoff was reasonably happy to help. As uncomfortable as it was for him, he had met with Dimitri previously and recognised that he was in a better position than others to help him settle in.

Geoff was not due to be in Manhattan until a week later, so the meeting was arranged to coincide with his trip. Veronica was great at taking multiple diaries and schedules and just making things happen in general. She was a real asset to the company and, more importantly, to Barry.

By the time of the meeting with Geoff, Dimitri had been on a whirlwind tour of the global facilities meeting with his teams. Although, it was clear that he was no stranger to such an important position.

Geoff was once again impressed with how Dimitri handled the needs of the company, even the legitimate ones, along with his command of the market and his ability to handle the stresses of the enormous responsibilities he held.

The meeting was going well, so much so that for a while Geoff had forgotten why Dimitri was appointed and treated him just like any other senior executive. Geoff occasionally felt his smile deteriorate when reminding himself of the dangers that lay ahead – the dangers this man presented and the people he was connected with – but he was careful not to let Dimitri see this. He was hoping that Dimitri would report what a great chap he was to the higher authorities and that his own appointment to the board by Barry was the right choice. It was a strange feeling. He was enjoying the discussion, although at the same time he was guarded by his conscience, just like any interview he had conducted.

Behind the veneer of his appointment, Dimitri was an excellent leader of operations. His credentials were amazing. Had he not been associated with the Ivanov family, Geoff was convinced that he would be François' natural successor. He needed to pause to remember that this guy's friends had created the bloody vacancy in the first place by murdering François. This thought swirled around his head for several minutes.

Dimitri recognised the instant change in Geoff's demeanour and suggested that they both take a break. It was just past four in the afternoon, so Geoff and Dimitri agreed to continue their conversation over drinks at the hotel later. A welcome break for them both.

Geoff went back to his office and watched the people in the high-rise block opposite. He was fascinated as usual about the many figures going about their day focused on whatever tasks they needed to complete, likening this to blood cells travelling around the body with each one having a purpose.

He stood looking with a glass of water in his hand. The cold liquid helping to calm his racing heart as he struggled to let go of the image of François being strangled, shot, poisoned or buried alive. Also, he was feeling guilty about laughing and enjoying time with Dimitri, which seemed hugely disloyal to François' memory. He was curious in a morbid way to know the truth about his fellow executive.

He needed some spiritual guidance, but he could not talk openly to his wife as his secrets would need to remain hidden from those he loved.

Dimitri was a drinker. By the time Geoff arrived at No.4 it was clear that he had a little catching up to do. Even though he was troubled by the disloyalty, Geoff was keen to join Dimitri in a few drinks.

The dinner was delicious as always, and Geoff was decidedly more relaxed now. The two men got to know each other, obviously avoiding the awkwardness of the illegal transactions as Dimitri also had a global operation to run. There were no pauses necessary as they had much to discuss.

Dimitri had the largest number of people in his teams compared to other executives, so professionally Geoff was in his element, particularly as he knew that much of his time would be working alongside Dimitri and his team of vice presidents of each function.

At one point, Geoff looked up and purposely glanced at two ladies at the bar. Their heads were at an angle, so he was prevented from seeing their faces.

Wearing his vodka goggles, his curiosity continued as he stared hoping to glimpse more of their beauty. The slender figures half-perched on a barstool was enough in itself to maintain his interest, not that he was the type to do much about it. They looked in their early twenties, so he was more than twice their age, yet he was a man like any other and continued to glance occasionally during his conversation with Dimitri.

Dimitri was charming, good-looking and younger than Geoff. Although, at this stage of the evening the barriers were somewhat lowered, so Geoff could tell that he was rather selfish, not exactly a family man and disrespectful towards women. Geoff was always respectful and women were not sexual objects to him. Despite his occasional curiosity, he was a decent chap and hugely loyal to his wife and family.

As Dimitri left to use the bathroom, Geoff saw him take a sudden detour towards the women sat at the bar. He mumbled to himself out loud, 'Surely he's not going to... Blimey, he's gone straight up to them.' *Wow*, thought Geoff, himself not having the same confidence.

He saw Dimitri soon revert to his original plan and head away from the bar. As he glanced once more, one of the women looked over. It was the same lady from the pool a few weeks ago. Geoff felt his heart in his throat, which could have been acid reflux given the alcohol he had consumed. He quickly broke eye contact before returning to glance again. As the woman smiled innocently with warmth, Geoff returned the gesture instantly as the two women continued their conversation.

By the time Dimitri returned to the table, proud of his attempted prowess at the bar, Geoff made a point of looking over once more. They were now approached by another man who was tall, handsome and super confident. Geoff sank a little and returned to his drink that had been unattended for at least fifteen minutes.

As Dimitri continued to impress Geoff with his views and opinions, he noticed the two women go their separate ways. The man was left standing at the bar, remaining there to hide his embarrassment of crashing and burning via their obvious rejection. Geoff looked up as he saw the woman approach him.

'Hello, would you mind pretending that I am with you, please? That man at the bar is being rather persistent and my friend has gone to her room to make a call. I really don't want to be on my own with him. I've seen you here before, but sorry if I'm intruding.'

Geoff stood up immediately to welcome the beautiful young woman to join them. The sight of her in front of him was instantly sobering. The two exchanged smiles as she introduced herself as Kristeena, a ballet dancer in a New York theatre on tour for seven months along with Anna, a fellow dancer.

Dimitri instantly began his charm offensive, yet Kristeena hardly acknowledged him as she continued talking to Geoff. Flicking her long black hair occasionally, she revealed more of her perfect young face and the neckline of her tight dark blue dress, which revealed the most amazing body even to the uninitiated. Geoff tried not to look despite having the burning desire to do so.

The conversation continued. Geoff was mesmerised by her southern European accent.

She was from Georgia. He knew this was not Georgia in America, as her accent reminded him of a couple of James Bond films. He was in fantasy mode for a matter of ten minutes until Kristeena's friend returned. Attractive as she was, her smile was hardened by life unlike Kristeena, whose warmth was of the sun itself whilst projecting a breath of fresh air in an otherwise stale environment.

Dimitri's eyes lit up once more. 'Great, a double date,' he suggested whilst acknowledging Dimitri with a smile as Anna greeted her.

Kristeena thanked Geoff as they said goodbye. Geoff was now back in gentleman mode shaking her by the hand, as if a business meeting had ended in a positive outcome. The two women took a table for dinner nearby. He watched her elegantly move across the room as he had done so in the pool several weeks ago, remembering her sweet scent emanating from her perfectly toned skin.

Dimitri offered a wolf-like smile and continued to offer his advice on pursuing Kristeena, like a predator plotting to lure its innocent victim.

Geoff shrugged this off as nonsense, yet in the back of his mind he felt that there was a connection, in some hopeful naive schoolboy fantasy.

At that point Dimitri received a call from Ricardo, which he made no secret of to Geoff.

Ricardo was helping Dimitri refine his views on how to achieve the needs of the somewhat dangerous and distant owners with the ongoing demands of running the legitimate operation, which eventually led to Dimitri walking out of the restaurant to continue the conversation. He indicated to Geoff that the call could be quite lengthy, which Geoff acknowledged as Dimitri moved out of view.

As Geoff moved to the bar on his own, he noticed Kristeena walking towards him. She was alone and seemingly heading back to her room with a key card in her hand.

'Goodnight,' called Geoff in a polite and innocent gesture as he glanced at the array of colourful bottles displayed in front of him.

Kristeena did not hear what he had said, so she took a detour to approach Geoff in order to clarify.

Geoff turned around to hear her warm brogue once again, embarrassed that the comment was saying goodnight rather than asking if she would like a drink. Geoff recognised her embarrassment and offered her a glass of champagne, which she charmingly accepted as if to be polite if a little uncomfortable at first.

Geoff continued to be positively paternal initially, which he recognised was confusing and uncomfortable. He apologised immediately, although he could not really recognise why she had accepted his offer to join him.

Once the barriers were chipped away, the two enjoyed each other's company and continued their dialogue into the night. Geoff forgot his age and weathered appearance. He was feeling like a thirty-year-old again as he looked at this charming and lovely beauty who had simply captivated him in every sense.

After an enjoyable evening, Kristeena ended it with an apology due to starting work early and needing to rest. Geoff escorted her to the lift, which they shared.

Kristeena's room was on the second floor, whereas Geoff occupied a much more palatial suite on the top floor. As the doors opened for her to leave, the two embraced in a kiss combining tenderness and passion. Kristeena said goodnight and hoped to see Geoff tomorrow, which he acknowledged with a gesture only, not believing what had happened.

As he caught a glimpse of himself in the polished interior of the elevator, he was shocked that this lady of twenty-two would be attracted to him. Had he done the right thing in letting her out of the lift? Should he have taken Dimitri's advice? He settled for being himself and smiled outwardly as if he had just won an award for being the most attractive man in Manhattan. He retired for the evening alone but happy.

On a Mission for Change

Ricardo had an excellent start to his new responsibilities. He was a seasoned negotiator and skilled in the many ways of business. He often reminded himself of his humble beginnings as a teenager growing up amongst poverty, being hungry and surrounded by corruption, which was his path to a 'better' life.

In those days, a lucky break was to be given an opportunity to commit a crime on behalf of someone with money, working for an unknown faceless family who were so far removed from the detail.

To have travelled so far from poverty to becoming a man of immense talent and value to the Ivanov family was a dream come true. He was now approaching the point of final success: to be part of the family's inner sanctum of business leaders, to see behind the mask of their true identity and a place at the top table in developing their global interests. Just one more risky assignment lay in front of him, but he was energised to make it work. After all, he had risked so much to date already.

For now, the company's facilities and distribution channels were legitimate and useful for him to build a secondary channel for the movement of the other 'white goods'. His proposal was to bring on new distribution clients in new territories, where the company would supply bulk quantities of fridges and freezers legitimately manufactured each with a stash of cocaine added prior to despatch.

The distributors, themselves part of the illegal set-up, would then move the drugs on to their clients whilst selling the electrical white goods to consumers. Therefore, creating a front of legitimate sale of goods to consumers.

Getting the drugs to the manufacturing facilities was a bigger challenge, however, as the goods were monitored and accounted for accurately for reporting and financial diligence.

The plan was to establish a recycling facility where the refined cocaine would be transported in old, disused and broken refrigerators sent back to the manufacturing facilities making the new models. Taking old units and disposing of the inert gases, and scrapping the metallic carcases and using them as recycled materials would in itself be a great green initiative and potentially award-winning.

The typical costs associated with gas disposal would be paid by the company aimed at reducing greenhouse gases and acting responsibly. Ingenious, yet ultimately corrupt as reduced profit for the company meant increased cocaine movement.

In the scheme of things, Ricardo would sell infinitely more new units using recycled materials. Beyond being a hero with the Ivanov family, he suggested that Barry could end up with his profile on *Forbes* one day. He knew how to stroke the ego of the man at the top – the corporate puppet in his eyes, with Ricardo pulling the strings.

Ricardo's plan required minimal investment, but he needed to ensure that Dimitri's teams were able to support the transition of cocaine into the new units prior to them leaving the manufacturing facilities, which was easy enough with the right people on his side. Bribing a few men on a production line whose salary barely paid the bills was hardly rocket science. A few cash payments could secure the kind of loyalty that people go to prison for without snitching. The family were well placed to use such people without remorse or concern for their well-being.

From a sales perspective, Ricardo's plan would take the company into several new distribution markets and achieve a sales growth like never before. To any large company this growth would be super impressive, but it was fair to say that such expansive plans do not require hard work and talented people skills. They merely require a corrupt approach to bribe those who were susceptible along with greasing the palms of governments who were themselves corrupt and ready to receive a bundle of undisclosed income, which was obviously free from scrutiny other than those paying it.

There was no shortage of officials, workers and politicians ready to help and do their bit in the countries connected to Ricardo. All Ricardo needed to do was keep them happy, explain the rules of the game and remind them of the risks occasionally by demonstrating their reach and influence.

Ricardo had done this previously. He knew the way they worked, their thoughts, their greed and often their desire to survive. He was no stranger to making an example of a few people in order to maintain a master and slave ecosystem. This way everyone knew what would happen if they stepped out of line, became greedy or attempted to speak out.

There were many times Ricardo would make examples of people even if they complied with the rules just to prove the point to everyone else. The stakes were always high and the risks needed to be understood.

Ricardo's job was to move the operation around different companies because a long-term singular distribution channel was easy to expose. People become complacent and mistakes happen. Authorities often catch up with corruption, but as hard as they tried sometimes things went wrong.

Moving their distribution from one company to another gave those in the organisations concerned a chance to one day extract themselves from risk whilst making a pot of cash. It allowed the continuation of supply while making it difficult for authorities to catch up with them – a moving target is always harder to hit.

Ricardo would have notched up a progressive body count in his continued quest for making this work on the ground. It was soon to be his time to move into a corporate role. A way of extracting himself from the risk of being caught with a great cover position. A position of corporate responsibility that would see him cruise to the point of early retirement having served the family well, amounting a good level of wealth and allowing another version of himself to move through the ranks, just like layers of skin replacing themselves on the human body after a defined period of useful service.

His fate was to take over from Bernard, yet he was still in the thick of it, exposed and on the ground until he had put a structure in place for the distribution channels. He would buy his way to success with a sickeningly charming personality and hiding a callous character that would stop at nothing to achieve his aims. Not even murder was out of the question. Although, he had not done this himself for several years. He left such things to those who were still to prove themselves, desperate for rewards, recognition and to move up the ranks just like he and Dimitri had previously.

Dimitri was Ricardo's role model. Once he achieved a position of huge influence, Ricardo would be legitimate, wealthy and pretty much bombproof regarding the corruption. Dimitri was more experienced than Ricardo and nearer to his end goal. He was also closer to the family and a continued trusted associate.

The intention would have been for him to retire from corporate life quickly after the family move their interests to another distributor, a three-to-five-year life cycle. This would take him from washed-up desperado to retired corporate executive over a twenty-five-year period having served the family with loyalty. With less than five more years to go, the risks were worth it.

His was an inspiring story for wannabe rogues in developing countries. Dimitri had done this, and no doubt he would succeed Barry once the family became concerned or worried about him. Hence, why they were monitoring him closely. Ricardo likened this to aspiring movie stars. For years they are prepared to bare all in photos shared on the internet, take on scenes some think immoral and step on friends to get what they want. Typically for greed, fame and adoration from fans, while in the process making more money in a year than most people would make in two or three lifetimes.

Ricardo was on a mission to take over from Bernard, but for now he needed to wait until the job was done.

Recycling and the Wolf

It was not long before the operation was in full swing; time was money for the Ivanov family. Each new fridge freezer sent to the new distributors carried twenty-five kilos of cocaine, with every weekly shipment consisting of fifty units. For just one facility, this resulted in around $15–$20 million per week of uncut cocaine, which could be worth three times this on the street when cut with other materials for end user consumption, and it was.

As an example, the South American teams would buy old fridge freezers, stash the cocaine inside and ship them to Indonesia for recycling. As these were regarded as leaky, broken carcases of scrap goods, they attracted little attention. At the other end, there would be a few blind eye inspections before transporting to the manufacturing facility.

The gases, if there were any left, were bottled and disposed of. Well, at least that was the process described in the corporate literature. This was not as stringent in Indonesia compared to the majority of other countries or continents. In reality, governments bought with regular cash payments gave little concern for how harmful environmental gases were released into the atmosphere. Their view was similar to that of other non-compliant countries such as China. Why should they be concerned when others did not care? Just release the bloody gas into the air! Who cares? The answer was no one at all given that they were relatively small amounts and pretty much undetectable like a fart on a mountain.

The cocaine was simply moved from one old unit into another new unit destined for the specific market channels. Careful attention was paid as to which unit the product went into, as this could bring the whole operation down if a legitimate retailer opened the door to their new showroom unit only to find twenty-five kilos of Columbian pure cocaine. Questions would be asked and it would not be long before the manufacturing facility was raided and closed down. It was not difficult to delineate the units, however, as the ones sent to the corrupt channel were clearly marked for the use of recycled materials with a big sticker on the side. Not that there were any differences in the materials used for the specific units. It was only a ruse so that the guys in the manufacturing facility could pop in the packages before sealing with cellophane strips.

None of the legitimate recipients of the fridge freezers would accept paying top dollar for goods made with recycled materials, so they were relatively well separated unless someone was malicious.

Barry's meeting with Alexandre started reasonably well. Alexandre had agreed additional funding for the recycling facility in Indonesia. How could he not? It was to support the movement of his bloody cocaine, a mere $300,000.

In reality, minimal impact was needed: clear out a warehouse or two, rebrand them with a lick of paint and employ a lot of staff to run it. There was no shortage of people willing to work, and a few carefully chosen were trusted to handle goods in and move packages around after hours. It was relatively easy.

There was no shortage of money on offer. Although, Barry was a straight businessman and needed to be satisfied that money coming in through the front door could be accounted for. Strangely, he was to continue pushing back on further investments offered by International Rescue as presented by Alexandre over the coming weeks and months. Money laundering is a crime, and he was in enough trouble without adding this to the list of things he could be arrested for.

Barry did not trust Alexandre at the previous dinner he attended nor today. He was aware of his involvement with the Ivanov family, but this was rarely discussed in the meetings that followed.

At this particular meeting, Alexandre was keen to explore the motivations of the other board members whilst looking for weak links and risks.

Barry was guarded as always and careful not to reveal that he was aware these bastards had his house bugged and goodness knows what else. He was also concerned that the next words from his mouth could seal the fate of someone else just to clear up loose ends for a faceless organised crime family who cared for no one except themselves.

Barry discussed one particular person of concern. A snooper. A man of real attention to detail and a potential corporate whistle-blower. This was the chair of the audit committee, Peter Parsons.

Even though Barry had no affection for Peter, he did not want him to meet his fate on a building site. He was careful to highlight his concerns, yet they were genuine as Peter was a generally curious person.

He said that Peter had been appointed to ask awkward questions by the previous owners. A thorough chap who liked to lift up rocks to find out what lurked beneath. Although this could be helpful, Peter could easily uncover something he should not.

Peter's role was more aligned to financial matters than the operational ins and outs of the warehouse, but Barry was concerned how Peter would perceive this with the constant push of money from Alexandre. He was right to be worried.

Peter was not a likeable person within the company. Barry was convinced that he would be great, yet he was a thorn in his side, a necessary evil, whilst occasionally helping to outline concerns early that would have otherwise caused trouble further down the line. Despite this, Barry failed to give him the credit he deserved. Perhaps their relationship would have been more constructive if he had offered his findings with compassion and support rather than his usual corrosive, acidic snipes that would enrage and irritate him.

Peter was in his early sixties, bald with small grey sideburns and was always neatly turned out. He wore his glasses halfway down the bridge of his nose in a judgemental manner as he stared and commented without emotion or humour. Yet Barry always knew that his intentions were on the right path, even though his views were often clinical, unemotional and rather pedantic at times.

The audit committee met once per month and Peter, as his title suggested, would chair this meeting along with a few non-executive directors, advisers and veterans from other sectors, who were appointed for a small fee each year to meet periodically and share advice on matters relating to corporate governance. This was a typical structure and followed the same rules as most large organisations. They discussed everything from salaries, supplier engagement, legal compliance and statutory obligations in various territories.

Therefore, Peter had enough to keep him busy even though Barry was constantly attempting to keep him contained. Peter's desire to get involved often saw them clash. Barry liked the opportunity of stamping on him. He was employed by the organisation and, despite his strength of character, Peter would need to back down more often than he liked because he did not have executive responsibilities.

Alexandre sat listening to Barry as he described Peter. His deep-set eyes, intimidating to most, caused Barry to be unnerved even though he was no stranger to forceful characters. His nickname, 'The Wolf', awarded by others was certainly fitting. Other than recognising that he was now his point of reference, his contact with the owners and realistically someone he reported to, he knew very little about him.

To Barry's surprise, Alexandre made no suggestion of how to reign in Peter and there was no suggestion of doing away with him. Instead, he suggested that such a person was good to have on the team. It would look good if they were ever investigated: another neck to hang.

Alexandre had the perfect opportunity to use his time with Barry to get to know him, but he made no attempt to do so.

In some ways, Barry was pleased by this as it allowed him some distance from the corruption. At least in his own mind despite knowing deep down that the owners would have no recourse at all when the shit hit the fan. It was him running the company and his name as the leader who would be challenged.

'Will I get to meet the Ivanov family?' Barry enquired. He was not necessarily bothered one way or the other, but he was strangely curious about them and had an unusual respect for their achievements, which he could only assume were great given the enormity of cocaine being shipped by his teams each week.

'No one meets the family, except those who are close to them or are running their operations,' replied Alexandre.

Barry thought for a moment. *Surely I'm running an important operation and rather close by default?* He challenged Alexandre with a playful smile – probably to see if the guy could open up, but he did not.

The meeting ended with Alexandre arranging their next discussion as clinically as it had started. Veronica then escorted him down to reception on his way out of the building.

Upon her return, Barry sat with her to discuss urgent messages and tasks. He was listening intently for the first part, but then his mind wandered thinking about his own security after recalling Alexandre's comments.

Knowing what the family was capable of, if the last two deaths were to be believed, he remained concerned that he could be next.

He was acutely concerned about Alexandre's ability to replace him. It was not unusual for a CEO or global president to be ousted in favour of a private equity company assigning their own replacement.

Veronica interrupted his thoughts when she reminded him to return the call to the NYPD regarding François' missing person's report. His attention was refocused immediately.

He was keen to move on from this and quickly made the call as Veronica left the room. He was surprisingly calm given his knowledge, their friendship and recognising that François would still be alive today if he had handled things differently. He possessed the gravitas and skills to easily outwit the detective whose job was to find a needle in a haystack. It seemed obvious to Barry that the officer had neither the time nor the energy to dig too deeply given the mountain of crimes piling up by the hour.

Barry was pleased that the conversation was on the phone rather than in person. Looking at the police officer face-to-face may have prevented him from withholding the facts that continued to burden him daily. Barry was asked to discuss the events leading to François' dismissal. Something that was easily explained in business and even easier to recognise in America as an everyday occurrence of an executive moving on. He attempted to convince the officer that he believed François had not taken the news well and maybe there was a mental health issue. He suggested that they check the alleyways for drunks and tramps knowing it was a wild goose chase, but he was convincing enough for now.

The Magician

Dimitri and Geoff were away from Manhattan for a number of weeks touring the facilities. After Geoff had seen the recycling facility for himself, he secretly admired what had been achieved in such a short time frame, although he despised his association with the movement of anything illegal, especially drugs. It was clear to him that the family's interest in the company was not a sudden knee-jerk reaction; it was carefully planned and executed. Although Barry had not said so, Geoff was convinced that they had been carefully chosen by the family for their investment.

Despite being thousands of miles from Manhattan, Geoff continued to remind himself of the kiss with Kristeena in the elevator. Had he imagined it? Did he read more into it than he should? There was no excuse not to call as he knew Kristeena would be staying at No.4 for several months, yet he dismissed the thought each time.

Geoff had a strange admiration for Dimitri. Given his passion and skill for interpreting people, situations and emotions, he could identify that Dimitri was well placed to take over from Barry and could even be better at the job. Initially, Dimitri was appointed to replace François, but Geoff recognised his broad knowledge and talent straight away.

Similarly, Dimitri knew that Geoff had been positioned as the potential fall guy by Barry. However, he was better placed to recognise Geoff's talents and hoped that further trust would develop as time progressed.

Geoff would be asked for input into many of the changes and challenges that were presented to Dimitri. Although this meant Geoff was doing his job for him, he loved every minute of it and felt an increased sense of belonging.

During this intense period of travel, Geoff stayed longer than usual in the different countries. He only returned home for very short periods and missed several weekends. Typically, Geoff would not have enjoyed this as he loved being at home. He viewed travel as the necessary exception, not the norm.

'The time has come, Geoff, for us to make some changes to the organisation,' stated Dimitri. 'I will be talking to Barry next week in Manhattan about dismissing Bernard and replacing him with Ricardo. Therefore, two things: One, I need you to help me propose this to Barry as he is still the boss and we need to respect that. Secondly, for you to execute the plan.'

Geoff had neither the time nor emotional attachment to Bernard; he really considered him an overpaid arsehole with an inflated ego. His recent knowledge of his misdemeanour in Indonesia made him even less popular, so Geoff agreed that he would find a way to help.

At the same time, Geoff's mind turned towards the word 'Manhattan'. To him this transported him back to the elevator again. He easily recalled the softness of her skin. Her hair so perfect and the way it fell over her face before she flicked it back. He could almost feel her tiny waist and the warmth of her smile as she said goodnight. What would he do? This flooded his mind beyond anything else. Perhaps he had enjoyed being on tour with Dimitri as this ensured he was on the other side of the world from her. So much easier than admitting his guilty feelings to himself, which helped him to sleep better at night.

Given that Geoff was feeling a little more at ease with Dimitri, he decided to ask a question hoping that he would receive a supportive response. 'One thing that has played on my mind for a while is the man I met after being apprehended by the FBI, following a misunderstanding. He gave no name, although—'

Dimitri interrupted, 'We both know that was no misunderstanding, Geoff. These things are arranged for a reason. It was arranged to get your attention, to remind you to treat Ricardo with respect. You should ask Ricardo about it.'

Geoff pursued questioning who the man was. He had no intention of asking Ricardo, the man who had enraged him for obvious reasons.

'He's a tough guy, Geoff. Do not mess around with this chap. Just let it go, stay loyal and forget about him,' added Dimitri in a supportive voice.

Geoff could not. He insisted that he was loyal to a fault, happy doing what he was doing and just wanted closure for his own sanity.

Dimitri stared intensely at Geoff as if to evaluate his mindset like a technical scanner feeding data into a computer. 'He is the family's security man in the West, a fluent American born in Russia or somewhere like that, connected by marriage to one of the Ivanovs. He is a troubleshooter, not a businessman like you and I,' Dimitri confirmed.

Geoff paused as he considered what a troubleshooter would do. He then asked the question hoping that the response would not be incriminating for either of them.

'He is known as "The Magician". He takes care of the family's unwanted problems and sorts things out,' replied Dimitri.

'Like getting rid of people?' Geoff gently enquired.

'I guess so, like magic!' Dimitri laughed. 'But also helping people, like he did for you, Geoff. A lawyer here and there, a favour or two for those who need it and taking charge of things when they go wrong. The less you worry about this, the better. If he shows up, something is wrong, horribly wrong, so it's best to keep out of his way.'

Geoff knew instantly that he was the person responsible for the murder of François and maybe Jaypee before that, but he was pleased to have a little more information now. He once again felt empowered and that he was moving in the right direction. Geoff knew that he would recognise the man they called The Magician if he saw him again. Obviously, he hoped he did not, unless it was to come to his assistance, then he considered the possibility that it was this guy instead of Ricardo who sent the rat to his home. Perhaps Ricardo was not as bad as he first thought. Geoff quickly dismissed this as nonsense; he did not easily forgive those who treated him badly.

Kristeena Balanchenko

Back in Manhattan after a full day of meetings, Geoff lived up to his promise that he would present a case for Bernard's demise in favour of Ricardo's appointment. He did not like either of them. Promoting this change would keep him in favour with Dimitri and those above him, but he knew that Barry would be uncomfortable making such a change so soon after appointing Dimitri following François' dismissal, disappearance and murder.

Barry agreed to share time with Ricardo to discuss this; after all, Ricardo did report to him even though Barry had given him a wide berth since joining.

He refused to axe Bernard immediately, suggesting that he would do this in three months' time when he was ready. Geoff feared this was not a good decision as he looked at Dimitri. He expected Dimitri to react, but he just smiled and thanked Barry for taking time to consider the proposal. Something did not seem right.

That evening, Geoff called home hoping to receive a boost and some attention. Nikki was giving him a hard time over minor things, so he switched off halfway through. He hoped that he could talk to her and have a friendly chat, something to cheer him up rather than being bombarded with more problems, making him feel inadequate and wondering why the hell he had bothered dialling the number.

The call was not positive. As he said goodbye to his wife, he was heading towards the bar at No.4 once again.

Despite being run by a slippery little shit called De Silva, he had to admit that it was the best place to stay in Manhattan. Probably better than the other establishments that welcomed him around the globe. Dimitri was a travel snob. It was always the swankiest hotels, so even by his standards No.4 was impressive and somewhat unique.

Geoff's heart raced looking around for Kristeena, despite worrying like crazy about meeting her again. He was secretly hoping for another close encounter with the raven-haired dancer from Georgia.

Geoff returned to his room briefly to freshen up. He was expecting a rendezvous and wanted to make sure that he at least made an effort.

At eight o'clock, Kristeena walked into the bar where Geoff was waiting. She was not dressed up as before, more casual, but looked simply stunning.

As she approached Geoff with a kiss on each cheek, he considered that she had forgotten their previous intimacy. He now worried that he had caused her some embarrassment.

It was clear that the attraction was still there for both of them as the conversation progressed, yet they merely continued talking into the evening. This came to a sudden halt when Dimitri joined Geoff at the bar.

Kristeena looked strangely shy as Dimitri introduced himself, as though having forgotten their previous meeting. His accent seemed to unnerve her like a criminal meeting a police officer unexpectedly in the street.

After making her excuses to Geoff, she set off to retire to her room. He followed her towards the elevator and they kissed once more. Although this time was much briefer as she was looking around not wanting to be seen. Geoff apologised believing he had overstepped the line.

Kristeena put his mind at ease with a mere smile and a grasp of his fingers. The two agreed to meet after he got rid of Dimitri, which Geoff soon attempted.

Not wishing to cut him down to size given Dimitri's importance, Geoff was receiving a barrage of questions about the young beauty he was with moments before.

Geoff used his remarkable people skills to wriggle his way out of their dinner to continue his fantasy with Kristeena. His heart pounded as he went back to his room. He knew her room number and plucked up the courage to call her.

To his shock, Kristeena arrived at his door shortly afterwards. He nervously invited her in for a drink, which she comfortably accepted given her rapid attendance to his room.

Geoff was nervous to comment, yet the look in his eyes spoke for him. She looked stunning as she gently slid into his room. With a nervous smile she stroked his hand as she passed by him.

Geoff's senses lit up like a bonfire inhaling her sweet scent as she turned to him. The door slammed shut. Geoff took her by the hands and kissed her passionately. A passion he had not experienced in years; his heart raced with excitement.

It was not long before his hands were exploring her every curve. Her part-naked flesh pressed against his as they undressed each other whilst moving steadily towards the bedroom. Geoff, looking longingly at Kristeena's beautifully shaped body, was easily led by the hand towards the bed, her lingerie clinging to her magnificent shape as she edged backwards. They once again engaged in a passionate kiss that tuned in to every ounce of Geoff's nervous system making his body tingle with desire.

As the two lay together, moving around the Egyptian cotton, Geoff could feel the movement in her body and breathing telling him not to stop as he pushed further, exploring her sex, feasting on her delicious body like a man who had been starved beyond his wishes, savouring her sweetness and taste of her perfectly taut skin.

As the two continued to cherish each other beyond the initial climax, the lovemaking continued as they held each other, stroked each other and continued kissing as if this were their first love.

It was clear that the two enjoyed each other's company. Even though Geoff confessed that he was married, Kristeena continued to encourage their intimate encounter. He carried on without hesitation.

Each visit to Manhattan, which Geoff manufactured to suit his cravings, involved a night together. Although he still loved his wife and family, he could not ignore the desires and hunger that Kristeena stimulated in his ageing body and rejuvenated mind.

Three months into their relationship, Kristeena was visibly shaken by something that had happened, something causing immeasurable pain, but she was unable to discuss her dilemma. Geoff went into business mode. He attempted to extract her concerns hoping to help in some way.

He knew that the relationship would soon end; her seven-month tour had one month to go. They had talked about it previously, but it was clear that this was not the problem.

Finally, Geoff's magic touch seemed to work. After twenty minutes, Kristeena revealed her problem.

'You remember the woman I was with many months ago? Her name is Anna. You met her that night when we kissed for the first time?'

How could he forget that night? But he genuinely did not take much notice of her friend at the time because he was completely fixated with Kristeena.

'She is my colleague in the Minsky ballet, if you remember. It is one of the world's-renown ballet companies, we are both proud to be dancers and teach others of our experiences. We are not friends. She is definitely not my friend, Geoff. She is connected to some people, bad people who want me to do things that I'm not happy about.'

'Then, don't do it, whatever it is,' Geoff said in a comforting but firm manner.

'You don't understand. My position in the ballet is all I have. Unless I do what they want,

I will be kicked out. I have nothing but my dancing. Nothing,' Kristeena replied, her voice emotional and her beautiful brown eyes full of tears and a sense of terror.

Geoff was now curious what she was being asked to do and by whom. He knew that the Minsky Ballet would not be insisting that she commit a crime or anything like that, yet looking at Kristeena's face it was clear that she feared for herself. 'So this thing they want you to do, is it dangerous?' Geoff asked almost unsure whether he wanted to know.

'My parents are poor, my place is funded by a grant set up by a wealthy family and I am very lucky to be here. Anna said that I must repay the favour from the ballet school in letting me stay as I hope to teach there. They expect me to act like a whore by luring some poor unsuspecting businessman into bed, then supplying him with a lethal dose of cocaine. I can't do it, Geoff.'

'Then don't. We will go to the police; let them handle it,' Geoff said angrily.

'If I don't, Anna said that bad things will happen to me and my parents in Georgia. I have no choice; I cannot go to the police.'

Kristeena's tears had subsided although her pain remained.

'Those bastard Russians, they're all alike,' he stated.

'The Ivanov family are well known in Russia, Geoff. They kill people, they—'

Before she could finish, Geoff placed his hands on his head. 'Oh my God!' He considered his position for a while. His thoughts towards Kristeena now moved from constant sexual desire to support and caring. Could he trust her with his own story? Was she a plant to get him to talk? Was he the businessman she was sent to kill? 'So, have they told you who the man is?' Geoff asked hesitantly, dreading the answer. Surely she did not know, otherwise she would have said. *No*, he thought, *it can't be me.*

'Yes, a man I have never met, an American man called Barry Isaacs. I have a photo and everything. How can I sleep with this man and then kill him? I also think that they will kill me once I have done this,' Kristeena blurted out in an emotional rage. She looked decidedly young and innocent, more like a teenager than a lover.

Geoff felt his heart thump in his chest, as though suddenly warning him of going into seizure mode. He gasped the air to reassure himself that he was still functioning properly before his rhythm returned to a level of normality. The acute light-headed sensation then began to subside.

Geoff could recognise Kristeena's innocence. He genuinely believed that she had no affiliation to the Ivanov family and was in an impossible position, which caused his own pain just looking at her.

Geoff told Kristeena about one of his connections associated with the family. He was thinking specifically about Dimitri but resisted the urge to tell her everything. This was partly because he feared that he would get himself into trouble and partly because he did not want to burden her with additional detail. She clearly had enough to worry about.

Geoff stayed with Kristeena that evening, but something fundamental had changed between them. He comforted her as a dear friend. They enjoyed each other's company without the usual complications or intimacy as there was too much else going on.

The next day, Geoff waited for Dimitri to finish his seemingly never-ending series of meetings before squeezing in to see him in one of the spare offices. 'I need your help, Dimitri. I don't know who to ask. It is rather sensitive and I'm completely out of my depth. The girl you saw me with last night, we…um…are…you know…seeing each other, pretty much now for a few months.'

'I knew it, you dirty old man, and she is more than half your age!' Dimitri said with a grin stretching from ear to ear. 'Those ballet dancers are the best, aren't they? You need help filling in for you while you're away?'

Geoff hesitated in his response. How did he know Kristeena was a dancer? He was certain that he had not mentioned it previously. And it was clear that Dimitri did not know her when they met recently. He chose to avoid questioning this and instead continued with his original plan. 'This girl is an innocent party, but she is being forced to take care of Barry on behalf of the family. There must be another way. Surely there is a better way.'

'So, you're okay with getting rid of Barry but not using the girl to do it?' Dimitri suggested.

Geoff suddenly realised how utterly insensitive this was. Killing his boss. How selfish had he been? This was disgraceful. All he had thought about was protecting Kristeena.

Dimitri merely highlighted that such things were not his decision. All he did was business; others took care of the clean-ups.

'*The Magician*, you mean?' asked Geoff.

'Maybe, although even the best magicians have glamorous assistants, my friend. And she certainly fits the profile,' added Dimitri in his playful tone.

'Okay, but how can I help her? She's my… Well…we're close friends. This will ruin her. Who knows, maybe she'll crack under the pressure,' Geoff said trying to convince his colleague that it was in his interests to help remove her from the process.

'It has been decided that Barry will be found dead after partying too hard whilst attending the conference in Germany next week. Your little girlfriend will make sure of it,' Dimitri said assertively and clinically.

'And you will take over as global CEO, I assume?' Geoff retorted impatiently.

'If the family believes this is right. It is up to Alexandre, I suppose, but yes, I should be in the frame for the job,' replied Dimitri. 'I suppose you could suggest another route, so long as it happens at the conference. Although, you don't really have the body for luring middle-aged men into bed like Kristeena does.'

Geoff suggested that he could simply negotiate with Barry to leave. He thought that Barry was sensitive to his eventual demise and was sure of a positive outcome. 'Is it because he has objected to Ricardo's appointment? If so, I'm sure I can talk him down on this. He will have reconsidered by now. He can be an obstinate old bugger and probably didn't like being told what to do. I'm sure he will have already reconsidered after thinking it through,' Geoff continued.

Just then, Martin walked past the office and saw the two men in a deep and private conversation. He felt hugely uncomfortable. Geoff was supposedly the fall guy for the operation if it all went wrong, so it was a shock to see them talking so intimately. He felt a sense of discomfort and wondered whether they were now plotting against another – him maybe.

'What are you two plotting?' he said with a laugh as he opened the glass-fronted office door.

Both men looked around a little sheepish, making Martin feel that he had indeed interrupted something sensitive or sinister.

Dimitri just stared at him without responding. Geoff looked away.

Martin, feeling unwanted, apologised and left the room, which did nothing to help his insecurities.

Geoff thought that he would no doubt be heading upstairs to tell Barry his views and spin some sinister plot. Well, he would be right to do so. He felt that he had a duty to protect both Barry and Kristeena. Protecting Barry was merely the decent thing to do. He was now implicated knowing the plan via Kristeena's pillow talk, so he felt the one responsible for ending his career and life by not taking action. For Kristeena, it was obviously a different story. Geoff was infatuated with her. This one act alone would transport her from lovely, young, innocent and warm person to no more than a prostitute and killer. Geoff could not shake this thought off no matter how hard he tried; he knew that inertia was not the right action.

A Stab in the Back

Back in his office, away from Dimitri, Geoff had the business card for John Maxwell at the FBI following his previous arrest. It was ironic that he had been forced to go through such an ordeal because Ricardo was a complete arsehole. Yet this had put him in touch with John, someone who could bring this whole bloody thing to its knees. Geoff smiled to himself, if only for a few seconds, while he considered what would happen if he went to the FBI.

He knew it was the right thing to do. His moral compass whizzed around as if he were in a magnetic field, stopping each time to remind him of both his confusion and the righteous path he knew he must choose.

He feared for his life in doing so, but he recalled the many movies he had watched, mostly in flight, where the FBI would offer witness protection programmes. He would certainly never see his darling Kristeena if this happened, but he once again considered the safety of his family as this was something he could not compromise. He knew he needed to talk to his wife. Knowing Nikki, she would not be pleased about going into witness protection, giving up her life to bring down a global crime ring, nor that he had kept this from her for so long. He worried that she would certainly leave him, even before she knew about Kristeena. She would probably castrate him if she knew about his feelings for Kristeena, even before acknowledging his affair.

Geoff was understandably divided on his next steps. Maybe talking to Barry would be the right way to go. Tipping Barry off on his fate may lead to protecting the innocent and let Kristeena off the hook. It seemed like a good compromise and a bloody good idea given his options. Either way, Geoff felt in it up to his neck. He was sensing the shit slowly and progressively rising towards his chin leading to his eventual suffocation. Time was running out. Geoff dialled Barry's extension.

'He's in with Martin, they've said not to be disturbed,' answered Veronica.

'This is really important and something they'll both want to hear,' Geoff replied in a stern yet soft tone, trying to appeal to her sensitive side.

'If you tell me what it is, I can relay it to him, and then see if he is able to see you.'

Geoff paused for a second or two. How could he tell her? Making a doctor's appointment meant telling the receptionist your ailments before a doctor would see you, it meant disclosure, but there was more at stake here than disclosing an embarrassing case of haemorrhoids. 'It's a matter of life and death, Veronica. I must see him urgently,' he demanded.

Veronica put him on hold while she ventured into Barry's office to interrupt his meeting. After a couple of minutes, she came back on the phone. 'I've asked him, Geoff. Sorry, but he's not available to talk with you.'

Geoff hung up feeling isolated and alone. He was sure that Barry and Martin believed him to be acutely allied with Dimitri and plotting against them. He had to correct this inaccurate perception that existed. He took to his email and wrote a detailed note about the conversation with Dimitri. He was sure to leave out the piece regarding Kristeena and the fate that awaited him. Instead, he highlighted that he had more to share, that there was a plot to remove him from the business in the coming days. He read it through carefully before sending it.

Geoff was avoiding returning his wife's calls. He could tell from her messages that nothing was wrong, so he continued to text her periodically to let her know that he was still working hard, all was okay and he was missing them all. The usual stuff really; lots of words without saying much. This was commonplace between them given the length of their marriage, so Nikki would not suspect anything untoward.

Following a series of short meetings, Geoff went to the kitchen to grab a coffee before returning to his office.

Dimitri walked in, helped himself to a coffee and approached Geoff. With his hand on Geoff's upper arm, he asked, 'I gather there is a problem. Anything you want to talk about?'

Geoff just shrugged and said, 'You might want to be more specific. I have problems coming out of my ears. No doubt the same for you, too.'

'Your note to Barry… Disappointing, Geoff, disappointing,' Dimitri said. His mouth moved to make a smile, but his lips pursed together in a serious look that had Geoff worried.

How the hell did Dimitri get hold of the email? It was sent in confidence. He considered Veronica may have opened his mail, yet it was marked strictly confidential. Veronica knew better than to open internal messages marked as such. Maybe Dimitri was monitoring emails himself.

Embarrassed, Geoff acknowledged this act of disloyalty to Dimitri whilst highlighting that he had withheld other more sinister facts.

Dimitri looked on as he left Geoff in the kitchen area alone stewing in his own compromising thoughts. He knew this was not the last word from Dimitri; it was only the beginning.

As he sipped the hot coffee, taking a seat on his own, he knew that all routes were now compromised. Angry as hell and feeling lonelier than he had ever felt before, he stayed there for a few minutes before deciding his next course of action.

As Barry's personal assistant, Veronica was typically someone in the know, well connected to the staff and teams, and offered a matriarch-like character that people could relate to and trust. Like most people in her position, Veronica was exposed to a myriad of sensitivities regarding the company, its people, finances and challenges. She would often be referred to as Barry's work wife. Sometimes it would seem that she made many of the decisions instead of him; albeit, low-level ones of course.

During the discussions around funding, the refinancing of the company, Barry became much more guarded and disengaged with her.

Her attempts to realign herself with Barry were met with roadblocks, pushback and more frost than warmth from the main man, which Veronica found difficult to deal with.

It was a very difficult time for Barry, having had new investors withdraw at the last minute. With much-needed funding, Barry's life went from calm yet exciting to frantic and stressful. He had attempted to shield Veronica from this latest set of challenges leading to appointing new investors, new owners, but in doing so had pushed away the one person he did not want to.

Veronica was aware that Barry had become unnaturally stressed. She saw it every day when she arrived. Longer hours, bloodshot eyes, tired from a lack of sleep and irritability beyond the man she had known for years.

Veronica was delighted when the funding terms had been agreed. At the time she recalled seeing Barry back to his gregarious, happy and charmingly assertive self. Someone she had secretly admired in many ways having demonstrated unparalleled loyalty towards him.

During Barry's darker times, which included his current state, Veronica felt unloved. Not in the intimate way lovers typically share, but a deep understanding, as if Barry no longer wanted her around. Her involvement in helping Barry had diminished to the point where her job was much less a personal assistant and more a general secretary. This was like a poke in the eye for Veronica. She had become quite unhappy about his behaviour towards her. Her isolation felt undeserved and unwelcome.

Barry was typically unapproachable. Not someone she felt comfortable to talk with the same way as they had previously. So much had changed, and now she was excluded.

Veronica suspected that Barry was taking some form of stimulant to help him through the day. Alcohol was the conclusion, as in her mind only pop stars and gangsters took drugs.

Veronica would observe her boss's mood swings throughout the day. He saved his best for those he needed to impress, and then shut himself away at other times. Shut himself off to her, which made her recognise that he was no longer the man she had respected for years.

Veronica hoped that Barry would return to his former self once the funding was in place. Barry had not intended to give so much of the company away to the new investors. This resulted in him becoming marginalised: a CEO without the real power to make decisions. He was now reporting to a higher authority; something he was not used to. This was the corporate politics part, which was painful even before considering the less than legal elements the job now demanded.

Veronica's commitment to the company remained despite her unhappiness, even though her emotions towards Barry had changed from admiration to pity considering his new positioning.

Veronica was no longer part of Barry's 'inner sanctum' amongst his closest associates for reasons unknown to her. But had she known that Barry was attempting to protect her from the sinister people he now found himself associated with, things would have been so much different.

After the completion of the funding, Veronica was approached in confidence by Carlos, the lawyer representing the investors International Rescue, to ask her out for dinner.

Veronica was a mature single woman and flattered by Carlos's approach, unaware of his hidden agenda and intentions.

The two discretely went out for dinner, with Veronica unsure whether his charm was romantic or just business.

After Veronica opened up about Barry's recent change of state, Carlos confided in her that Barry was in trouble. 'He's in way over his head, taking cocaine and who knows what else. We're really worried about him.' Carlos was setting the scene for future events, knowing that Veronica's loyalty needed placing somewhere. He was just ensuring it was on his side rather than Barry's.

As the two became closer, Veronica's loyalty clearly transferred as Carlos continually set the scene for Barry's self-destruction and the need to find his future replacement. It would be easier and significantly cheaper to dismiss Barry for an act of gross misconduct than asking him to step down. His death would cost the company nothing at all.

Veronica continued to feel sad for Barry, yet it was no shock that he was a changed man. It was easy to believe the stories from her charming new friend. She also believed that her association with Carlos was no bad career move, despite not knowing who she was really dating or being aware of the atrocities committed by those he represented – maybe even by himself directly.

It was clear that Veronica filled the void in her life left by Barry's changed state of mind with another man of similar status; someone she could admire and receive admiration and attention back in return this time.

Therefore, it would not have been viewed by her as disloyal reporting to Carlos anything that had happened in the executive team that day. Just like normal office gossip after hours. After all, she was merely talking to Carlos who was ultimately representing the new owners. *So what could be wrong with that?* she thought to herself.

Acutely aware that Veronica could be working against Barry, Geoff stormed into the executive offices. He walked straight past Veronica to Barry's office.

Despite her best efforts, Geoff continued undeterred opening the office door without knocking and pushing her aside as if she was a flimsy curtain blowing in his face.

'What the hell…Geoff. What is wrong with you, man!' exclaimed Barry, who was sitting on his sofa talking to Martin. The brown leather squeaking as he moved to see Geoff forcefully enter the room. 'It's okay, Veronica, I will see Geoff,' added Barry in a calm but assertive tone.

She acknowledged his request and closed the door behind her.

'Did you get my email earlier, Barry?' Geoff demanded.

'What email? What are you going on about? Are you off your head, old chap?' Barry responded.

'My email discussing the plan to get rid of you. That email was sent to you in strictest confidence, yet within the hour Dimitri had seen it!' Geoff said, talking down to him, believing that something was not right at all. He was going to get to the bottom of it, and fast.

As the three men stood talking to each other, Geoff relayed his conversation with Dimitri both in the kitchen and behind closed doors, which was something that Martin had his own views about.

'Yes, that conversation earlier, Geoff. It was clear to me that you were very cosy with Dimitri – no doubt plotting this between you. What has he promised you, you lying shit?'

Geoff reacted instantly. 'Lying? Me? I'm the one telling you, you ungrateful bastards.'

Looking at Geoff and hearing his forceful emotions, Barry needed to take him seriously. It was obvious that all three men were uptight and concerned about their own futures.

Geoff cautiously explained his friendship with Kristeena and that she was expected to lure

Barry to his room, sleep with him and at some point serve him a cocktail of drugs that would see him checking out in a body bag and a free taxi courtesy of the German mortuary service. It was a shock to Geoff just how calmly Barry was reacting to this.

Barry was expecting something to happen, although he did not know the details. He gave a surprising smirk as he commented, 'At least I get to sleep with a pretty girl. A decent last request, at least.'

Geoff did not join in for obvious reasons. Kristeena being referred to in this way was not a conversation he was willing to find amusing at all. 'Why not still attend the conference, Barry, but despite Kristeena's best efforts you turn her down. That way she doesn't need to do what they expect and you get to live.'

Barry shrugged off the gesture as a waste of time. He believed that either way the family wanted him relieved of his duties and they were not prepared to do things within the boundaries of common legal practices. He was suddenly resigned to the fact that he would need to go to the FBI and bust this whole thing wide open.

Geoff was pleasantly surprised and agreed that this was the best option. He handed him the business card for John Maxwell.

Once Martin and Geoff left the room, Barry was set to make the call. As he moved towards his desk, he saw that the intercom light was on. Someone was listening. It was Veronica.

'Please can you come in, Veronica?' Barry asked in a stern tone.

Veronica arrived with her notepad as she did countless times each day.

He greeted her by asking, 'Why were you listening?'

Veronica instantly went to pieces. In a flood of tears, she apologised to her boss.

Barry was unsympathetic, yet he remained calm whilst demanding more from her.

Under pressure, Veronica began to talk about how he had changed, pushed her away and made her feel unwanted, isolated and no longer a confidant. Eventually, she opened up about her friendship with Carlos. Also, how he was concerned about Barry's drug abuse, his mood swings and his ability to run the company.

Barry felt the time had come to talk to her openly because he could see that his actions had hurt her. He needed her to understand what was going on, as she had clearly misplaced her loyalties. He was forgiving of this, but her naivety was a surprise. He needed to correct this immediately.

He wasted no time in dismissing the mystery surrounding his alleged drug habit: there wasn't one. He confessed, 'I must admit that I consume my weight in alcohol each week. Also, I apologise for my somewhat distant demeanour of late.' He continued to explain his actions, which were driven ultimately by an unprecedented amount of stress due to involving International Rescue at the eleventh hour as their saviours.

Barry reserved no caution in telling her about the Ivanov family, the new backers of the private equity company, and the type of people they were. He took great pleasure in disclosing her beloved Carlos's connection, the deeds they had committed so far and the threats they had made to those closest to him. Barry looked up from his rant to see Veronica holding her hands over her mouth in horror and disbelief.

As Veronica looked at Barry, her eyes reddened and swollen from her earlier tearful tirade, she saw his eyes filled with pain, fear and disappointment. She began to feel terribly guilty and disloyal.

Barry had a knack of either making people feel exceptional or as though they wanted to shoot themselves. The latter emotion was now felt by Veronica as she listened to his every word. She once again saw the man she had trusted for so long; he was there all along.

When Veronica realised that Barry was trying hard to protect her from those very people he knew had threatened others, she began to weep once again. This time not due to being found out, but she was sad to hear how he had tried so hard to keep her from the burden of the truth, the people who called the shots, those who pulled the triggers, and the illegal transportation of cocaine, which came as the biggest shock of all to her. As if she had heard it all by now, the company she worked for was now transporting class A drugs. Something she despised as much as Barry.

How could she be taken in by Carlos's story, his lies and attempts to get close to her?

As she sat in the chair opposite Barry, Veronica remembered a number of instances when she had given up detailed information to Carlos. Now feeling sick with anger, she beat herself up over her actions and naivety. She wondered how she could make this right, if at all.

Barry shared his concerns over what had happened, but he was keen to forgive her actions as he truly believed that he had contributed to her behaviour. However, he was once again angry about how the family could manipulate the innocent to achieve their desired outcomes.

'What can I do to make this good again, Barry, to help you?' she asked.

'My fate is already sealed, Veronica. I am being replaced, probably by that shit Dimitri, although I won't be resigning.'

'How can they sack you after all you've done?' Veronica asked, unaware that his fate was not falling on his sword in professional terms.

Barry elaborated about the planned event awaiting him.

Veronica insisted that he go to the FBI. They discussed this at some length, including the ramifications of a negative outcome for him and others.

It was clear that Barry cared for Veronica. It was natural after all the years they had worked together. He had trusted her with both sensitive work and personal situations more than anyone else in the company.

Barry asked Veronica to resign as he felt it was no longer safe for her, but she refused explaining that he needed her now more than ever. This was something she had always wanted, as if such a need expressed an emotion better than any love affair.

As Veronica left Barry to his obvious pain, the moment had passed to call the FBI – at least for now while he continued to weigh up the various scenarios.

A Pleasurable Goodbye

After all the stress he had experienced recently, it was a pleasure for Geoff to invite Bernard to a meeting for a discussion about the future – Bernard was not going to have one with the company.

The meeting commenced with Bernard rattling on about how stressed he was, something typical to Bernard. He always felt that he had the rough end of the stick with those around him earning more, despite himself earning a small fortune. He was always in negotiation mode, always seeking something more than he had.

In terms of his commercial position, this was a typically selfish characteristic that Geoff understood and recognised as necessary to perform his job in sales. It continued to frustrate Geoff. He was aware of others' earnings, and Bernard's was inflated beyond other executives given his regular bonuses based on sales and profit.

Whilst historically Geoff could not comment out of turn on Bernard's unhappy lot, he was now one of his peers, a board member and had equal status, which added to his confidence in dealing with him. Geoff typically did not like Bernard, so the meeting to dispose of his services gave him a little more happiness than he had been used to over recent weeks.

Bernard, on the other hand, failed to recognise Geoff as an equal. The newcomer to the board was just that and yet to earn his stripes; whereas, he was an established executive.

Bernard continued with his selfish rant not realising the agenda for the meeting.

'Bernard,' cut in Geoff, 'I have been asked to meet you today to talk about some changes that the new owners wish to make, which may involve changes to your job.'

Bernard being as arrogant as ever replied, 'Then tell Barry to get off his arse and talk to me about it. I report to the group CEO, not some new boy like you. So if it's all right with you, I'll say goodbye.'

'No, it is not all right,' Geoff replied. 'I have equal status to you regardless of whether you like it or not. My job is to deal with changes and people, and that is something I am paid to do. So sit down and take this seriously, as what I have to say is going to affect you. Your attitude towards me will determine how much you get.'

With the inference on money, Bernard was attentive once again.

The two men talked for thirty minutes to ensure they were aligned in their thoughts. Bernard was not happy for obvious reasons and demonstrated greed in order to move on and let Ricardo take his position.

Geoff had the authority to negotiate a deal with Bernard, just to make things smooth, but he was aware that the matter may be taken out of his hands should this fail.

Despite his circumstances, Bernard was feeling on top of the situation. He believed his negotiating position was far superior to that of the company and his experience in such areas was streets ahead of Geoff.

Even though Bernard was used to negotiating supply contracts via his team, Geoff was hugely experienced in legal matters of restructure. Therefore, to Bernard's shock, he proved to be a worthy adversary.

As Bernard offered to bring down the company upon his exit, Geoff was quick to remind him of his misdemeanours abroad that may compromise him. He chose to place the Ivanov family at the centre of his argument and was secretly pleased to use this ammunition to shoot Bernard down quickly. As he squirmed over his words, Geoff took great delight in reducing this sixteen-stone, red-faced executive to rubble by turning his own argument against him.

Bernard looked at the terms offered by Geoff. 'You must be fucking joking – this is not even respectful. If you want me gone without a fuss, you will need to treble this figure.'

Geoff had offered him a sum equivalent to one year's salary. It was generous given that his entitlement was only for six months.

The two men took a break from each other with Bernard refusing to budge. Geoff had the ability to pay more, but he had no intention of Bernard profiting from this further.

They agreed to meet again in one hour, which would allow each person to reconsider their position in confidence.

Dimitri knocked on Geoff's office door during the adjournment, which was unexpected and certainly unwanted. Geoff did not hide his feelings. He gave him an unwanted look, not something that could be interpreted any other way.

'Has Bernard agreed the deal, Geoff?' he asked.

'No, not yet. You know Bernard, typically argumentative and greedy to a fault,' Geoff replied without looking directly at Dimitri.

'May I sit in on the next meeting? Can we see him today, together?' Dimitri asked.

Geoff looked up to see him appearing genuinely supportive. For an easy life, he agreed.

As the meeting reconvened, Geoff set out the offer in professional terms by reiterating the initial deal, which had not increased.

As Bernard continued his stance of extreme arrogance believing the company owed him wealth, Dimitri chipped in, 'Okay, Bernard, you greedy bastard, we will reduce the offer to six months. Nothing else, no negotiating.'

Geoff looked as surprised as Bernard, but he was secretly pleased of the support in making him less wealthy.

Dimitri handed Bernard a letter addressed to the company. 'This letter comes from the authorities in Malaysia following your involvement with a dead hooker. They want to investigate you.'

Bernard's chubby red cheeks turned decidedly pale as he read this.

'Obviously, I can make this go away, given the family's contacts with the local authorities, or I can sell you out and make sure you get what you deserve – an unpleasant life sentence,' Dimitri added.

Geoff suspected that the letter was not real. Even if it was, he was not entirely sure that the whole corrupt thing would have stood up that well. He kept quiet as he watched Bernard crumble to dust; his arrogance now destroyed leaving a regretful, pathetic shell of a man in his place. Geoff also wondered if Bernard had killed the girl in the first place, or whether this was a glamorous charade to entrap Bernard. Geoff knew the extent of the family's reach and abilities; he knew that nothing was to be taken at face value.

Bernard knew that this was a set-up and his DNA was at the scene of the crime. He had little choice but to trust in Dimitri's authority and agree to the terms.

Dimitri left the room leaving Geoff to tie up the signing of the document.

It was the same document he had used many times in exiting people who had become surplus to requirements. The same document François refused to sign, prior to him ending up dead and buried somewhere on a construction site. Surely Bernard understood his predicament.

Swearing as he read the terms again, he looked at Geoff and muttered, 'I look forward to being there when it's your turn. It will come, Geoff. I hope you know this.'

Geoff was acutely aware of his own dilemma. He acknowledged Bernard and accepted his signed copy of the agreement, something that would prevent him from talking about his time with the company, their staff or shareholders. Basically keep your mouth shut about everything or you will be in breach of contract, sued for large sums of money and no doubt become unemployed, penniless and ruined in the process.

The agreement was obviously not referring to the other option of being shot, poisoned or whatever else the family chose to carry out at the time. François' disappearance was still a mystery to most; a subtle threat to all others and a missing person's report at the local precinct that would no doubt go unsolved.

Bernard, as always, insisted on having the last word. As he exited the room having waived all his legal, moral and contractual rights, he shouted, 'At least I'm free from this illegal crap that you're now all caught up in. Hope you're all arrested and go to fucking jail!'

His words felt chilling to Geoff as he watched Bernard hand over his company effects and security pass.

Bernard's red face seemed almost scarlet as his anger superseded his jolly yet aggressive manner, like a traffic light about to explode. Whilst Geoff felt little sympathy for this obnoxious, self-centred and overweight adversary, he recognised that Bernard was right: there was a high degree of risk in being caught. It was yet another sign that he needed to expose this whole thing wide open to free himself and protect those around him.

It was time to talk to his wife, but not over the phone.

Homeward Bound

The flight home for Geoff was like any other. The hospitality in business class always welcoming as he gulped his first glass of chilled champagne. Glancing around, he reminded himself of the hundreds of people sitting in standard class. His status upfront in the aircraft reminiscent of his status in business.

However, this was no ordinary journey; it was to be a sleepless night. As the flight commenced, his mind flooded with scenarios of how events could play out at work, with the FBI, his own safety and how the Ivanovs would preserve themselves at any cost, which could result in devastating events for him.

Not even the alcohol had the desired effect of helping him to sleep. His thoughts turned to the conversation he was to have with his wife. He rubbed his face firmly in some kind of refreshing ritual. He knew that her stance would be critical of his behaviour regarding the illegal transactions he was aware of and not having reported them so far. He would have difficulty explaining his actions, his reasoning and concerns. Once she started, it was typically difficult to get his point of view across to her closed yet wonderfully naive mindset.

He remembered an event whilst at a previous employer when he had become ill. He was unable to work for a few months due to a serious illness, which left him in a difficult position because his employer would not allow him to return. He felt that his illness would create problems for them. Despite a steady recovery, his employer refused to let him come back. This resulted in Geoff going to court to fight for his rights.

At the time, Nikki continually pushed him to sue his employer, an unrelenting quest for satisfaction, but Geoff took a more practical view. Having been to court numerous times, he understood how painful the process could be, and how utterly demanding and often pointless the outcomes were. A moral victory in court could be damaging to your health as well as your pocket, which Nikki failed to recognise in her own innocent manner.

At the time, Geoff's lawyer briefed Nikki on how she would be required to give evidence at the hearing. She was a principal witness to his health, recovery and emotions, but Nikki refused to take part citing that she did not want to be cross-examined. Geoff remembered understanding his wife's reluctance and was supportive as anyone could be in the same situation.

The case settled out of court for much less than he was entitled to, but a result nonetheless. Yet she criticised the outcome despite her withdrawal weakening his case and suggested that he could have achieved so much more. In reality, he may have got less without any witnesses to support him had it not settled out of court, but this was brushed under the carpet as such a confrontation would have achieved very little.

On this particular and immediate problem, he knew that he would receive similar input: lots of self-righteousness and pushing for action without her substantial support or involvement. This was his dilemma. He knew he should talk to her, but would she actually listen? He knew he would have taken a similar view if the tables were turned; it was a typically well-balanced marriage.

His anger was boiling over when he thought about Kristeena. The pain the family were putting her through: to kill an innocent man, his boss, and make it look like a drug overdose after partying with a prostitute. The thought of her behaving like a hooker made him mad beyond belief. How could he allow his beloved Kristeena to go through with either act? While he could never consciously leave his wife for Kristeena, he cared for her deeply and she made him feel like a man again, desirable, sexy and excited to be alive.

Despite being happy growing old together such feelings had not existed between himself and Nikki for a number of years, so he was making the most of the attention from his stunningly beautiful and talented dancer. He had to pinch himself each time they were together to remind him that this was real life and actually happening – yes, him, an ageing businessman. He was somewhat short and lacking the physical profile of the kind of men he would place her with, such as a male model, a dancer or someone with a six-pack abdominal structure and chiselled facial features. He knew it would not last forever, but for now he could live out a real fantasy and just enjoy it.

Geoff woke with a jump as the plane landed at Heathrow. He sat upright, his body feeling heavy and worn out as he rested his head back onto the seat. He was saddened that his sleep had ended.

A driver was always waiting for him as he emerged from customs with chocolate for the children and perfume for Nikki bought at JFK in a hurried attempt to let them know he was thinking of them all. The handwritten sign caught his attention as the driver helped him with his bags to the waiting silver Mercedes E-class diesel.

In just over an hour, he would be home. Some nine hours had already elapsed since he pondered on the story he would be sharing with Nikki, yet he was no clearer in his mind how he would start the conversation despite knowing her reaction in advance.

The driver, mindful of Geoff's weary look, refrained from conversation. Something Geoff was truly appreciative of as he was in no mood to make small talk with a stranger, certainly not an hour's worth anyway.

The car arrived at home. As the children were at school Nikki was at the door to welcome him, which she often did when not busy working. Nikki volunteered at the school for an odd day here and there on the payroll or on a commission basis. Not exactly the height of capitalism, but it kept her busy and provided a little income to retain her independence. Her life was hectic beyond this with friends galore. The opposite to Geoff who had little time for friends outside business by comparison. Not that this was his preference, but his work-life balance was not established.

Geoff sat down with a cup of tea while Nikki went into typical download mode relaying the events of the past few days, the children, school, friends, gossip and the next holidays that needed decisions.

When she went to her email to show him a quote received from the travel agent, although still talking, he saw his opportunity.

'Work is just awful at the moment, darling. I have a few things on my mind that are causing me some major problems…'

'So are you saying not to book another holiday? You said we could. What's changed?' she muttered.

'Yes, the holiday is fine. I just have some things going—' Geoff tried to continue but Nikki just carried on talking about holiday destination choices without acknowledging her husband's obvious pain.

It was no wonder that Geoff found comfort in Kristeena's arms. His life was lacking attention; today was merely a reminder of what his life at home had become.

It was not Nikki's fault. Geoff had thrown himself into his work for years. Despite blaming work for everything, he loved it, loved being part of something good and loved the attention of having seniority. He was even happier now that he had reached the heights of an executive director. This did present some problems at home though. He was hardly there for his children, at least he could never guarantee it, and he was never there when his wife needed him. Essentially, they still loved each other yet had grown apart. It was nothing intentional, just something that happened.

'Will you just listen to me for one minute, please?' Geoff exclaimed throwing the holiday brochure on the table in front of her to make the point. 'I'm in trouble at work. Things are happening that are just terrible, and I don't know what to do.'

Nikki looked understandably perplexed while her husband continued to talk a lot about nothing, circumnavigating the reality of his situation. 'You're not making any sense, Geoff. What trouble? Are you just stressed and tired?' she asked.

Geoff paused as he stared into her worried eyes. He wondered whether to give her the warts and all version or a sweetened snapshot. He knew that after all these years of marriage that he should spill the beans, the only reservation being his relationship with Kristeena as this would create unnecessary pain with no benefit at all.

As he continued to relay his painful story, jumping from point to point and reverting back and forth trying to get all the facts across, Nikki just sat there taking it in not saying a word, which was unusual.

Nikki saw a side to Geoff that she had not remembered for many years. He was usually strong in his resolve and dealt with major problems in his stride. Now his vulnerability was exposed, his guard down, and his emotions laid bare in front of her. Such a weakness would usually have been hidden from all those around him, so it was apparent that this was not an easy thing for him to do.

With tears in his eyes, he spoke of the Ivanov family's capabilities, the crimes he was aware of to date and his fears of what would happen if he ever decided to oppose this corrupt, criminal regime that seemed to stretch the world over.

As he paused for a second whilst sharing his knowledge of Barry's house being bugged by those closest to him, Nikki placed her hands onto his. This acted as both a calming influence and a reassurance that he had not felt for some time.

He looked at the floor scratching the corner of his eye as though to discretely wipe away a tear. He was now telling her about a young lady 'in his team' called Kristeena and how they were blackmailing her to carry out an appalling act.

Nikki's other hand raised to her mouth as she attempted to hold back her expression of horror thinking about Barry's pending murder.

As Geoff relayed to her his impossible position, he reminded her of all his achievements, what he would give up, the potential threats that would follow and the risk to his own family from those hell-bent on protecting their own. The Ivanovs would stop at nothing despite his obvious business status. He was a mere pawn in the bigger game and a sacrificial lamb to the higher beings.

'You must go to the police, FBI or whoever you need to.'

Geoff reminded her of François' fate, the joke threat made to her by Ricardo and how the Ivanovs knew where they lived. He emphasised their children's security and his own involvement in appointing several people associated with the drug distribution process and how this would look to the FBI if he was arrested or implicated.

He then decided to mention the previous arrest at the airport, which he explained was the work of the Ivanov family and a reminder of their devious and potentially dangerous ways.

Nikki viewed it differently. 'If they wanted to hurt you, they would have. You were let off without charge. Surely this shows that they're not in control of everything, or that they still need you,' she added offering a practical opinion.

'They need me to keep digging my own hole, darling. Can't you see? Everyone I hire that is associated with the drug process digs me in deeper and deeper to the point where I'm so involved and implicated. The whole thing is a weight hanging around my neck,' Geoff replied, his hands raised in exasperation and defeat.

Nikki went over to the drinks cabinet and poured them both a small vodka and tonic. 'Here, something to take the edge off, I think we both need it. I had no idea you were involved in all of this. You bloody fool, you idiot! How could you put us all at risk like this? You selfish bastard, all for a promotion! Why didn't you get another job like most normal people? No. Instead, you choose to get into drugs and murder and prostitution!' Nikki summarised holding her husband responsible for her obvious anger and disappointment, her tears now flowing as both her tone and volume increased.

'Do you think I volunteered for this? Do you? When I was appointed to the board, we were revelling in the excitement and potential wealth. Barry then shared with me the journey: five years and we're all out as rich men. I knew nothing of the murder, prostitution or the lengths the bloody Russians would go to, or how I would be implicated if it all goes wrong. Barry, Martin and Paul are all involved as well, you know.'

'So, Barry will be murdered by some prostitute. Where does that leave your precious Paul and Martin then, eh? And yourself, too? Do you think that Barry is the last change they will make? You could be next! Well, the way I see it is that they'll kill each of you. Do you not see this?'

She had moved on her previous stance, yet she was right. Geoff was not keen to accept it, but deep down he knew that his time would come. Regardless of whether he lived or not, he stood little chance of walking away a rich man. The dilemma was what he should do about it.

As the two sat together talking things through, sipping the drinks Nikki had prepared, he knew that the pain he had caused her was not intended, yet it felt that he had purposefully set out to do this. In her mind there were no alternatives but to report it and finally put an end to all of this.

Geoff went to the small antique table in the hallway where he placed his wallet and keys when returning home. He reached for the business card from the FBI stowed carefully in a zipped pocket in his wallet. 'Special Agent John Maxwell, FBI,' he read out loud as he handed it to Nikki. 'This was the man who arrested me at the airport. He seemed to be aware of something sinister at the company and suggested I talk to him.'

'Then do it, Geoff, before we all end up shot or knifed to death by these maniacs,' she retorted without hesitation.

Geoff knew that this was his only real option. He would not be in Manhattan for another week, but he had to do something quickly before Kristeena was compromised and Barry was murdered.

Thinking that his phones may have been tapped, he borrowed Nikki's mobile and went into his office to make the call. Phones being bugged. A crazy notion, but he knew that life was beyond normal for him right now.

His heart raced as he dialled the number. He could feel it thumping in his chest as the operator attempted to connect him. The ringtone was decidedly different as the call connected; he was obviously in transit somewhere.

'Special Agent Maxwell.'

Geoff announced himself in response and attempted to explain who he was. John Maxwell greeted him immediately as he recalled his name.

'I think I need to talk to you,' Geoff said hesitantly.

'You think or you know?' questioned Maxwell.

'I think I have no choice. You see it's about the company and their connection to something terrible. Something that is—'

'Okay, not on the phone, you never know who's listening in. Let's meet somewhere neutral in Manhattan. Where are you right now?'

'In England. I'm not due to be in Manhattan for a week, but this will not wait, Agent Maxwell,' Geoff stated in desperation.

'Any way you can get here sooner? I cannot help you until I know what's on your mind, despite having a good idea of the situation. I need to hear it all from you first-hand,' Maxwell said, stating the obvious.

Geoff knew that he needed to move quickly. 'Leave it with me. I will call you when I have a flight sorted out.' After disconnecting the call, he immediately dialled Barry's office number. He had his own plan.

When Veronica answered immediately, Geoff announced himself playfully to her. He tried to play down his stresses in favour of presenting a business reason to call, a happy level of normality, but he was concerned that Veronica would still be listening in.

As he was put through to Barry, he immediately asked him to call back on Nikki's mobile and offered the number without an explanation. Barry happily obliged.

As the phone rang, Geoff could see that he was calling from a different number. Barry obviously knew that the call had some level of sensitivity and kept it from the landline where he also suspected Veronica of eavesdropping.

'This conference of yours, Barry, I have an idea. With your support, I can arrange for you to bump into another woman, an escort girl, something I will arrange, leaving no opportunity of Kristeena getting to you first. You go off with her and keep yourself busy out of harm's way. Kristeena won't need to compromise herself and you survive the night. At least it will buy us some time. I will be meeting the FBI to spill the beans. I know it's risky, but I fear that we will all be killed off one by one unless someone does something.'

'Geoff, this could work, but I cannot expect you to expose yourself to the risks of the FBI. These people will not be able to protect you against the Ivanovs. Do you realise what you are risking?'

'I fear I have no choice but to do this. Too many people's lives are in danger,' Geoff quickly pointed out.

'You do understand that we might all go to prison? We will all be out of jobs and all those in the company could be at risk of unemployment.' Barry's words reminded Geoff of his previous dilemma, but he promised Nikki and he had committed to reporting matters to the FBI despite his unease.

As Geoff eventually ended the call with Barry, he glanced over his shoulder to see Nikki standing there with a reassuring smile. A smile that was comforting and loving, reminding him of why he enjoyed being at home.

He returned the reassurance in his own facial expression and watched Nikki leave the room. He made sure that she was out of earshot before making the call to Kristeena on Nikki's mobile phone.

He was hoping that Kristeena would answer. Surprisingly she did, seemingly happy to hear from Geoff like a love-starved teenager. He discussed the plan for her to book into the hotel, where she would no doubt be watched, and then to approach Barry as he retired to the bar along with other conference delegates. Kristeena would of course look elegant, stunningly so, and ensure that she made herself noticed by Barry. He would then engage with her given his natural dominance and affinity for attractive females whilst on business.

Geoff asked for her help in arranging an escort girl to get there first. She had not done anything like this before, but Kristeena knew there was no other option and readily agreed. He explained that he would send her a file with Barry's photograph and venue details.

He acknowledged that he did not know whether they would see each other again as he would be meeting the FBI whilst Kristeena was at the venue. He could be taken into witness protection along with his family, but there was also the possibility that he might go to prison, but he believed he could avoid this considering what he had to offer the FBI.

Geoff felt the uncomfortable silence as the two knew they would not see each other during his next visit to Manhattan. It was clearly difficult to say goodbye, but they agreed to talk again once Geoff had met with the FBI. He would no doubt use code words to describe either a positive or negative outcome. He asked the same from Kristeena, so he knew that she and Barry were both safe, who Geoff felt would be an ideal witness in the campaign to bring down this tower of corruption.

Federal Investigation

As Geoff set off on his flight the next day, he was sweating profusely as all the passengers moved through the cabin to take their luxurious bed-sized seats. Knowing he couldn't put it off any longer, he texted John Maxwell.

The two men discussed meeting at a different hotel than No.4. They agreed on the Stacato Intercontinental Hotel. This was not as exclusive as No.4, but it was somewhere that Geoff knew and he thought free from connections with the Ivanov family.

After arranging to meet in the lobby, he hoped that he would recognise John Maxwell. He also hoped that he would not be wearing his blue jacket with the bright yellow lettering of 'FBI' on it, something that was indelibly etched in his mind from their previous encounter.

He knew that by the time of his meeting with Agent Maxwell, his beautiful Kristeena would be checking into the same venue as Barry and it would be too late to stop anything by then.

As the airline steward served his meal and drink, Geoff pictured an image of Kristeena entering the bar. A red dress clinging to her perfect shape, her raven hair in a French plait and wearing red lipstick enhancing her perfect white teeth and smile that would turn the most loyal of husbands, or indeed wives. He felt jealous of the men who would be staring at her and breathing in her perfect innocent elegance as they watched her every move. He wished he could see her tonight, to be with her and that she was safe with him.

He had saved a text message from Nikki sent before he boarded. *Good luck darling, thinking of you. I love you, Nikki xx.* This was enough to dampen his excitement whilst dreaming of Kristeena. Rightly so, he needed to protect his family. The lovely Kristeena was to be saved from her ordeal; this was as much as Geoff could manage to do for her.

As the flight was during daytime hours, he was wide awake and not able to shut himself away from the thoughts of the scenario to come. What would the FBI actually do? How long would they take to construct a plan to bring down the Ivanovs? He then reminded himself that the FBI only had jurisdiction in the US. At least that was his belief, and that Interpol or some other force would need to be involved.

What if their action only amounted to closing down the company's business in the US while other things were looked into. This could lead to further problems for him, including not being as well protected as he would like. He was fearful of the process that he would need to follow after his meeting tonight.

As the aircraft landed and people began to disembark, he was desperate to call Kristeena. He refrained and decided to text Nikki to let her know he had arrived safely, just as she had asked.

Upon arrival by yellow taxi at the Stacato Intercontinental Hotel, Geoff entered the lobby that doubled as a lounge area with piano music in the background. He looked around for someone resembling the man he had met previously under somewhat different circumstances. Geoff was aware that the ground-floor lobby had several hidden tables tucked around each corner, so he attempted to conduct a full reconnaissance of the whole area. As he did so, there came the welcome sound of a man's voice.

'Hey, Geoff, good to see you again.' It was John Maxwell accompanied by another man.

The image of John Maxwell was different in his mind, but he recognised him after a few seconds. He had already spotted the other man whilst walking around but discounted the table of two as he could not see John's face. As Geoff sat down with the men, all dressed in suits and ties, none looked out of place as they ordered three coffees from the waitress who swiftly approached them.

Geoff was on edge. He knew the risks of being there and glanced around trying to determine if anyone was looking at him rather than being swept away with the hotel's natural ambiance and gentle music.

'No one here will be interested in us, I can assure you. They're all here for themselves. Just relax and tell us what's on your mind. Oh, this is Agent Simmonds, he's also a John,' said John Maxwell.

Geoff referred back to the airport arrest where he and John Maxwell were introduced.

The two agents sat in silence as they listened to Geoff's story while looking at each other as John Simmonds made notes.

'Let's go upstairs,' said John Maxwell. 'We have some recording gear up there, so we can get this on tape formally. I just needed to see where this was going, you understand?'

The three men left the table with no regard for the drinks yet to be delivered or indeed paid for.

As they entered the meeting room on the mezzanine floor above the lobby area, Geoff could see a case containing a recording device and video camera, tools of the trade for informants.

Geoff began to go on the record to give his initial statement of what he knew, which he believed was substantial.

The two agents then began to question his involvement to determine his motives and understanding of the illegal and unsavoury practices he had found himself party to.

'You know what I think, Geoff? I think you're up to your fat neck in this shit and you will face charges whichever way you go. It will be up to you how far you're prepared to go in order to bring this thing to a close,' John Maxwell concluded.

'I will do what I can. Surely though my cooperation and information will be useful in getting to certain people and ending all this?' demanded Geoff as he attempted to seek protection for himself and his family.

He also offered Barry as a potential witness along with Kristeena whom he knew he could count on. Geoff highlighted the immediacy of his boss's compromising position further afield at the conference in Germany, without the honeytrap part. He was keen to expose both the wolf-like man Alexandre and the slimy shit of a lawyer Carlos, who he felt was the brains behind the ground operations.

Geoff continued to recall his exposure to The Magician, who he met in the car that picked him up along with the lawyer appointed by the Ivanov family following his arrest. He realised these were loose descriptions and not things they could use as hard facts, although he could place them in an identity parade.

Despite the download of information and names, Special Agent Maxwell was keen to explore the details of the cocaine transportation. They pressed Geoff for more as this was the basis of their interest before using the additional characters to pursue those at the top of the food chain – the big boys, the Ivanov family themselves.

It was clear to Geoff that the two agents had prior knowledge of the family and their operations, as though most of this information was not a real shock to them. But he felt listened to and believed, which was both comforting and gave him a sense that they were taking him seriously.

'Would you be prepared to wear a wire in order to provide conversational evidence with Barry or this Carlos chap?' Simmonds asked.

'Well, okay, if it's essential, but I don't really deal with Carlos anymore. That's more Barry, but I think I can set up Ricardo, the new president of sales. He's the slimy chap who sent my wife a warning message in the post.'

'Okay, that would be useful. So how do we get to Barry? Will he give evidence?' asked Maxwell.

'The FBI or the Ivanov family have bugged his house anyway. If you can tap into these things, you will soon have evidence for sure.'

Geoff continued to talk about the events at No.4 in Manhattan, his exposure to De Silva and the cover of one of them for money laundering at least, which was something that Maxwell seemed unaware of judging by his uncomfortable body language.

Special Agent Maxwell left the room to make a few calls.

Geoff felt comforted by his sudden absence and thought of Kristeena hoping that she was safe and uncompromised by now.

The Conference

As Kristeena entered the bar area after the conference, heads turned to watch her sit at a small table in the middle of the room. Barry noticed her as if there were no other guests, as did many others.

Kristeena smiled at him keeping up the appearance of her character for the benefit of anyone watching. She was sure that someone was there keeping a check on her actions.

Barry stood at the bar with others from the conference ordering himself a drink when a beautiful blonde girl stood beside him. Kristeena looked on in excitement as the escort she had paid to lure Barry away for the evening effortlessly flirted and played with this captain of industry. He put up no resistance; the two enjoyed a drink together. They talked intimately to hear each other against the background noise, the girl luring him with her low-cut dress, body language and comments.

Kristeena had chosen well; she was a high-class beauty at the height of her profession. She was suitably impressed as the two made their way out of the bar clearly 'together' and assumed they were heading to his room.

Barry looked back at Kristeena and gave her a wink over his shoulder, a gesture acknowledging his understanding of the situation and that he was safe. He appeared to look forward to a pleasant evening, which was of no cost to him financially. Happy days indeed.

Kristeena texted Geoff immediately: *A quiet night at the hotel bar, hope you're having a good day.*

Geoff saw the text and showed it to Agent Simmonds. 'It seems that Barry is safe tonight. We should get to him in the morning and ask him to come forward. I will call him in his hotel room first thing.'

He smiled to himself knowing that Kristeena was also safe, her dignity intact and that anyone watching would see she was pipped to the post by another woman, which was something beyond her control and would allow her to remain safe from the family's henchmen.

As the session continued without Maxwell, Geoff once again asked about witness protection, cleverly doing so whilst the camera was on.

'Special Agent Maxwell is making some calls. This is something that will require planning and execution and will take a while, but we will keep you safe and secure,' Simmonds confirmed.

It was now dark outside. Geoff had provided everything he could, yet they craved more and kept going over old ground. He had watched the odd film on the plane showing how the FBI worked, which all seemed par for the course, so he just went along with this as it seemed logical.

Geoff looked and felt tired and he was hungry. Simmonds offered to get a sandwich sent up to keep him going. It was the least they could do given how much help he was offering.

As Simmonds left the room to arrange some food, Maxwell returned following his calls and asked for a coffee. He then said, 'Good news, Geoff. The department will arrange for you and your immediate family to go into protection as your wife is clearly aware of the Ivanovs. It will need to be stateside, so it's best you arrange to put them on a flight in the next few days. Obviously we will not arrange this ourselves to avoid suspicion, just in case. We will pick them up at Florida airport. If you can tell them on the phone, your regular phone, that you're taking them away for a few days, we will do the rest and unite you guys at a safe house somewhere. You are not to mention anything else.'

'Thank you, John,' said Geoff as he leant across the table to shake his hand.

'Let's not be too hasty here. Save your gratitude for when we all get what we want. If you back out now, you will be on your own again. We don't do free protection for life unless we get what we want, capiche?' John stated.

As Maxwell left the room to take care of another call, Geoff rang home. Nikki answered immediately even though it was late evening.

He disregarded Maxwell's advice and gave her the good news that they would be going into witness protection. As he said it, they both recognised what this would mean: their lives would become unrecognisable and for now at least they would leave behind their families, friends and everything they knew to escape the wrath of the Ivanov family for this act of disloyalty towards them.

Despite the obvious pain this would bring, they both felt a sense of comfort that their children could go on in life without fear or approach from these assassins.

Nikki used her skills as a keen traveller to book the flights. She would surprise the children when they returned home, but then only disclose the truth when they were in protection.

John Maxwell returned shortly before the food and drinks arrived with Agent Simmonds. They both maintained a serious demeanour.

'Now the fun starts. We will set about digging up the shit on these people as hard evidence. When can you set up the meeting with Miss Balanchenko and Mr Isaacs?' asked Maxwell.

'I will call Kristeena tonight and Barry in the morning as he will be busy tonight!' he added with a smile thinking of the pleasure Barry would be having with his transient lady. It was the first smile he had managed in days.

As they continued to talk through the witness programme, Geoff attacked his ham sandwich like it was his last. It was nothing special, nor interesting, just simple food to relieve his hunger.

The two agents continued to clarify a few points as they sipped their hot coffees, slurping with no refinement as the men shared the events yet to come.

'Miss Balanchenko will not be offered protection. Although we still need her statement, it seems she is not that integral to the evidence we need. We will suggest protection for Mr Isaacs because it seems he is a threat to those he will be providing evidence against,' Maxwell added.

Geoff merely acknowledged the statement as fact rather than attempt to negotiate or demand. He felt he had done enough to help Kristeena. Besides, keeping her away from Nikki felt the right thing to do in case they were all shoved together in the same safe house.

'So, is this it?' asked Geoff. 'Do I need to meet anyone else in your FBI team?'

'We always try to make sure that witness protection programmes involve as few people as possible for obvious reasons,' said Simmonds.

Geoff left the hotel and retired to his room at No.4. It was now eight in the morning. Even though he was exhausted, he texted Kristeena. *A good day at the office. I will need to arrange seeing you.* She would have understood this to mean that the FBI need to see you and they are hopeful that you will be okay.

There was no response, so he dialled her number. It went straight to voicemail. He balanced his concern with his own exhaustion and need for sleep whilst recognising that Kristeena would also be tired.

He went to bed to get a few hours' sleep. Barry would no doubt still be in bed as his flight home was not until late afternoon.

Meanwhile in Berlin, Barry woke with the sensation of an almighty hangover. He sat up but instantly sank back down onto his pillow. Trying again to lift his head, he turned to his left to see the slender curves of the woman he had slept with. He noticed the small of her back exposed by the sheet that had moved with him as he glanced at her shape with intent once more.

He began to move closer to the young woman although his head was pounding with pain. As he touched her tanned shoulders to pull back her blonde locks, she felt cold, very cold. Upon closer inspection, once he had rolled her onto one side, he could see that she was dead.

In a panic, Barry bolted out of bed and paced around the bedroom whilst getting dressed in the process. He was sure that this was just like the stories Bernard had shared. Almost identical, in fact. He called for the hotel manager.

Whilst staring dumbfounded at the pretty young woman remembering the night they had shared and trying to make sense of things, there was a knock at the door.

Barry hesitantly opened it expecting a corrupt character like De Silva. The manager who, for a favour or two, would make this disappear and force compliance for his freedom despite knowing he was incapable of harming her. Instead, the manager was accompanied by two German policemen and a security officer from the hotel.

As Barry started to explain that he had awoken to find the girl dead in his bedroom, the police placed him in handcuffs and read out what he believed to be his rights. The hotel manager offered no comment or deal. This was really happening.

Barry believed that the Ivanov family were behind this, yet he could not prove anything. A doctor entered the room at the request of the police.

He sat his bag on the floor beside the bed where the woman lay. She was still and lifeless as he conducted his brief yet conclusive statement. 'Death by strangulation. Although I will need to carry out a post-mortem to check the toxicology reports,' said the doctor as the hotel manager acknowledged his words.

'Check my toxicology,' snapped Barry. 'I think I was drugged. I did not hear a thing. I did not kill her!'

No one cared about his plea for innocence and continued to follow formal procedure. The police officers awaited the arrival of their colleagues who were shortly on the scene before escorting him away to the local police station, where he would be formally charged for murder.

The hotel did their best to preserve their reputation and prevent the press from reporting this scandal of prostitution and murder. They were desperate to preserve their status as a business venue of choice, from which they achieved twenty-five per cent of their profits.

At the police station, Barry was held in custody in a room much different to the accommodation he was typically used to. It was cold, grey, clinical and lacking any comforts.

An hour into the ordeal, a policeman opened the door to his holding cell. 'Your lawyer is here. Come this way.'

Barry was pleased for the interruption and that he would be seeing his lawyer. *Wait a minute*, he thought. His lawyer was in Manhattan; this was Germany. *How the hell did he get here so quickly? And how did he even know?* Barry had not made his phone call yet.

As he entered the room, the lawyer introduced himself as Harry Delaney. Barry seemed to recall the name somehow although he had never met him before.

'I am the man sent here to help you, Mr Isaacs,' informed Delaney.

'How did you know? I mean, how could you know that I am in trouble?' Barry asked in a pleased yet confused manner.

'Never mind all that. You are in big trouble, but I am here to help you. Tell me what happened.'

With that, Barry relayed his story. The two men then discussed his options, which on the surface did not look good for him.

'No forced entry and only the two of you in the room. She was an escort with no money on her. You can see how this looks, Mr Isaacs. She demanded money, you got into a fight after having sex and things got out of hand – it happens. If I am to help you, I must know the truth,' Delaney demanded.

Confused and still unaware of the depth of trouble he was in, Barry knew that he must get his lawyer to call Geoff. He would be able to explain that Kristeena had paid the girl for the night and the reasons why.

The lawyer agreed. Barry constructed his statement before he was due to be interviewed formally. Delaney exited the room and asked the police to call Geoff and Kristeena at Barry's request.

Geoff answered his phone. He was expecting a jovial Barry after spending the evening with a beautiful woman and surviving an elaborate death plot. Instead, it was the German police calling to ask him questions.

He was able to support Barry's statement that the escort girl was not paid for by Barry and that Kristeena Balanchenko, who was also staying at the hotel, would be able to verify this.

He was of course unable to offer any support or explanation regarding the girl's death. He thought it best to talk to John Maxwell as he was investigating the Ivanov corruption story.

John was full of concern speaking to Geoff. A star witness now in custody for murder. His credibility as a witness if found guilty would be zero, which would not help the case against the Ivanovs at all.

Geoff felt pleased with himself; he had played the right move. He hoped to give evidence in support of his boss, and Barry would stand a good chance of bail with the FBI on his side.

'Geoff, we need Mr Isaacs' statement to be credible. Without this, your case is weakened. Our protection might not continue if we drop the case,' Maxwell suggested.

Geoff's skin went cold. He had put himself at major risk. The plan must work – he had no option but to make this work. The alternative of the FBI throwing him back on the streets without protection was unthinkable.

Geoff's next calls were to Martin Brinstein and Paul Newark. It was the early hours of the morning, but he hoped they would be able to take his call.

Both conversations happened quickly. Despite the time, they were happy to speak to Geoff when they learnt of Barry's sudden arrest.

Immediately, Paul reacted supportively and believed that the Ivanovs had struck once more. He was prepared to offer a statement to support Barry's innocence, although he would not refer to the corruption or the Ivanov family.

'Paul, Barry needs support not a character reference. Unless we can work on this together, Barry is going to be put in prison for murder – something we both know he didn't do.'

'Well, let's be honest, Geoff, neither of us were actually there. I for one am not prepared to spill the beans on the Ivanovs. We all agreed not to do this, including you, Geoff. Barry was the one asking us to keep a lid on this. It is Barry's wishes that we support his leadership and instructions,' Paul continued.

It was a similar conversation with Martin. It was as if both men had already spoken and decided their positions. 'There is nothing I can do. We must respect Barry's direction on this and stick to it firmly,' Martin offered.

'That was before he was arrested for murder. Will you not stand firm against these people? I have met with the FBI and provided a statement. Will you now back this?' Geoff pleaded.

'No fucking way! Are you crazy? You know what they're capable of! You of all people have seen the impact of the Ivanovs, yet you still put yourself out there as an enemy. You are on your own, my friend. I cannot stand with you on this – and I will just deny any knowledge if questioned by the FBI,' Martin concluded before hanging up.

Feeling exposed, Geoff decided to call Kristeena, this time in her hotel room. It is a typical human trait to hear a friendly voice after a few non-friendly ones. He was only human and ultimately wanted to see if she was okay.

As the receptionist answered, Geoff's attempt at a few words in German prompted the man to converse in English. Clearly he was not that good at speaking German after all.

'I am afraid that Miss Balanchenko checked out early evening, sir,' came the polite and friendly response. 'We have a note saying that she left to visit an elderly relative. Are you a relative or co-worker?'

Geoff hung up on the call and quickly dialled her mobile number. It rang several times before diverting to voicemail. He convinced himself that she had gone back to Georgia to see her mother. Perhaps there was a genuine family issue and she was on a plane not able to answer.

However, he was more concerned that something bad had happened to her because she did not act on the specific instructions to kill Barry. It seemed like another Ivanov magic trick.

The King is Dead,
Long Live the King

Back in the office, after the sad news circulated regarding Barry's arrest, an emergency board meeting was called. It was a sombre event, led by Alexandre of course, with a statement produced by Alexandre on behalf of the board of directors:

> As you may now be aware Barry Isaacs has been charged with the murder of a female in Germany. We are uncertain of the details, but Mr Isaacs will not be returning to his position in the near future. Until such time as this is resolved, the investors International Rescue, whose interests I represent, have appointed myself as acting global CEO and chairman

with full responsibility for the company's ongoing and future activities.

We will of course send our messages of support to Barry. In the meantime, I can assure you of the ongoing security of this firm despite Barry's absence and it will be business as usual until further notice.

Huh, business as usual, Geoff thought to himself. *Illegal business as usual. Killing as usual. Drug trafficking as usual.* He was hopping mad at how Barry's semi-innocent rendezvous was to become a circus event, set up by the Russians as some light entertainment whilst flexing a tiny muscle or two. Yet another relatively innocent life ruined by those who only served greed and crime.

Despite his hatred, Geoff knew how to stay composed, how to mask his inner feelings whilst maintaining a supportive veneer to those around him.

He could see the obvious fear on the faces of Paul and Martin now Dimitri and Ricardo were both flying the flag flaunting 'the king is dead, long live the king' in their obvious support for Alexandre's promotion. Something that was both unexpected and undeserved in the eyes of the others.

United We Stand, Divided We Fall

Nikki had booked the flights with no accommodation at the earlier request of her husband in readiness for their next chapter in life together.

Two days to go until the trip. She explained to the school that Geoff had won the break as a corporate treat, something that was easily believable. She was surprised just how well she enacted the story; it was almost an award-worthy performance.

The children were unsuspecting and fed off her excitement despite her obvious fears, which she kept well hidden. However, Nikki did decide to tell her mother, which Geoff had instructed her not to do. It was her way of saying goodbye as she was in her early eighties. She did not want her brother and sisters thinking she had vanished of the face of the earth without a good and justified reasoning.

Seeing her for what would be the very last time, Nikki's mother began to break down. Her acute realisation that her daughter was taking the grandchildren away, never to be seen or contacted again, was too much for her.

Nikki began to think of ways that may give her some form of contact with her family: a secret mobile phone, a holiday destination they could all go on, meeting up in the depths of the African continent, a private residence in India or maybe on her brother-in-law's small yacht.

She knew all of these options would be prohibited by the FBI once in the confines of their protection, yet she was not prepared to give up that easily.

When her mother suggested that divorce was an option, Nikki purposefully ignored this even though she had considered it herself recently. She was angry to be giving up a life that was largely comfortable for something unknown with no friends, based on a lie and circumstances that her and the children had not sought or deserved.

Talking things through with her mother, she began to think of the hatred from the children once they knew that their home, friends and school were all to be left immediately based on a poor decision that Geoff had made. She felt he could have walked away from this whole situation easily, yet he failed to do this. He had failed to keep them safe, which was something he had always promised as a husband and a father. He had put all their lives in danger for the sake of his burning greed and complete selfishness to gain promotion.

Nikki also thought that all of this was nonsensical. Like most innocent people, she was unaware of the reach of such criminals. She refused to believe that they would actually kill anyone and believed her husband was being over dramatic.

Her support for Geoff was weakening in favour of them having a few years apart. They were reasonably secure financially and her mother would help. This was becoming more of an option, especially sitting in front of her elderly mother seeing the pain this was causing.

This was not their problem – in her eyes,

at least. Ignorance was bliss. Protecting the children from harm also meant not travelling to some far-flung place across the Atlantic Ocean with no friends, family or life. This was not her idea of protecting them.

Her view was that Geoff should battle this out for a few years and then join the family once the dust has settled. It was a kind of logic that assumed they would all be safe once the criminals were put in prison; therefore, negating the need for witness protection. Neither she nor the children were witnesses to anything. A dead rat in the post maybe, but other than that it was only Geoff who was implicated.

As the conversation with her mother continued, Nikki began to convince herself that Geoff would soon return to the family home without any need for disruption or life-wrenching changes after a brief period of absence.

She had been talked around mainly by her own thoughts, but her mother did not waste a moment jumping on the bandwagon and kicking sand in Geoff's absent face.

Her concern for her husband was bypassed by her concern over how to pay the household bills, how long their savings would last and if she would need further help to support them.

At the end of their discussion, Nikki recognised that they could survive for about seven years even without the support of her mother with careful planning and modest living. This would mean taking on part-time work. A small income could push this into what she viewed as early retirement age, although the luxurious holidays would need to stop.

Nikki recognised Geoff would be kept safe under witness protection and still believed that he would be able to call the children easily enough. After all, they were used to him not being at home night after night.

At the school pick up later that day, Nikki greeted the children each in their own way. The children were understandably excited about the prospect of a trip to Florida, a holiday to Disney World and missing school.

In the car while parked in the school car park, Nikki began to explain that the trip was not going ahead as Daddy needed to go on another business trip. The children understood their father's work commitments, as they always did. There was obvious disappointment on their faces as they thought about returning to school telling their once jealous friends that the trip was cancelled, and how they would be mocked and teased in the process by those who liked to dominate and bully.

As they drove home, the children's saddened faces stared silently through the car window with Nikki maintaining her story despite feeling upset at the thought of their separation from Geoff. Yet, in her mind, this all made sense. She was pleased that he would be in the safety of the FBI and felt he would not be absent for long.

Looking in her rear-view mirror, she could see the two little faces whose short-term dreams had been shattered and hoped that her act would one day be understood by them. She had no idea how to explain the next chapter once they realised their father was not coming home at the weekend as usual. It was something that may need the support from her mother as only grandparents could provide.

Unaware of the family plans, Geoff remained cool-headed as he settled back into semi-work mode just doing the minimum required to get by. He could be living a different life within the next few days protected from those who would harm him and united with his family in a strange yet secure location.

It sounded easy to cruise for a few days; it would have been under Barry's leadership. His activities were becoming difficult to hide now Alexandre was in the big chair calling the shots along with Ricardo and Dimitri as his trusted executive guards. He had to justify his every move. He recognised that Martin and Paul were in a similar position as they were seen as supporters of the previous regime, the old guard, and loyal to a man since displaced by some act of manufactured crime against him. His once respected name now purposefully disgraced.

Geoff knew that his last-minute trip to Florida was not going to be easy. He still believed that Nikki and the children would be meeting him and the FBI at the airport, ready for an adventure like no other. Therefore, he had to find a way of getting away from the business without giving the game away to his new boss.

There were no legitimate reasons to travel to Florida as the company had no facility, staff or distributors there, but the FBI had asked him not to raise suspicions. He knew that faking an illness would not be a good move given his typical workaholic behaviours, so he either had to position it as a last-minute holiday or a business trip.

Geoff went to see Martin, who he had always seen as his superior. Even though they did not have a tight and open friendship, he needed someone to talk to and his options were rather limited.

Once Martin offered his time in an email response, Geoff arrived at his office door within a few minutes. He passed a distressed Veronica on the way as he dropped off his expenses, which he was keen to complete as it was for £6000. Money was money regardless of whether it was funded by drugs or a legitimate employment contract. He had used his Amex card, so he needed it back.

As he opened the door to Martin's office, a worried man sat before him. 'You okay? You looked stressed,' said Geoff as he walked towards Martin who was busy looking down at his laptop screen.

Martin glanced up only for a few seconds and then returned to his work. 'Alexandre needs some data. I usually report it at the end of the month, but he needs it early. Typical!'

Geoff sat in front watching Martin rub his eyes, the action creating a set of wrinkles that seemed to age him immediately before the elasticity of his skin sprang back.

'Okay, so what's on your mind? As if I didn't know… Barry's arrest, am I right?' Martin asked.

'Kind of, but my thoughts go way beyond Barry's situation.' Geoff began to describe the events leading up to the arrest, details of Kristeena, her ballet colleague, the escort girl and Barry's agreement to a plan that would keep him alive until he could go to the FBI.

Martin listened intently not uttering a word while resting his hand under his chin.

Geoff continued the story that Barry was clearly set up and somehow the family were aware of the plan. They had infiltrated the plot and found another way of ensuring he would be the prime suspect.

The two pondered on the scenario for some time. Why had the escort girl been murdered, not Barry? Surely if one of the family's henchmen had entered the German hotel room, they would have had ample opportunity to carry out their plan to 'remove' him easily enough. What would happen now he was in custody? He would be in a position to tell the German police all about the corruption. He was under suspicion of murder, so he would have nothing to lose.

Something did not add up. When Martin suggested that Kristeena was involved in some way, Geoff was quick to discuss her own dilemma and the threat to her family in Georgia, which he was convinced still existed given that she had not carried out the murder herself. He knew that she had returned home due to a family problem, so he wondered if they had already got to her mother as punishment. Either way, he knew Kristeena. He knew he could discount her involvement even if Martin continued with conflicting views.

With Geoff still there, Martin buzzed Paul asking him to call Barry's lawyer for an update.

It was not long before Paul entered the room. 'Just spoken to Harry Delaney. He's convinced of his innocence regarding the girl's death, but the only evidence on file shows Barry and the girl entering the lift together clearly with the intention of heading to his room. Sadly, no other footage exists despite all floors having CCTV in the corridors. It seems that the recording on his floor was erased or corrupted. Harry has asked me to offer anything I can to support Barry's claim of innocence.'

Geoff began to download the salient points with Martin pushing and filling in the gaps he may have overlooked. It was a good double act.

Whilst useful, Paul knew that such a story would not be believable in isolation and without the statement of Kristeena, who would no doubt be a useful witness for Barry along with Geoff's comments.

Geoff agreed to call Kristeena again and arrange for her to provide a statement to Harry and the local police. If nothing else, it was a good excuse to pursue her again, to hear her warm, innocent voice and remind him of happier times.

Geoff reluctantly opened up about his agreement with John Maxwell, the witness protection programme and his evidence that would justify their investment in him and his family.

The whole reason for Geoff talking to Martin initially was to ask how he could manufacture a reason to fly to Florida at a time of intense scrutiny from Alexandre – the man with deep-set dark eyes, 'The Wolf', the man who represented the Ivanov family and could potentially make a man rich or make him disappear with one call.

In all Geoff's years of reading body language, he would never have trusted Alexandre. Even less now that the slimy shit Ricardo was in a position of power along with Dimitri, his trusted ally, by his side. The power shift in the company was extraordinary.

With three of the six board members now under the control of the Ivanov family, even Martin's loyalty and experience was now diluted from the freedom he once knew. Despite it being business as usual, the environment was colder, less enjoyable and with a sense of fear that put him in a tight box. He recognised that stepping beyond this confined space would result in pain or discomfort, which would be monitored by those who now controlled the company both operationally and financially.

Paul considered the implications for the company whilst discussing Geoff's agreement to give evidence against International Rescue and the Ivanov family. 'Geoff, do you realise that you will compromise the security of all the staff here, including Martin and myself?' asked Paul.

'Obviously, I didn't want to compromise you, I don't want to cause a problem for you, but look at my situation. Barry agreed to step forward. He was willing to give evidence. He recognised that it was the right thing to do, to come clean, report these bastards for the lying murdering criminals they are,' replied Geoff.

'If what you say is true, Barry had no choice. We, on the other hand, do. We can choose to carry on living, submit counterstatements and sink you,' Paul snapped, revealing his corporate lawyer experience and training in the expression of a few words.

Martin calmly intervened, 'Hang on, Paul, let's consider this for a minute. We could support Geoff's statement in return for protection. It would help Barry, maybe not clear him completely, but it may raise concerns over his circumstances and allow the police to consider that he's telling the truth. I recall saying that we were in this together, Paul. We said this to Barry – all of us.'

'We agreed to keep our mouths shut as we were in it together, not to blow this wide open. Geoff has gone feral and decided to backtrack,' Paul continued.

Neither person wanted to back down. The recent events were causing an understandable divide amongst the three men with raised voices, aggressive body language and gestures overriding the dialogue.

'So, do we just let Barry rot? He believed in me and he has made both of you rich, yet I'm the only one prepared to help him. At least he's alive because of my actions,' asserted Geoff.

'You mean facing murder charges for killing a prostitute whilst saving your mistress!' Paul retorted without hesitation.

It was clear that such feelings of emotion had been building up. The tensions were obvious and the atmosphere was one step further than the aggression Barry promoted in his boardroom.

'How would Barry handle this? I mean, he dealt with our conflict every day and always seemed to sleep at night. Why can't we see a way through this?' Martin queried.

He was right. A common action was needed and now was not the time for divided opinions. There was no way the three men could consult with Barry. They were alone and isolated from the other three board members for obvious reasons, so they needed to agree on something, and fast.

Geoff was due to go into protection in less than two days. His statement had already been provided; the clock was ticking.

Martin and Paul needed space to talk. With so much at stake, they would need to consider their next actions very carefully.

Red-faced and disappointed at not getting the support he wanted from Paul and Martin, Geoff left the room to call Kristeena from his office.

The dialling tone of her mobile phone was different denoting that she was out of the country, which he expected if she was still at home in Georgia.

Geoff's heart raced when she answered. He felt uncomfortable calling despite all they had shared together. It was like trying to talk to a stranger; there was more than geography in the distance between them.

'How's your mother?' Geoff asked politely trying to break the tension.

'She is dead. She was dead when I got home. A heart attack. The funeral is on Monday,' replied Kristeena matter-of-factly.

Relaying his condolences, Geoff was pleased to hear that she was safe. Well, alive at least. Although, he knew that furthering this relationship was rather pointless; he would be meeting his family in two days.

Geoff told Kristeena of Barry's circumstances, as if to remind her of the freedom she continued to enjoy following his intervention to help remove her from such burdens placed by others.

It was the point needed for Kristeena to respond. Her coldness thawed instantly.

If they had been together, Geoff knew they would have fallen into each other's arms in the blink of an eye as the two continued their discussion.

He attempted to reason with Kristeena about making a statement to the German police, which she agreed was the right thing to do. Doing so would help lock up those whom she so detested. She insisted that this was done in Manhattan with John Maxwell. He agreed, hoping that the FBI would accept this.

'And your family, Geoff, are they going into the protection process with you?' Kristeena asked. She knew the answer, knew that their relationship was not forever, yet her voice exhibited a sadness and loneliness that Geoff had always been attracted to. A vulnerability that he found innocent and lovely. Something that was strangely unique in his life and certainly rare in Manhattan.

'Yes, we'll be meeting in two days. Then, that's it. Hello new life; farewell old. I shall miss you dearly. Not just the…you know, but the friendship, kindness and warmth I have felt every time we were together, and the longing for you in between.'

Geoff's words broke her delicate shell. She burst into tears as she reciprocated her feelings.

'Why did you ever want to be with me anyway? You are beautiful. You are the loveliest person I have ever known. You are talented and kind. You could have any man, anyone at all. I am a middle-aged family man, with grey hair, a bit of a tummy, certainly not a dancer's body and...' Geoff waffled on, fishing for compliments and genuinely unsure of the attraction.

'Because every other man looks at me for what they want. None of them looked at me for what they could give in return. I got that from you. You always treated me like I imagined it would be as a teenager growing up. A fantasy, I guess, being loved, protected and feeling safe. Not as a sex object or a trophy girlfriend on show for their self-esteem, but because you liked me for being me.'

This caused Geoff's tears to flow. He would miss her terribly, more so having realised her affections were sincere.

Kristeena suggested that this meeting in Manhattan would be their farewell to each other. Their relationship would then become a wonderful fading memory. She knew Geoff would soon rekindle his life with Nikki when they were reunited, being the family man he was.

They agreed to meet in Manhattan in the presence of John Maxwell to receive her statement, which Geoff was to arrange. The two said their goodbyes in their own way, knowing how difficult this would be in the presence of his family and the FBI.

A Very Special Agent

Geoff met with John Maxwell that evening, once again at a neutral venue. He was hopeful that Kristeena's statement could be provided to the German police via the FBI, which John agreed to. This would be handled by Interpol, someone who Geoff would meet on the day of the witness protection before reuniting with his family.

Given his difficulty of breaking free to meet in Florida, Geoff asked if they could change this to Manhattan. John initially refused given that arrangements had been made. His frustration at the request was obvious, and Geoff could see that any modified plans would not be well received, but he eventually conceded. Geoff was convinced that Barry would be at least a credible witness for the FBI with Kristeena's statement.

Sitting together, John took time to explain, 'On the day, Frank Hildreth from the DEA will be leading up the operation to bust the cocaine ring wide open. If you could just make sure that nothing has changed in terms of the transport – I mean, make sure the drugs will be where you say they will be – so we can catch these people in the act. We need this, Geoff. One false arrest could push the investigation back months and we'll lose all hope of catching these bastards red-handed.'

Geoff confirmed that things were on schedule and that the cache would be everything he had promised.

'How do you know?' John continued in his typical federal quizmaster manner. 'Who is telling you this? I think you should give us some more names. We are risking a lot and putting faith in you, so I need to be sure. Similarly, contact with you will be rare once you're in the witness programme, so I need to know who the good guys are, people who we will arrest and the ones to let go.'

It seemed a logical request, yet Geoff had promised not to compromise the people on the inside helping to keep him informed, the whistle-blowers, as they wanted their anonymity to safeguard them longer term with Geoff taking the risk and protection.

'Okay, I can see the logic, but I hope you won't make it obvious, you know, not to…give everyone a reason to think…' Geoff waffled on.

John Maxwell let him, despite knowing what he meant. 'We will take care of things, Geoff. Names, please?' Maxwell demanded politely.

'Okay, so the good guys are as follows: The logistics manager Dylan who is based in France. The security guard called Matt Arthur in Detroit. The HR manager in Malaysia, Sarah Rayang. And the inventory clerk, John Queen based in Manhattan. They are all willing to make statements after you make the arrests, not before. They are good, loyal, hard-working guys caught up in this shitstorm. They will not volunteer statements like myself. They will tell you what they know at the point of arrest. You see where I'm coming from? They just don't want to be seen as enemies of the Ivanov family. From each of their statements, you will be redirected to others who will come forward once these people know the bad guys are locked up. There are some sixty people in total.' Geoff felt good. He was playing the game cautiously and making sure that the FBI kept to their part of the deal, each part opening up another and so on. He was sure that this game of dominoes would reach a momentum big enough to bring the whole thing down. 'What will happen to the company? Will it go bust?' asked Geoff, now sounding concerned.

'That's not for me to comment, but I would imagine the only person who can answer this is your finance guy who's probably implicated somehow,' John suggested.

'On that subject, Martin Brinstein is the chief finance man. He can be swayed to support all of this,' Geoff quickly offered.

John looked confused. 'Are you certain? I thought he was tight-lipped?'

'I met with them today. They're mulling it all over knowing that I'm coming forward,' Geoff confirmed, pleased with himself. He felt a sense of accomplishment like a politician getting their policy approved in the House of Commons.

Maxwell continued to query, 'They, who's they?'

'Oh, sorry the legal executive, Paul Newark,' Geoff continued.

John Maxwell looked perplexed as he continued to explain without referencing his previous comments. 'So, Frank's team will set up the sting operation. His guys will be in the right places at the designated time. Frank will give the order to strike all the points at the same time. My colleagues will be ready to strike this office and International Rescue, alongside the IRS who will be all over your head office. I will co-ordinate with the Interpol team to blow open the other locations. There is a lot resting on your contacts, Geoff. If the drugs are not there, all of this is for nothing. There will be no protection, nothing. You understand? That's why we need to make sure we know who's with you.'

Geoff felt a chill across his shoulders as if a door had opened to the outside, with a breeze stroking him gently. Yet it was merely the feeling of concern brushing over him, warning him of his risk, his boldness and his one-way journey to the unknown.

There was no way back now. He was edging towards the river with no sight of a rescue ship, as if on a slippery slope, unable to clamber back up. The next step was inevitable. The outcome and safety of his family was still uncertain and based on so many variables, mostly beyond his control. His mind flooded with fear and insecurity. He was saddened to strip his family of their lifestyle, their school friends and even breaking connections with the family they so dearly loved.

Returning to his hotel that evening, Geoff paused as he waited outside to make the call home. He was excited to talk to his wife, but he felt it might wake her as it was early in the morning. He recognised the huge sacrifice she and the children were making to be with him, supporting him, but his guilt over his secret affair with Kristeena was overwhelming.

Geoff did not want to call home from his hotel room; his suspicions that someone was listening had been heightened since the recent death of his colleague.

He put aside his guilty feelings as he dialled. As it went to voicemail, he could only think of Kristeena and their farewell comments. It was not his wife who he was longing to talk to in reality.

Kristeena was still on his mind. Her last words had hit him hard and acted as a reminder of a special relationship. Something he craved for, like a drug addict craving their cocaine. At the very thought of his addiction for her, he thought of the millions of people who the Ivanov family were supplying their drugs to, their death sentence. As if woken by a cold shower to the face, he once again displaced his selfish desires to help end this large-scale conveyor belt of drugs.

He happily visualised a production line of white powder ceasing. Its employees redundant and the facilities once in their prime halted by one man. A man of integrity, boldness and prepared to do what no one else had the gumption to do. Himself.

As he waited for a call back from Nikki, he stood under the dark cloudy night sky looking up at the tall buildings surrounding him. Imposing structures that lay awake at all hours, like guardians of a prison, the prison called business, and he was one of the inmates.

It was a poignant moment for Geoff as he reminded himself that he was not free. He was not really living a life without restriction. He was imprisoned in this life of corruption, a life of loneliness, and it was the next chapter that would put him in the confinement of witness protection.

He was naturally concerned about the witness programme being restrictive and limiting, but he was convinced now more than ever that he was making the right choice.

His mobile phone rang as he entered his hotel room. He looked at the word 'Home' on the screen and recalled the years of memories they had created in their house together.

As he answered, his tired and sleepy wife was clearly not in a good mood, which he convinced himself was merely due to her being woken up.

As the two pieced together snippets of a conversation, Geoff asked her the inevitable question, 'All packed ready to leave for the airport, darling?'

Her delayed response was expected. This was not a trip to the Maldives for three weeks of sunshine and good living, but a heart-wrenching and life-changing decision that he could not expect her to be excited about.

'Are you sure this is the right move for us, Geoff? Once the Russian people are in jail, surely things will settle down and return to some normality. I'm not sure we're being fair to the children,' Nikki said with a concerned hesitation. She clearly knew that her words would be destructive to her husband's state of mind.

'We talked about this. It's the only way I can keep you all safe, to protect you and make sure we can be together,' Geoff added convincingly.

'We have done nothing wrong – nothing. It's this bloody job of yours that's the problem. You've decided to take these people on, not us, yet we end up needing to walk away from everything we love,' she continued, recognising what she had said.

'Everything…? What about me? You wouldn't be walking away from me. We would be together.' Geoff was not trying to settle an argument, merely seeking clarification as to what she meant while carefully not pushing too hard.

'We don't want this, we never wanted this, we just want to go on living our lives. We don't want to live in America with new identities. This is not who we are, not who we're meant to be.'

Her concern immediately raised alarm bells for Geoff. *What is she trying to say? She's about to jump on a plane this evening with Thomas and Alice. Surely she's not changing her mind.* 'When we talked this through, you were the one who pushed for me to go to the FBI, for fuck's sake. You were the one who told me to give up my selfish greed and not support this crime-ridden company that was poisoning and ruining lives with drugs. You were the one who told me to do this!' Geoff was in no mood for games. He was right. She was the one who reminded him that what he was doing at work was wrong, very wrong. That he was aiding and abetting criminal activity at best. At worst, he was a drug trafficker on a massive scale.

Whilst she was right to remind him of the person he was, and to keep him on the path of righteousness, he thought she was with him. Literally that she would be with him.

'Are you still coming...? I need to know whether you're just having last-minute nerves or whether there's more to this. It's natural to be uncertain, nervous and worried. I'm scared shitless of what's happening. I'm responsible for uprooting my family, responsible for their safety and above all else about to expose one of the biggest crime families in the world. I'm scared. Nikki, but I can do this if I know you're with me.'

Nikki continued, 'I'm just not sure. You need to see this from my perspective. I can't see that we're in any danger. We haven't seen anything or done anything, whereas you're the one who's been in the middle of it all. I think you're doing the right thing, honestly I do, and knowing that you will be protected will be a good outcome. I just don't think we need to go through it, too. I really think that in a few months or a year the dust will settle, and then we can be reunited. It's not as if you're home every night, is it?'

'I won't be able to call you or the children. This could be forever. These bloody people have contacts everywhere. I cannot sit back while you put yourself and the children in danger from these people; they might well come after you as revenge for my actions,' Geoff said, passionately believing that they would be vulnerable.

'No, Geoff, I'm not the one placing us in danger. I'm the one thinking of us being separated for as long as it takes to be safe, life as usual, our life, but then you wouldn't know about that. You've always been so busy with work. It's me who has brought up the children, taking them here and there, nursing illnesses, making a life, a social life, with my friends and support network that I'm loathed to give up,' Nikki added, hearing her words echo a conclusive statement to her husband.

His pause on the end of the phone spoke volumes and confirmed that he was under no illusion that her departure from life in the UK was neither comfortable nor agreed.

Seconds seemed like hours as the two held on for the other to finally speak.

'Okay, sounds like this isn't going to the plan I had in mind. I'm sorry that you may feel shoehorned into this scenario. I didn't create it. I merely found myself an innocent victim caught up in this web of deceit and criminal activity – and I wish I hadn't been, but I am. You have your tickets. I love you all and hope to see you tomorrow evening as planned. If you don't show, I'll assume you don't feel the same way and will be staying there without me. I just hope you know what you're doing,' Geoff said solemnly, knowing that he had no control over her actions or emotions. Both hung on in silence until Geoff added, 'I hope to see you and the children tomorrow. Love you.' He hung up staring longingly at the screen, playing with the functions on his smartphone, not knowing what he was doing, with no purpose other than to distract himself from his acute pain.

How would he cope on his own? He liked being married and loved his children dearly. Okay, he had been entangled in an affair with Kristeena, but he had since recognised that this was not right and no longer an option for him.

His feelings were once again selfish, feeling alone more than ever and believing that he would become depressed, isolated and give up everything he had worked for over the fear of persecution from people he neither knew nor cared for.

As he settled down into bed, he remembered recent times when he seemingly had everything. The home others envied, a debt-free life with money in the bank, an executive lifestyle, a loving family and his casual arrangement with Kristeena, which just iced his delicious cake with decoration, desire and made him energised once more.

This package seemed far from the version he would soon inherit from the FBI. Regardless of their generosity, his life would be marginalised in all respects.

He understood his wife's fears and thoughts, but he still believed that he would see her the next day. Then everything would be on the right path to safety and security once together.

Although he had the weight of the world on his shoulders, he slept well, like a child with its parents watching over them. Perhaps the FBI represented a parental connection for him. Tonight, at least, he felt safe despite sleeping in a hotel owned by the same people he was soon to help destroy. He often used a rubber doorstop in hotel rooms, which even though fallible gave him some peace of mind.

The Final Push

Waking up the next morning, Geoff felt sick, exhausted and stressed to a level never experienced in his life. Breakfast was always a highlight of his day, yet he could only handle a few slices of toast with his morning Earl Grey.

He felt tearful as he made his way a few blocks north of the hotel to his office, looking up as he stood outside as though to view this for the final time and say his goodbyes.

He saw Paul Newark roaring into the underground car park in his black Mercedes S-class, always immaculate and a familiar sight early in the morning before others arrived on the scene.

He was pleased to see him and hoped to get to Paul and Martin before the stresses of the day took hold. He had just a few hours to convince them to join his crusade and help Barry out of his painfully distressing captivity at the same time.

Ideally, he would have loved to talk to Barry, but the German authorities did not allow it. He had been formally charged with the murder of an escort girl and remanded in custody.

In a matter of hours, his life would become a whirlwind of activity. He would say farewell to Kristeena, meet the FBI, Interpol, the DEA and who knows who else before being in the loving arms of his family once more.

As Geoff walked into Paul's office, he was stressed mopping up the coffee he had inadvertently spilt on his keyboard and swearing as he attempted to dry out the keys with a paper towel. He looked lost without his PA to help him, like a young child trying to wash itself.

'You know why I'm here, Paul. I'm sorry to hassle you about this, but tonight is the big one for me. I was hoping to have your support to make a statement to the FBI and help bring an end to all this shit and hopefully get Barry back on the right path,' said Geoff, optimistic that Paul had talked to himself and grown a conscience that would overtake his greed.

He could tell that the bad mood was not due to him spilling a cup of coffee, as Paul responded, 'Some of us have been running this fucking business well before you got the key to the executive washroom. Barry, Martin and I have all put our necks on the line to invest in this company, the company we built up. Do you know that I have a mortgage on my house that helped to buy up my shares? Do you? You go around trying to do good, yet you were happy to take up the big chair, the big bucks and the share options that would make you rich. It's what you wanted, so don't try to appeal to my compassion. This whole damn thing changed when your little whore was asked to compromise her fragility and do something she—'

'To murder our fucking boss. Murder is hardly a compromise to anything I've ever recognised,' Geoff responded angrily.

Paul sat up recognising that his choice of words were perhaps misplaced.

Geoff continued, 'Have you forgotten François, Jaypee, Bernard, Barry and how the family have their claws in each of us, including you?'

'You stand to lose nothing, my friend. You know absolutely nothing of my risk, my life. If this company goes under because International Rescue are being investigated for money laundering, I am stuffed. My house, my job, my life all gone up in smoke while you sit in your cotton wool bubble of protective witness shit. Blow the rest of us. No, Geoff, you need to keep this in perspective.'

Geoff recognised Paul's genuine pain. He could see that he was knee-deep in debt and there was every chance the company could fold. 'How about talking to the IRS? I could ask Maxwell to arrange it. I'm sure they would give you some guidance.' As he watched Paul turn to the window and look down at the street beneath him, Geoff wondered why the FBI had not pursued his statement. He could be a credible witness and the FBI would be more persuasive than himself. What had he missed? 'Have the FBI asked you to come forward, Paul?' he asked in a gentler manner, trying to appeal to his less aggressive side.

'No, no one has contacted me, and I prefer it that way. They no doubt have enough with your witness statement. I for one will not be volunteering anything. Please don't implicate me. I think you should leave now. I should be calling Alexandre and snitching on you. After all, you're not here for my benefit,' said Paul making his way across the office. He opened the door for Geoff to leave.

Geoff recognised Paul was in an impossible situation and that he was not going to help. 'Are you going to tell Alexandre?' he asked whilst passing Paul on the way out, his head lowered fully expecting Paul to blow the whistle on him.

'I'm not a bad person; I'm just unable to move in the way you want me to. I don't like what you're doing, but I'm not capable of pushing the button that gets people shot,' Paul whispered as he closed the door behind Geoff, expecting this to be the final time he would do so.

As Geoff wandered down to his floor, he saw Alexandre walking into a meeting room with two other colleagues. He had no reason to be suspicious of the meeting, but he was careful to avoid eye contact as he slipped past the frosted glass. He was desperate to avoid meeting up with Alexandre.

Alexandre had the knack of seeing through your eyes and into your soul. Well, that was the view of some in Geoff's team. They neither trusted him nor found him approachable. Geoff had a similar distrust, but his views were formed through a deeper knowledge.

The next few hours were a series of internal meetings with his team members. Meetings that dragged on, compounding every element of stress and pain making his day more unbearable.

Geoff found it difficult facing them, talking about the upcoming month, when he knew that in twenty-four hours he would no longer need to concern himself with such matters.

The FBI wanted him to maintain his focus as normal, leaving nothing to raise suspicion and to perform his duties as diligently as ever, which he was keen to do.

In a perverse way, Geoff seemed to be enjoying the meetings. It was like the day before going on holiday. Obviously, he was under pressure and quite stressed, but he was a little more carefree than usual, just like tying up loose ends at work before jetting off long haul. One has to detach to an extent, otherwise the ticket is wasted and the plane takes off without you.

It was difficult agreeing to actions knowing that he would not actually complete them, not something he was ever used to. He was a company man, loyal, hard-working and focused on results. Yet today was a charade. He was a fake and all the things that he would fire someone for if he were managing them. This was why he needed to avoid Alexandre. He would see through him like a glass windowpane. *Just a few more hours to go*, he thought to himself.

To kill time and get out of the office, Geoff nipped out for lunch taking a full hour. He clock-watched like no other time in his life.

As he sat on a bench surrounded by tower blocks, Dimitri saw him and approached. 'Had enough of corporate life? Glad to be getting out?' he asked.

Geoff naturally jumped to the conclusion that Dimitri was on to him.

'Had the same thought myself. Just needed to get out for a while. Mind if I sit with you?' Dimitri said as he sat next to him not waiting to be invited. 'Fancy dinner tonight? I'm staying over, leaving tomorrow,' he added.

Geoff was sure that Dimitri knew he was leaving via FBI Airways. 'Stacked up, Dimitri. May need to give it a miss. Talking of which, I need to get back to it...' Geoff made his excuses as he set off towards the office again, this time fast-paced trying to avoid eye contact, conversation and direct questioning.

At six in the evening, Geoff put his laptop, phone and a few personal effects in his laptop bag and walked out of the building. He was due to meet at 7 p.m. at the Stacato Intercontinental, thankful to avoid No.4 for obvious reasons.

His walk to the hotel was a brisk twenty minutes, thirty if he dragged it out. He called Nikki en route, but it went straight to voicemail.

He glanced at his watch and thought she may not have landed yet, so he was not overly concerned at this stage. He left a message saying that he loved her and was excited to see them all soon.

Before he knew it, he was at the Stacato. Agent Simmonds was in the lobby reading a paper. Geoff was previously asked to wait at the bar until seven o'clock before heading to room 1512. He nervously ordered himself a vodka and tonic.

Although he had left his work colleagues behind, he was in no mood to drink champagne just yet. There was no reason to celebrate until he was tucked up away from the henchmen who would no doubt be tracking him first thing in the morning. He only had a few hours to escape.

He texted Kristeena hoping that she was okay, safe and had now given her statement to the FBI. Her phone would be switched off. Even so, it was a kind, sweet gesture that let her know he was thinking of her.

He was suddenly worried that his brief meeting with Kristeena in the presence of the FBI would include a rendezvous with Nikki and the children. How could he disguise his feelings for her? He knew that she would not give the game away, yet he might. He was certain that there would be such high emotions that anything else going on would just be swept along with the other major events: staying alive and moving from life number one to life number two.

Thinking about it some more, he wondered if they would actually put them in the same room.

He had arranged it so he could say goodbye to Kristeena. Maxwell agreed to let them have a few moments, so that would suggest he knew the circumstances. Surely he would not let him give away his goodbye emotions in front of his family.

Either way, it was a distraction from sitting at the bar constantly looking at his Rolex and checking it against his mobile in case the Swiss timepiece was wrong. It rarely was, but it was a ritual he performed given that the time seemed to pass so slowly. The watch barely moved in between his frequent glances at it.

Agent Simmonds carefully watched him at the bar taking in the surroundings and making sure he was alone. Geoff noticed this immediately after taking his first sip of drink, which may be his last for a while. How long 'a while' would be was uncertain to him. For now he just made the most of it.

He knew he could not acknowledge Simmonds. It was protocol suggested by the FBI. He must remain completely detached until meeting in the room at the specified time.

A man approached the bar and stood next to Geoff. He went cold with fear as he noticed the man's muscular physique. He believed this to be the look of a killer. With his heart racing, Geoff looked around the room before glancing at the man trying to look less obvious. He then noticed him reach inside his jacket as he caught Geoff's eye.

Geoff was convinced he was armed and placing a hand on his shoulder holster. Instead, he pulled out his wallet and gave Geoff a look of concern.

'What the heck are you looking at?' asked the bemused stranger.

Geoff looked away again realising that his paranoia was not doing him any favours. Turning away, he proceeded to a small table on his own where he could do what he was good at: observe and relax. Well, as much as he could considering the circumstances.

The waitress brought over another vodka and tonic, which he paid for with a twenty-dollar note. Staring at the glass, he wondered whether he should drink it, whether it had been poisoned. When he was standing at the bar, he could see the drinks being mixed from source rather than a glass served by a stranger. As pretty as she was, he did not trust her. He was obviously aware of the Ivanov's tactics by now;

nothing would surprise him. Neither would using a pretty young lady to distract him while he sipped away at the poisoned mixture served conveniently away from prying eyes. He doubted anyone would notice a man slumped at a table in a bar. Time was running out for the family if they were to bump him off.

His senses were heightened; he suspected everyone.

He decided to nurse the glass for several minutes and examine it rather than drink from it, knowing all that separated him from safety was a hotel lobby, seventeen minutes and fifteen floors in an elevator, which was several hundred yard's walk away and out of his line of sight at this time.

Dozens of people moved in and out of the bar, each one with their own purpose, in their own little worlds going about their business, laughing, joking, kissing in the greeting sense and shaking hands as they attempted polite conversation.

Geoff was keen to keep half an eye on Simmonds as he people watched, a pastime he often adopted in hotel bars and restaurants.

Tonight was exceptional as he fully expected someone to be watching him. Not out of general curiosity, but watching with the intent to kill him and stop him from disappearing into the care of the FBI.

He had replayed such a scenario in his mind after seeing this on many a movie played on the airline film selection. He was aware that the family would stop at nothing to preserve their affairs, which was no doubt why John Maxwell was keen to maintain such discretion, secrecy and to plan everything just so.

Although he had every faith in the FBI, he had not met the people from Interpol or the DEA. Although he recognised that all of these people would be involved considering the reach and complexity of such an operation.

He called Nikki again. Once again voicemail. He went online to check if the aircraft had landed. The Delta airlines information page showed that it had, just five minutes ago. He checked his watch again, not that it had moved since he last stared at it. It was still ten to seven. Five minutes or so and he would need to make a dash to the elevator.

The time seemed to move faster now. He discarded his drink touched only by his hands and felt a sense of achievement in not being poisoned; something he convinced himself was going to happen.

He did not want to leave too early, as per the specific instructions of the FBI. He wondered what they were doing up on the fifteenth floor. He hoped and assumed that Kristeena was there just finishing her statement and excited to see him in the safety of the authorities.

She would have just as much to lose as Geoff. She was an employee of the family, just like him. Her disloyalty would be viewed as a knife in their backs, so he was hoping that the FBI was not going to renege on their deal for either of them. If they were cast aside by the FBI, they would certainly meet their deaths in a no doubt unpleasant manner.

Another look at his watch. Five minutes to seven.

Geoff rose quickly from his chair and took one last discrete look around the bar area before setting off on his short journey to the elevators. He knew that the best course of action was to focus and not be distracted by strange faces, to move swiftly yet confidently and to avoid arousing attention.

As he did so, he even forgot to look at Simmonds. Geoff continued to look ahead avoiding eye contact with anyone.

At the elevators, his heart raced as he pushed the button to take him up to the fifteenth floor. The ding of the bell confirming the elevator had arrived seemed shockingly loud as he began to sense that others were behind him. He had no idea if they were genuine guests going about their evening or someone holding a weapon ready to strike at the right moment.

Geoff felt a wet sensation under his arms. The movement of his moist blue shirt reminded him that his blood sugar was low. He quickly unwrapped a sweet from its foil wrapper before consuming it. Stress always sent his sugar level crashing, so carrying a few sweets was always his instant remedy for such events. Not that tonight was comparable to a business meeting or his typical worries.

As he entered the elevator, he thought of his children and how he longed to hold them tight once again. He turned around to see four others in front of him facing the doors. No one looked at him. There was a couple in their mid-fifties, a man in his early forties and a hotel staff member. He used his expertise in body language to read their behaviours. He saw nothing that would disturb him as the elevator gently cruised to the eleventh floor before the doors opened.

After the hotel staff member exited, Geoff stared intently at the other three. The doors closed and his body continued to pump out enough heat to dampen his shirt further.

On the twelfth floor, out walked the couple. He watched as they walked down the long corridor between rooms before the doors closed once again.

This was it; the guy left was the assassin. Geoff prepared himself for the assault. He felt claustrophobic as if the walls were closing in. The few seconds for the elevator to reach floor fifteen seemed like minutes to him.

The doors opened. The man stood aside to let Geoff pass. Glancing at the control panel, he saw that floor sixteen had been pressed. Was this just a ruse or genuine?

Geoff's legs struggled to move past the man, out of the elevator and down the corridor. From behind, he sensed the man looking at him. He turned around to see his potential assailant before he could pull the trigger. The man disappeared behind the closing doors.

Geoff arrived safely, sweating and feeling sick with anxiety. He quickly sought to find the hotel room, no assailant, no gun, just another innocent person. He counted the room numbers looking up to see 1520. His room was now in sight some five doors away.

Nothing suspicious caught his eye as he approached and there was no one in the corridor. He glanced behind; it was clear.

After knocking on the door, which Maxwell opened immediately, Geoff sprang into the room as though crossing the finishing line in a race. His stress lifted instantly shaking the hand of his saviour Special Agent John Maxwell.

As Geoff took a seat in the lounge area of the bedroom, he noticed Maxwell looking concerned. 'So, I'm guessing that something has gone wrong, John. What is it?'

Maxwell paused before saying, 'It's your wife and family. They didn't board the plane at London. I'm sorry.'

'Are they okay? I mean, are they...you know...?'

'They're alive and well, Geoff. As far as I know, they just decided to stay put,' Maxwell added.

'I spoke to my wife, so I knew she had doubts. She did say she might not come here, but I didn't think she would go through with it, really I didn't,' said Geoff, his demeanour thoughtful and solemn.

'Now, think carefully, is there anything your wife knows that could be of benefit to our investigation? Anything she could add to your statement that might help us?'

Geoff responded with a sad look and shaking his head. 'Nothing at all.'

'Miss Balanchenko has provided her statement; she has been a credible witness. Thank you. She provided much more detail than we had hoped for. We will need her to go into witness protection also, which she has agreed to. I said you could say your farewells. She's next door.'

The adjoining door was slightly opened as he was shown into the room, presumably number 1510. Geoff noticed that Kristeena had been crying as he hurried towards her.

She stood up to embrace him, not as lovers but good friends.

Maxwell turned away and moved back into the other room allowing them some privacy.

'Are you okay? I hear you're going into witness protection having given your statement?' Geoff asked excitedly.

'Yes. Where's your family? Are they with you?' Kristeena asked him.

'They're not coming. They're staying in England. Nikki thinks it's the best way of protecting the children, not to mention putting some distance between us as well.'

'Does that mean you're starting over on your own as I am?' enquired Kristeena in a caring tone.

Geoff quickly seized the moment and asked if she would be with him to start their new lives together. She gladly agreed as the two kissed and held each other.

Maxwell returned and requested they hand over their ID, phones, computers and anything else that would identify them as they were about to be moved.

'Agent Maxwell, Kristeena and I want to stay together under the new identities you're providing us. Can you make this happen?' asked Geoff.

In the blink of an eye, Maxwell agreed. They were both excited, if not a little surprised by his immediate response. Geoff knew how big a deal this was bringing down the Ivanov empire.

'Where are your DEA and Interpol friends?' queried Geoff.

With a confident look, Maxwell replied, 'We're meeting them at a warehouse on a pier by the Hudson in about thirty minutes. Simmonds is just getting the transport arranged, which we will soon be moving you into. The sting operation is being co-ordinated by them. It's my job to get you to safety and ensure that you leave no trace of yourselves beyond this point.'

The Path to Freedom

Geoff and Kristeena felt safe for the first time in months. They were together and setting off on their journey. Not alone as previously thought, but in each other's company, rekindling a love that was meant to be.

They made their way down the fire escape and into the service elevator on floor ten. Then they made their way out of the back of the hotel and into a laundry van waiting to take them to their new life together.

The van was light blue, scuffed, damaged and badly treated. Geoff smiled to himself as he helped Kristeena into the side door; it felt like the van was a reflection of his life over the last few months.

Both agents put on a cap and an old grey polo shirt with the laundry logo 'Clean &

Fluffy Towel Services'. As Simmonds drove with Maxwell beside him, Geoff and Kristeena sat insecurely on a batch of towels, which were thankfully clean and neatly folded. The van was stacked with large laundry bags, some used and screwed up as though they had been thrown in.

The journey was forty-five minutes of discomfort yet one of the happiest he had known, with the security of two armed FBI agents, a new life and his beloved beauty in his arms.

He gave no thought to Nikki or Barry, but he was heartbroken to leave his children behind. They were not old enough to make their own decisions, yet Geoff was convinced they would stay with Nikki even if they were.

He knew there was no turning back. His old life was now dissolved and a new life was set to begin.

Kristeena smiled at Geoff. 'We did it! We have beaten those bastards the Ivanovs!'

Geoff responded with similar warmth. 'Tomorrow we'll be in some far-flung place, and they will be counting their losses, being interviewed by Interpol and hopefully being arrested.'

The van slowed down but did not stop fully as Maxwell jumped out to pave the way for them to enter the warehouse. As they did, the skylight on the van's roof lit up. They saw artificial light beaming through. The engine noise denoted that they were inside the warehouse before the ignition was turned off.

The door flung open and Maxwell ushered them out quickly towards some offices up a flight of old metal stairs with the side rail rusted. The two looked around to see a vast amount of pallets, boxes and goods waiting to be shipped somewhere, just like them.

As they reached the top of the staircase, they saw dozens of warehouse workers below carrying out their jobs. In a ground-floor office, Geoff caught a brief glimpse of someone he knew. It was someone from the company. The FBI had him in cuffs and were pushing him around. The process had started.

'Excuse me, Agent Maxwell, that man down there, is he, you know, being arrested and questioned?' Geoff asked.

'People who break the rules always get caught,' Maxwell responded with a curious smile as Geoff attempted to read his body language unsuccessfully.

'Is that allowed, to physically attack prisoners?' Geoff added.

Maxwell chose to ignore his question.

The office door was opened by Simmonds as the four of them entered before sitting down in a small back room. There was nothing in there except for a few chairs and a desk. There was no phone, no windows, no pictures on the wall and it was very cold.

Agent Maxwell smiled at them both and said, 'Okay, Simmonds and I are in the next room. You're safe here. We will shortly rendezvous with the Interpol representative to arrive on the boat somewhere out at sea. He will explain the next steps of the sting operation, just so you're aware. I have some things to arrange, and then Agent Simmonds will take you to your safe house far away from here by boat. I can assure you that no one can get to you here – you have my word.'

That was all Geoff needed to hear, but he was still low on sugar and asked for a sandwich or biscuit to eat.

When Simmonds said that there were provisions on the boat they would soon be boarding, he felt able to wait a few minutes more.

As the door closed behind them, the two were left alone sitting in the uncomfortable chairs holding hands.

'Looks like the Feds are already breaking up the chain, so it won't be long before others give up on the boss. Ricardo will soon get what's coming to him,' Geoff said with sincerity before kissing her hands gently.

Kristeena smiled. 'Do you think our new lives will be like this, in a room with no windows, unable to leave. Will we be prisoners? I've had a life of imprisonment in one form or another; I don't want that again. I need to be free, Geoff.'

'Once we have our new identities, we'll be placed in a house somewhere and they will connect us with jobs. Okay, they won't be the jobs we had, but we will be free, away from anyone who knows us, away from the Ivanovs and their associates, and free to be us for always.'

'I have a vision of you and me at the weekend sat by a lake in our log cabin home. You fishing for our lunch in a boat and me preparing a fire. You would teach. I would give dance lessons to children in the local village.'

'Well, I don't know about me teaching, but that sounds lovely, just perfect and something for us to aim for,' Geoff said not knowing where they would be or how much money they would have, although the log cabin idea was one he also shared.

Either way, they were certain that their life of fear and terror was over, even though it was to be replaced with some immediate uncertainty. At least they had each other.

Geoff could not believe his good fortune. 'Did you mean what you said about me and how I look at you differently than other men?'

'Yes, you are most special. I feel safe when we're together. All my life I've been vulnerable, at the mercy of others, forced to be what others demand. With you, I'm free to be myself,' she added sincerely.

Geoff used his mastery of body language and looked into her eyes to determine her sincerity for himself. He was in no doubt that she meant every word as he kissed her gently once more whilst holding onto her for dear life. However, he was curious. 'Maxwell said you gave him more detail than he had hoped for. What was it that was so important?'

'I gave away the identity of the man they call The Magician. He was well known at the ballet school I came from; he was the Mr Big Fix It for the Ivanovs. He once blackmailed my friend, a fellow dancer, into prostitution. She was called Karla Bychkovia, so beautiful, so pretty.

'We shared many stories together and she told me of this man who came to see her in our dressing room. I would recognise him easily. She told me that he was arranging a special performance for Josepf Ivanov who had turned eighteen. We both knew what he meant by "special performance". Josepf had taken a shine to her at a recent performance and wanted to meet her in person. How else do you describe it other than forced drug-fuelled prostitution?

'Josepf has a terrible reputation, just like his father, and the guy they call The Magician fixes things for them. She was taken away screaming by his men. They injected her with drugs in front of me, which immediately subdued her as they dragged her out through the back door.

'I never heard of her again until her body was washed up. Reported in the newspapers as a junkie prostitute, worthless – this was a lie. The Magician made me a deal to keep my mouth shut. They would sponsor me through appointing me in the Minsky Ballet and I would have a job teaching at the end of my show career travelling the world. So, here I am.

'The most important thing I know is the identity of The Magician. He's not aware that I know his real name. Karla told me before being taken. He's a Russian living in America. His real name is Boris Valentin but lives under false credentials as David Stevens. You're the only person other than the FBI who knows this.

'I checked him out once when I was in America. He lives as a venture capitalist in a fancy mansion. This is a cover for him being a global assassin running the Ivanovs' Western security, which is what Karla's boyfriend told her before being found thrown off a bridge near our Ballet.'

Geoff merely sat there listening to her story. He was amazed that she could identify him and knew where he lived. This was the man who gave orders to kill, hired assassins in the Ivanovs' name and could link the Ivanovs to the very crimes they had got away with for years, assuming Interpol could get to him of course.

The door opened. It was John Maxwell. 'Time to get you two on a boat, you'll then meet the Interpol team offshore. Let's go!'

Kristeena held onto Geoff's hand and arm tightly, suggesting that she was scared. Geoff smiled reassuring her that they were going to be fine.

'As soon as we get you on the boat, your old life ends and your new journey begins,' said Maxwell.

They exited via the opposite end of the warehouse avoiding the workers. Simmonds made his way first to the boat before signalling that the path was clear to continue.

Maxwell led Geoff and Kristeena towards the boat, steadily buoyant against the dockside, its lights on providing just enough luminescence to see where they were going. A gentle humming from the engine and bilge pumps whooshing indicated that it was ready to depart.

Maxwell remained by the side of the boat, smiling whilst saying goodbye as Simmonds hurried them onto the narrow gangway to board the waiting vessel.

'You'll be pleased to know that we've begun the operation to deal with all those who threaten our way of life, Geoff,' Maxwell added with a smile.

Simmonds ushered them downstairs to a room of some comfort compared to the one they had just left behind. There was a drinks cabinet, fruit, comfortable chairs, TV and a bed. As soon as Simmonds left the room to meet Interpol, they could hear the engines speed up and the boat felt in motion.

Kristeena looked delighted to be free as she threw her arms around Geoff to kiss him. Geoff knew that their troubles were over.

As he sat there devouring the fruit to satisfy his insatiable hunger, Kristeena looked out through the porthole window. She could see that they had left the metropolis behind and it looked like they were heading for open water. It was a wonderful feeling as the boat maintained its steady pace and continued away from New York. She was excited about her new life and glad to be sharing it with such a lovely man, with whom she had shared so much love.

Geoff answered a knock at the door. It was Simmonds.

'Okay, so Interpol are here. They're just giving instructions to the captain by radio as we are to rendezvous with a bigger ship in open waters. You will be in their care and taken to Alaska where your identities will be provided and you'll be given further instructions. Don't worry, I'll be staying with you until then.' As soon as he delivered his message, Agent Simmonds left the room again.

They heard the engines rev up. The boat was now beyond the estuary and heading east. Bigger waves were now impacting the boat and forcing them to sit down as the vessel moved in all directions.

Five minutes later, the boat began to slow down. Kristeena rushed back to the window and saw a large cargo ship ahead as the boat proceeded to move alongside.

A few minutes later, there was another knock at the door. Geoff opened it while Kristeena remained fascinated at the window.

'These are our colleagues from Interpol.'

Geoff extended a warm greeting to the man speaking. He felt a glimmer of recognition but could not place him in all the excitement.

Kristeena turned around and gasped in horror.

Geoff raced over and held her tight.

'It's him!' she shouted.

Geoff turned to look at him once more. It was The Magician. There was no Interpol, just representatives from the family.

The two looked into each other's scared and teary eyes as they awaited their fate.

At least Geoff's family were safe.

Nikki had made the right choice after all.

30850075R00255

Printed in Poland
by Amazon Fulfillment
Poland Sp. z o.o., Wrocław